Early Praise f

"A top-velocity cliff-hanger, and a thriller with heart. Brantley is the real thing." — Timothy Hallinan, Edgar-nominated author of the Poke Rafferty and Junior Bender Series

"A compelling, complex and emotionally connected story! The tension kept building and I couldn't stop reading. Well done! — L.J. Sellers, author of the bestselling Detective Jackson series

"No sophomoric slump here after Ms. Brantley's first successful outing—RED TIDE.... Another 'unputdownable'." — Jack Quick, Reviewer

"As a novelist, Peg Brantley has done the equivalent of winning Rookie Of The Year with her debut, and MVP with her sophomore novel. It exceeds all expectations as a detective story, as a suspense thriller, and as a police procedural. I declared in the review of RED TIDE that she was a force to be reckoned with. Now, with THE MISSINGS she has proven herself a nuclear super power of the thriller genre." — Robert Carraher, The Dirty Lowdown

"Brantley handles the polemics of race without ever getting preachy, and has a deft hand when it comes to character. She's populated her book with a sympathetic, full-blooded cast, coloring the lives of the key players with detailed back stories." — Michael W. Sherer, author of Night Blind

Praise for RED TIDE

"For fans of the serial killer genre, RED TIDE is an engaging, well plotted story with characters you won't forget. — L.J. Sellers, author of the bestselling Detective Jackson series.

"The characters were engaging and as the stakes kept rising, I worried about them as if they were old friends....Brantley manages to cover a lot of ground and gives her characters depth and complexity." — Jaden Terrell, author of RACING THE DEVIL and A CUP FULL OF MIDNIGHT

"This book will go a long way in introducing Brantley to readers as a force to be reckoned with in the thriller/mystery niche." — The Dirty Lowdown, Blogcritics.org

"Just enough technical stuff to show Ms. Brantley has done her homework but not enough to take you out of the story....Definitely 'unputdownable.'— Jack Quick, Reviewer

"The main characters... have a good balance of haunted flaws and gutsy strengths, and the plot involves a lot of danger and risk..." — Kingdom Books, Mysteries-Classic to Cutting Edge

"The text is fast-paced and sharp, which will appeal to thriller readers. Colorado comes through in this story, much as it does in Diane Mott Davidson's beloved 'Goldy' series"— An Amazon Reviewer

"Hard to believe that RED TIDE is Peg Brantley's first book. The story grabs you from the first page and holds your attention throughout." — An Amazon Reviewer

"[A] fast-paced, easy read that is well-written and well-researched, with a cracking good story that satisfies on many levels..." — An Amazon Reviewer

"Peg Brantley's RED TIDE... depicts strained but vital family relationships."— Confessions of a Mystery Novelist...

THE MISSINGS

PEG BRANTLEY

THE MISSINGS

PEG BRANTLEY

BARK
PUBLISHING
LLC

2012

THE MISSINGS
Copyright © 2012 by Peg Brantley

ISBN: Electronic Book Text: 978-0-9853638-2-6
        Paperback: 978-0-9853638-3-3

Published in the United States of America by Bark Publishing, LLC

Edited by Jodie Renner at
http://www.jodierenneredinting.com

Cover Design by Patty G. Henderson at Boulevard Photografica, www.boulevardphotografica.yolasite.com

To George, Love of My Life, you patiently ate dinner alone while I worked, or stood ready to help me find the right word...you are deeply and truly my most important reader. I hope you like this new story.

And yes, it's done-done.

"Recognize yourself
in he and she
who are not like
you and me."
–Carlos Fuentes

Chapter One

Main Street, 400 block
Wednesday, September 19

Senior Detective Chase Waters pulled his car up to the alley. Crime-scene tape stretched like flexible neon ribbon across the entrance, popping in and out of the light from his headlights. The shadow of the tape bounced against the snow in a sort of bizarre striptease, with falling snowflakes adding a glittering special effect to the surreal setting. Chase hoped the uniforms who confirmed a body in the dumpster hadn't messed up the scene.

He'd know in a minute.

Chase pulled on latex gloves and cloth booties and climbed out of his car. His evidence bag over a shoulder, camera in hand, he dipped his long frame under the tape. About two inches of fresh snow made him slip, and he wondered if the old rubber-band-over-the-soles trick would have been a wiser move. Only September, and the snowfall held promise of another record Colorado ski season. It didn't, however, do much for his footing at this hour of the morning, when he could have been lying in his warm bed next to the woman he loved.

The Crime Scene Unit van puffed exhaust at the other end of the alley. A door opened at the end of the CSU vehicle, and he saw Akila move with cautious deliberation down the steps, carefully holding a pan in front of her. The pan billowed steam from its heated contents. Chase thanked the heavens that his case had drawn Akila Copeland from the crime unit. Known by other detectives, district attorneys, and more importantly, judges, as one of the most meticulous Crime Scene Investigators in the area, Akila made him feel a little better about being out here in the early morning hours processing a scene.

"Hey, Chase. We got lucky. The uniforms were careful and approached the dumpster from the sheltered side next to the building. We have a couple of really great footprints in the snow from the alley. Plus some tire tracks."

"You need any help?"

"I could use your assistance for this last cast. It's in an awkward place and looks like it'll be the best one for this set of prints."

"How many prints?"

"Two distinct sets. If you get their footwear we'll have some cool evidence."

"Too bad there isn't contact information on the sole of every shoe."

"You mean like an owner's code? One day, my detective friend, one day. I sort of hope I'm not around to see it, though—too much Big Brother for my taste." Akila laughed and led him to the far end of the dumpster where a clear footprint was formed in the snow halfway under the metal container.

As the two bent to pour the hot sulfur into the print, Chase worried about the fragile nature of sulfur casts. He knew that, surprisingly, the snow wouldn't melt when the liquefied sulfur hit it, but the resulting beautifully detailed impressions were like sandstone—one false move and all of the beautiful evidence could crumble into a thousand pieces.

"Don't worry." Akila read his mind. "I've got plenty of photos from all angles. We're good to go. There's just this print in this impossible place I'd really like to capture. And as long as we can keep the casts together, we've got perfect 3-D evidence."

"You must've gotten here fast." Usually Chase had to wait for the CSU van—if it was available at all.

"I just got back into town from Snowmass when the call came in."

"Snowmass? Did someone lose their platinum ring again?" Last summer a woman vacationing in Snowmass had called demanding every department in the area provide a full effort to find her half-million-dollar platinum ring. That included the CSU van.

"Actually, something completely different demanded our attention tonight—a dog and pony show for the brass and politicos. Some Hollywood production team is in the area to film some mountain scenes and wanted to get an authentic feel for a crime-scene vehicle. Some asshole volunteered me. I figure they needed to show another 'face' of our fine mountain community."

"You're kidding, right?"

"Nope. This fine African-American skin of mine is more than just something to hold my brain in. Not only did I get overtime, but I got two offers to test for a walk-on role."

"All right! Why so late?"

"My shift didn't end until eleven. And they didn't want us out there until eleven-thirty. Something about a late dinner and entertainment. Hey, I wasn't complaining. I can use the money."

Ten minutes after pouring the sulfur into the impression, the CSI carefully pulled up the cast. She flashed a smile at Chase. "Perfect. I knew this was the best one, but because of its position under the dumpster I couldn't get all the photo angles I wanted."

Time for the body. Chase worked to move his mind toward a professional and pragmatic place. It was important to work toward justice for each victim, and while observing a body whose life had been taken by force made him angry and depressed, he needed to trump those emotions. He needed to let the dead body begin to tell its story.

He cranked his neck. "Did you get photos of the DB?"

"Yeah, but you'll want to get your own. Jax is on her way."

"Great." They were lucky to have a medical examiner as good as Jacqueline Taylor based right here in Aspen Falls.

"Anything interesting?" Chase asked, as he moved toward the dumpster with his camera.

Akila stopped and looked directly at him, her expression somber. "You have no idea."

Chapter Two

Main Street, 400 block
Wednesday, September 19

Chase shook off the creepy-crawlies Akila's words carved into the night. They'd worked a lot of cases together, and for her to tell him he had no idea what to expect didn't bode well.

He directed his flashlight into the dumpster. At first he wasn't able to spot the body. The Pearls of the Ocean Chinese Restaurant had enjoyed a busy Tuesday night. They were supposed to bag their garbage but it looked like the kitchen help must have been in a hurry and just dumped everything. Then he saw it. The carved-up and mutilated corpse lay in bizarre repose among the detritus of bok choy and egg foo young. Chase fought a wave of nausea and wondered if he'd ever be able to enjoy Chinese food again.

At first glance, the body looked like a badly carved-up side of beef. Huge, vacuous, gaping holes were where he might have expected critical wounds, if not solid pieces of intact flesh. The body cavity was laid open from the groin to the neck. Skin hung loosely around broken and missing ribs. Chase stepped away from the dumpster and fought to keep his professional composure.

Akila was watching him. "Don't feel bad. If you think you're going to hurl, you can add yours to mine—around the corner. Just get there in time. I don't need your reaction to mix with whatever evidence might still be here for me to uncover."

Chase swallowed, took a breath and looked around. The clear places in the snow. Only those few prints—tire prints in the alley, shoe prints around the dumping place. The obvious lack of blood evidence. There hadn't been a struggle—not here. "This isn't the scene of the crime."

Akila shook her head. "Nope."

Chase leaned deeper into the trash container while speaking into his cell phone recorder app. Later, he'd be able to make sure he didn't miss any details in his notes. "Male. Nude. No clothing in evidence. No visible identifying scars or tattoos. Most of his upper torso has been cut out. Looks surgical, not like some animal. A knife did this. Someone who knew what they were doing." He made the comments more for himself. The CSI would have already seen everything.

"His face is intact. Young. Looks Hispanic, or some kind of Latino origin." Chase thought about the relatively large undocumented population of illegal Mexicans living in Aspen Falls. He also thought about his other new case. A Hispanic male—no ID—found on a hiking trail. The kid hadn't been carved up like this one, so other than sex, age and race, there didn't appear to be a connection. No information, regardless of the queries he'd put out there, had come in. They were still waiting on autopsy results.

A hand shoved him gently away. He turned to see Jax Taylor. "Hey, Chase. Let me get to my body, will ya? I'm dead on my feet and I don't need you taking up one more second of the sleep I'm gonna get back to when this night—strike that, early morning—is over." She held a pen and a notepad in one hand and carried a flashlight in the other. A camera hung around her neck.

The medical examiner looked into the dumpster and uttered something Chase couldn't quite make out. But he understood exactly what Jacqueline Taylor had said.

She turned to Chase. "Without a liver—or much else, for that matter—TOD is gonna be a problem."

This case had just begun and already it was going downhill.

Chase stood back and let the ME get to work. He turned to Akila. "Where are the uniforms?" He had some questions for them.

Akila nodded past the CSU van. "Kirk Wheatley caught the call."

Chase felt better about the support he'd lucked into. Wheatley had enough experience and street smarts to keep from messing up the evidence.

He headed over to the patrol car and looked in the window. Kirk was filling out his report, using the computer to diagram the scene. Chase knocked on the passenger window and the officer waved him in.

Chase climbed in to the passenger seat. " Hey, Kirk. How did you draw this shift?"

"I'm kind of baching it since my wife left me. I figured I could build up some points if I want some time off later—or need a favor."

Chase nodded. Personal relationships were tough to maintain in this line of work. He'd been lucky with Bond, but they still had to navigate rough terrain from time to time. "Sorry to hear about the breakup."

Kirk shrugged his shoulders. "Bound to happen sooner or later."

"Who called in the DB?" Chase asked. He didn't mention the pristine crime scene. Professionals expected nothing less.

"Skizzers."

Chase sighed. Skizzers was a doper. Townspeople provided him with food, and in bad weather, a warm corner in a heated garage. But as careful as they were not to give the Vietnam veteran money, no one had quite figured out that by giving him food and shelter, he could parlay his disability check into whatever street products he could find.

"Shit. Skizzers."

"Yep. Said that two giant bats swooped in with their Batmobile. Morphed into vampires and one of them split in two, leaving half of itself in the dumpster—which, for some reason, he referred to as a gift box."

"Someone listened to him?" Chase couldn't believe a call like that had been taken seriously.

"Not until he got specific about the location, and lucid for long enough to state the fact that two men had dumped a body, and we'd 'better, by God, check it out.'"

"Did he get a license number?" Yeah, right. Like that would ever happen.

"Nope, but we've got a BOLO for the Batmobile."

"Video surveillance?"

"A couple of cameras. That doesn't necessarily mean they're working cameras. Or that they taped anything we can use."

"We'll check the local businesses tomorrow morning." Chase looked at his watch. Four-fifteen. "I mean, later this morning." He needed to get his notes in order and try to catch an hour or two of sleep.

Chase got out and walked up to where Jax and Akila continued to work both the scene and the body. Akila stood inside the dumpster and looked almost comical decked out in baby blue protective gear. She rose to her full height and tugged down her face mask. "I should have taken the walk-on offers. This stinks. Literally."

"Good, you're here," Jax mumbled after glancing in his direction. "I'm ready to secure the victim and could use your help. Akila requested uniform assistance to bag the garbage and haul it to the crime lab, but she could use some muscle now to haul the body out."

Chase donned protective gear, like it would do any good, and jumped in the dumpster with Akila. "Shit."

"Welcome to my world."

The two of them struggled and slipped in the slime to place the body in the bag. Chase fell twice, in awe of Akila's more sure footage, but stayed on his game. With Jax's help on the outside of the dumpster, they got the body out intact and ready to roll.

Before he could offer his assistance, Akila put a leg up over the edge of the dumpster and dropped to the ground, covered to her knees in unidentifiable lab specimens. Chase elected to wait a few minutes until he could make the jump out of the dumpster without an audience. His bad knees and questionable back made him more of a target by co-workers than he liked. He also wondered if he could strip down to his skivvies and trash the rest of his clothes so Bond wouldn't have to deal with them. He didn't want to show up in their home with pants slimed with unidentifiable goo and bacteria.

One thing at a time.

He wondered if this body had anything to do with the other John Doe on the books. Bad things happen everywhere, even in the idyllic Colorado mountain town of Aspen Falls.

But really bad things, especially here, tended to be connected.

Chapter Three

Aspen Falls Police Department
Wednesday, September 19

After he put his notes together into a Word document, Chase went home and fell into bed. An hour later—it felt like ten minutes—he got up, shaved, showered and poured himself a cup of French roast. It didn't have the desired effect. Maybe he should try mainlining it.

Jax had scheduled the autopsy for nine, a full hour later than usual. Chase managed to cut through the damp fog in his brain and focus on business. Jax swore under her breath a few times, lack of sleep impacting her usually good nature.

Pending lab results, the only information involved things he already knew. All of the young Hispanic male's internal organs had been cut out, like some kind of frog on a slab.

After the autopsy, Chase paid a visit to the Chinese restaurant and three other businesses in the area, none of which yielded much information. Only one of them, Cobalt Mountain Books, had a working camera. Unfortunately, the snow had made a mess of the lens and only fuzzy movement could be seen. Still, he requested the tape and booked it into evidence. Maybe the crime lab could make something of it. They'd been known to do more with less.

He needed help and made a request through official channels, directly to his lieutenant. Chase's money was on not getting an answer anytime soon. In Lieutenant Butz's mind, all murders were not created equal, especially if the victims had brown skin and uncertain social status. If necessary, Chase would go directly to Chief Whitman, but he hated to jump over Butz's head. Because of Chase's personal friendship with Whit, Lieutenant Butz tended to take every interaction between them as a direct threat to his job, so it would make an already strained working relationship worse.

Terri Johnson walked into the squad room bearing gifts. More sustenance from The Coffee Pod, not the sludge machine down the hall. *Coffee. The woman has a halo on her head. Tilted and a bit tarnished, but a halo.*

She handed him a cup. "I saw you earlier today and you looked like shit. You're working on the dumpster DB, aren't you?"

"Yeah. Thanks for the coffee."

"Need help?"

"I've asked Butz."

"What he doesn't know... " She set a bag down on her desk. "Want a muffin?"

"Thanks, no. The sugar would be nice for about five minutes, then I'd be in real trouble. And thanks for the offer of help. Don't need to stir up more with our lieutenant than is already stirred."

"We've got a squad meeting tomorrow. Maybe he'll come through."

"We'd have better luck if my DB had blue eyes."

"Tell me about it. Even breasts wouldn't be enough for Butthead." Her cell phone rang and she checked the caller

ID. Without a word, she took the call and walked out of the room.

Chase took another sip of his coffee and tried to figure out what to do next on this case. He'd looked for Skizzers earlier when he'd gone to the businesses, but the doper had disappeared and no one seemed to know where he hung out during the day. Chase made a note to call Patrol. The uniforms usually had a handle on the more interesting characters who called Aspen Falls home.

Chase clicked another file in his computer. It was dated four days ago, Saturday, September 15. Some hikers from Lakewood had found a dead body on a trail just south of town. The trail, rated difficult, didn't get a lot of traffic, and if the body hadn't been discovered that weekend, the young man's remains might not have been found until next summer—if at all.

As with all of his cases, Chase had attended the autopsy. Other than the fact the man had undergone a nephrectomy within the last six months, the ME had found nothing unusual. *Kind of young to lose a kidney.* Right now, she'd listed the cause of death as undetermined. Some of the autopsy results should be back next week.

Two unidentified bodies in less than a week. Both Hispanic, both male, both young, both of whom had missing organs (one planned, the other not so much), and both in Chase's caseload. He needed to find something to link them. Two cases with unidentified victims in a small mountain town were two cases too many.

His life had become complicated. Again.

Chase picked up the phone to call the patrol sergeant. A doper might be his best lead. A doper who thought he'd seen the Batmobile.

Chapter Four

The Benavides Home
Wednesday, September 19

General unease fanged into dread as it licked the edges of Elizabeth's thoughts. Pulling her thick mane of dark wavy hair, she haphazardly knotted it out of the way then tried Rachelle's cell phone again. Voicemail.

Rachelle never ran late. Elizabeth's younger sister set her watch ten minutes fast and arrived at her appointments twenty minutes early. *Rachelle phoned to let people know she'd be on time, for crying out loud.*

The two hours she had pretended that her sister—who never wanted anyone to worry about her, who always thought of others before she thought of herself—would walk in the door breathless and contrite, morphed into four hours. Then Elizabeth sat and called each one of Rachelle's friends, her sociology professor (whose class she had gone to that morning), and everyone else she could think of. Her shoulders tightened with each call.

Finally she called her mother. Ramona Benavides didn't have a cell phone, so Elizabeth had to call Aspen Falls Elementary. After explaining that it pertained to a family emergency, the receptionist forwarded her call to the kitchen where her mother worked.

"Do not talk to anyone else, Elizabeth. I will come home now. You wait."

Elizabeth paced until her mother came racing in the door, tears streaming down her face.

* * *

"Mamá, quit crying. We have to call the police." Elizabeth trailed her mother into the family room. She sat on an ottoman while Ramona Benavides fell into a chair and tugged shoes from swollen feet.

"No," her mother said between sobs. "We are not calling the *policía*. Not until we talk to your father. That is final."

Elizabeth could barely control the frustration she felt toward her mother. "What time will Papá be home?"

"Not until late. They got a new piece of equipment for the cows that needs to be set up by tomorrow. We raised you to respect your parents. Watch your mouth. *No me gusta tu actitud*. We will wait. Your father will know what to do."

Carlos and Ramona Benavides shared a traditional Mexican marriage. Elizabeth's father, as head of the household, revered her mother and treated her like his queen. But all decisions were his to make. Period. Getting her mother to take action without his okay was like kicking a brick wall. Barefoot. Submission to male authority—*all* male authority—came as natural to Ramona Benavides as breathing.

Elizabeth's hands fisted. "If Robert were here, you'd listen to him." She wished, not for the first time, to hear her brother's voice tell her mother what she needed to hear. Tell her what they needed to do. Make Mamá listen.

Instead, her brother had a uniform on in the war zone. Robert Benavides was fighting for his country.

And Ramona Benavides sat in her favorite chair in her own home in the land of the free—afraid to call police for help.

Elizabeth rubbed her neck. *Some country.*

"Roberto isn't here. Your father is. Show some respect. No *policía* unless he say so."

"The police can help us."

"They can bring us trouble."

"What trouble, Mamá? What trouble?"

Elizabeth's mother stopped rubbing her feet and looked at her with sad eyes. "You know the trouble I'm talkin' about."

She was getting nowhere. Her mother would not listen to her.

Elizabeth tried again. "Rachelle is missing, and we need more help than a few friends—and a tiny search—can give us."

Her mother's shoulders slumped. A strangled sob ripped the air. "My Rachelle. My baby."

Elizabeth watched her mother rock back and forth, her movement punctuated by moans. She saw the head of gray hair, the familiar face filled with wrinkles, the swollen red eyes, and wondered when her mamá had gotten old. She moved to wrap the small woman in her arms.

Together, mother and daughter swayed.

"At work they say it is the policía who are behind the other missings," her mother said. "We do not need to bring more trouble."

"Mamá!" Elizabeth punched to her feet and began to pace around her mother, arms slicing the air. "We are legal. We have rights."

15

"Our rights *cesan* when friends would be in danger if we got your police involved. Our rights cease when we could bring pain to others."

"But it's Rachelle. Our Rachelle. What about *her* rights? She isn't just playing games. She's in trouble. And no one we know has the power to help her."

Elizabeth sat back down on the ottoman and reached for her mother's hand. "Will you at least call Papá and let him know?"

Her mother's brow wrinkled and tears welled again in her world-weary eyes. "It is a bad day to call him at work. He is busy and his boss need for him to get job done today."

"Please, call him."

"We must wait for your father and not bother him at work. It is in God's hands." Ramona Benavides stood. "We go to start the dinner."

Elizabeth went to the coat closet by the front door and pulled out a light jacket. *I need to get out of here.*

"Where you go?"

"I'm going for a walk. I need to get some air."

Twenty minutes later, Elizabeth walked into the Aspen Falls Police Department and asked to speak to someone to report a missing person.

Chapter Five

Aspen Falls Police Department
Wednesday, September 19

Chase met with Elizabeth Benavides for the better part of an hour, drank one cup of coffee and two Red Bulls like they held the secret to youth, and ran some checks while she sat—somewhat impatiently—at his desk. While she told her story, he made notes and searched various databases to confirm her information. At the end of that hour, Chase thought there might be something to what she said. A young girl, who had every reason to return home to her family and no reason to run away, had gone missing.

Chase thought about his two John Does in the morgue and wondered if there might be a connection.

Rachelle Benavides, Elizabeth's younger sister, just seventeen, a part-time student at the Aspen Falls Mountain College Outreach Program, hadn't returned home when expected. The girl had graduated high school early and enrolled in the program without skipping a beat. She had chosen to focus on economics and social work, and was very serious about her future. The only boyfriend in her life attended CU in Boulder. Chase got the contact information, but instinct left him inclined to believe Elizabeth when she told him she didn't believe her sister had run off to see him.

"She is a dedicated student, Detective Waters. She is not a flighty teenager. And Anthony is equally dedicated to his education."

Rachelle had plenty of family and friends who loved her. And that included a very determined sister.

And she was Hispanic.

When you have a dead body with no ID and no one looking for him, plus no fingerprint matches, you've got a cold case before it even gets warm. And Chase had two of them. Two male unidentified DBs that were going nowhere fast.

And they were both Hispanic.

Chase stood and stretched his back and shoulders, ran both hands through his hair, then reached for his sports coat by the door. He didn't really need the jacket, but guns made some people nervous, and the coat hid his weapon well. Fingering the inside pocket he pulled out a package of red licorice twists. "Would you like some licorice?"

The young woman shook her head. Her shoulders sagged and she closed her eyes. Chase knew what had happened. He'd seen it in interrogation rooms. He'd seen it disciplining his kids. He'd experienced it personally when David died. When people give up, they visibly deflate. Whatever force holds them up and keeps them going escapes with an exhale. He stuck a twist in his mouth and bit off the end.

"I need to talk to your parents and see your sister's room."

Elizabeth stiffened in her chair, shoulders pulled back again, but made no move to get up. "I should probably tell you that my mother doesn't know I'm here."

"Why is that?"

The girl blushed and for the first time since she'd been escorted to his office by the desk sergeant, wouldn't meet his eyes.

Chase understood. He'd dealt with suspicion and distrust while working on cases in the past, especially where minorities were concerned. There were plenty of cops who hadn't helped race relations in the past. Hell, his own lieutenant ranked as bad as any of those idiots.

"If you think something has happened to your sister—and I'm inclined to agree with you—the sooner I get the information I need, the sooner we'll find her."

The girl nodded and rose to her feet while Chase picked up his phone and punched a couple of numbers.

Chase finished off the strawberry-flavored licorice twist and spoke into the phone. "You working on anything right now?" He looked at Elizabeth and smiled. Hoped he looked reassuring. "Good. Meet me at my car. We've got a missing girl and I want you to come with me to check out her computer."

Chase didn't really need Detective Daniel Murillo to check out any computer. He could bring the computer back to the station for that. He needed Daniel Murillo as eye candy. Maybe keep the situation a little more in control. Maybe get a few more answers.

Daniel would hate it if he knew.

Chapter Six

The Waters Home
Wednesday, September 19

Bond Waters carried her iPad toward the kitchen. She wanted to review the agenda for the library board meeting and make sure her Realtor could meet her at a possible site for her antique store on Saturday. She passed the entrance to the family room and could hear Angela and Stephanie. Her Mom antennae picked up a frantic element to their whispers, and then she heard a sob. *Time for a detour.*

The second she entered the room both girls fell silent.

"What's going on?" Bond sat on the couch between her daughters. She waited. "One of you needs to start talking."

Angela, fourteen, pinched her lips and folded her arms. Stephanie squirmed. Although not always the case, eight year-old Stephanie was the weak link in whatever the two sisters had been discussing this time. Bond squared her body toward her youngest child and waited.

"It's a secret, Mommy."

Something cold and shard-like shook loose from Bond's memory, but with a skill honed from years of experience she slammed it back and closed the lid, almost but not quite able to pretend nothing had happened.

"Some secrets are good to keep, some are not."

Angela sniffed. "A secret is a secret, Stephanie Marie."

Bond shook her head. "That's not true."

"What's the difference?" Stephanie asked.

"Well, there's the present kind of secret. That's a good one, right?"

"Uh-huh. Like birthday presents."

"Then there are the kind of secrets that might be bad to keep."

Stephanie shoved her hands under her butt.

Shadows dipped in and out of Bond's vision and a heaviness pressed on her chest. Her nose wrinkled at a remembered scent. *Please God, not my daughter.*

"If either one of you are ever hurt, or worried about something or someone, those are not the kind of secrets to keep. Those are things you need to talk to us about." Bond paused. "Me and Daddy. Not each other."

Angela tipped her chin higher and Stephanie inched closer to Bond's side.

"Some girls are being mean to Angela. They say she's a narc because of Daddy."

Bond reached out and held Angela's arm. Her relief about the scope of this problem made her want to laugh but she also recognized that to Angela, being called a narc was right up there with being a nerd. "Stephanie, leave your sister and me alone for a few minutes, will you please?"

Twenty minutes later, Bond scrunched the phone up to her ear with her shoulder. "Mother, I really don't have time for this." She nodded at the clay sculpture Stephanie held up to her for approval, and went back to putting some kind of dinner together for her family, phone still pressed against the side of her head.

The refrigerator door open, she watched McKenzie, their Bichon Frise, rush up, grab something from the lower shelf, and run like four-legged lightning out of the room. She had no clue what he had snatched. Meanwhile, her mother continued to drone.

"Darling, you need to be exposed to culture again. You need to be around important people. You *need* to come home."

"Look, Mom, I can't just drop everything and go to Chicago to visit you and listen to all your reasons for why I should leave Chase. How many years has it been? Oh, yeah. Eighteen. I'm happy. Get over it." Bond pulled out an egg and the milk and set them on the counter. She closed the refrigerator door. Her mother could make it hard for her to breathe.

"How can you be happy living where you are? Without any cultural stimulation? Without people to bring out the best in you? Without David?" The mention of David stopped Bond in her tracks. *Crap!*

"Don't go there, Mother." Bond swallowed and reached for a mixing bowl. Her hand shook.

"I'm just saying that lives go through different seasons. And seasons change. People outgrow each other. People of a certain breeding come to realize they need more. They need their own kind."

Her mother had called her three times today. *Three.* Her first message had been when Bond had been reading to a kindergarten class at the library that morning. The second had been during her two o'clock library board meeting.

Her mother's messages both times had sounded petulant. Manipulative. Guilt-inducing. Bond had managed to avoid contact until this phone call. She'd been distracted enough to answer without noticing the caller ID. *My bad.*

"Mother, what's so important you've called me three times today? Is Daddy okay?"

"He's fine."

"Let me talk to him."

"He's not here, Bond. He's *fine*." Celeste Wentworth did not like sharing the spotlight. While her mother prattled on about some half-forgotten classmate and his accomplishments, Bond made a mental note to call her father in the next couple of days.

Stephanie walked up with a drawing this time, and something that resembled either a permission slip or a Parent-Beware teacher's note.

"Mother, really. I don't have time to talk right now."

"I suppose Chase isn't home and you're having to do everything without any help. Has he even bothered to call?"

"As a matter of fact, he isn't, and he did. And frankly, we make it work for us. It doesn't need to work for you too."

Silence.

"Well, darling, I'm only trying to—"

"Yep," Bond said. "*Well* is right. We're doing *well*, so thank you for asking." She took the drawing from Stephanie and anchored it to the refrigerator with a heart-shaped magnet. Then held her hand out and waited for her youngest daughter to hand her the other piece of paper.

"Okay, darling. I get this isn't the best time to talk to you. I'll try again in a few days. In the meantime, you know I'm always here for you."

"I know, Mother. Thank you. Good-bye."

Bond hung up the phone and breathed a sigh of relief. "Stephanie, go tell Angela that dinner will be ready in fifteen minutes."

Bond looked out the window and wondered about the black Mustang parked just up the street with two men inside. They'd been there when her mother had called. They were still there. Lost? On a break of some kind? As she opened the door to go see if they needed something, the driver glanced in her direction, made eye contact, then started the car and drove away.

Chapter Seven

The Benavides Home
Wednesday, September 19

Chase stepped between mother and daughter, the silence split only by the visual daggers Ramona Benavides hurled in her daughter's direction. The four of them stood on the front porch, Mrs. Benavides effectively blocking entry, while Elizabeth, Chase and Dan Murillo did a kind of strange dance in front of her.

He bowed his head a little and held out his hand. "Mrs. Benavides, I'm Senior Detective Chase Waters." He kept his hand out while he made eye contact with the gray-haired woman. She looked away, then back again. When their eyes met a second time, her hand came into his. Slow, hesitant, more out of respect than anything. He did his best to return the respect by giving her hand a gentle squeeze. He dipped his head again and let his hand fall to his side.

"I understand and appreciate your concerns," Chase said. "But our only reason for being here is to help find Rachelle."

Chase watched her gaze move from him to the man standing just behind him. "This is Detective Daniel Murillo."

Daniel reached forward to also offer his hand. "Ma'am."

"Come in. Before the whole world see."

Mrs. Benavides backed through the entrance and held the screen open. Daniel grabbed the outer door, allowing her to move ahead of her uninvited guests.

"Please. Room for everyone in kitchen." The woman moved slowly, giving Chase an opportunity to look around. He had noticed the tidy yard when they walked up to the porch, and the inside reflected the same loving care. Small, but well-maintained. Framed photographs covered almost every surface of the living room as they walked through it to the kitchen. Crosses, from rough-hewn to ornate, and paint-by-number oil paintings blanketed the walls.

Chase itched to begin asking questions related to the case, but knew that would not be the way he'd get any answers in this home. "Do you paint?"

"My husband. Painting the numbers help him to relax."

The four adults almost filled the room. Chase noted a new microwave tucked on the counter next to an old oven. A large, scarred table dominated the space. It reminded Chase of the well-used, well-loved table in his own kitchen.

He waited for Mrs. Benavides to sit.

"May we?"

"Course. Would you like some cold tea?"

"Very much. *Gracias*."

Chase watched Ramona Benavides shake her head as Elizabeth walked over to retrieve some glasses out of a cupboard. With a nod to acknowledge her mother—who

Chapter Eight

Aspen Falls Police Department
Thursday, September 20

Squad meeting. Chase sat with Daniel Murillo and Terri Johnson. The three detectives in the Aspen Falls PD—plus Lieutenant Butz, who hadn't investigated squat since 1987 and wouldn't know a bloodstain pattern if it had a label, and whose last name inspired more than one deserving joke—sat in the room. All three detectives had better things to do, but when your superior called a mandatory meeting, and you liked your job, you went.

Welcome to my world. Chase kept capping and uncapping his pen, a dead giveaway to everyone who knew him that his brain had processed Lieutenant Melvin Butz's carefully planned detective squad meeting outline, and it no longer mattered. Chase knew all of the questions and all of the answers, and the total waste of time galled him.

The officer-involved shooting Chase had just closed wouldn't come to trial for months. He'd already met with the DA's office and turned over his file. The court case would take a chunk of change from his day, but what else was new? Detectives often spent more time in court than on any other part of the job.

The delay before trial gave him time to focus on his other workload. He had two open missing persons cases. One was a probable runaway. Chase suspected the seventeen-year-old boy would either come back home or turn up on another town's police blotter. He hoped, for the sake of the kid, the first scenario won.

The second one, the Rachelle Benavides case, worried him. That one had kept him at his desk far longer into the night than he'd wanted. He'd gone back to the Benavides home and talked with the father. Carlos Benavides was a quiet man with a defeated posture. As he considered all of the things that may have happened to his daughter, his already collapsed shoulders curled in toward his heart even more.

Both the patriarch's wife and daughter seemed surprised at his willingness to do whatever necessary without question. Chase knew about family secrets and miscommunication. He guessed those issues weren't exclusive to one culture. He understood the feeling of helplessness Carlos Benavides must be experiencing at this moment. It sucked.

Chase had spent the morning with Rachelle's friends from school while Daniel interviewed the neighbors. They'd both come back to the station empty.

For the thousandth time he hoped they would find no connection between the girl's disappearance and the two other corpses discovered earlier. Both of those were also young. But they were male. Hispanic. One mutilated. One not. No IDs and no families looking for them—at least not through official channels. Only two facts connected Rachelle to the murder victims—age and origin. He hoped the fact that she was a *she*, that her family was clearly involved in finding her, and that at this point she was only missing, would be enough to keep her on one list and off another.

Butz's voice cut through his thoughts. "Waters, you got anything more on that missing? Not the boy, the wetback."

Chase pushed down the words he wanted to use to put Butz in his place. This wasn't his battle to fight right now. He set his pen down and the silence stretched. He wanted to give Daniel a chance to say something. To give the Hispanic detective a chance to stand up and be strong for his heritage. He waited. Nothing. He wanted to kick Daniel—make him speak up, but Daniel's position wasn't Chase's battle to forge either.

When no one moved, Chase answered, "Rachelle Benavides is a young woman with close ties to the Hispanic community. She's a part-time student at the college and not likely to be a runaway. She attended her economics class yesterday. Nothing unusual. Daniel and I have interviewed her family, her neighbors, and a few of her friends from school. Daniel is going through everything on her laptop but we don't have anything yet. There's no reason for her to have left on her own, and so far, there's no evidence of foul play."

Chase paused, then: "What exactly did you mean by 'wetback', Lieutenant?"

After an initial clueless look the man at least had the grace to flush crimson.

"My apologies for not being *PC*," Butz said. He gave a perfunctory nod in Daniel's direction. "Especially considering."

Chase closed his eyes and shook his head. The man was a relic. His pension couldn't come soon enough. How he'd managed to hold on to his job for this long, particularly with an African-American chief of police, proved a testament to the collective bargaining system.

"I don't know how you cut opening a case when the spi—uh, *señorita* has been MIA for less than twenty-four,"

Butz said. "If it weren't for those other two DBs, you'd figure along with the rest of us that she was just movin' on like those people do. You waited for the juvie white boy but not the Mexican. This world is gettin' stranger and stranger."

"Lieutenant, I did not delay any search for the 'juvie white boy.' His parents didn't make a report until he'd been gone for two days." Chase rarely chose a wait-and-see attitude when a person went missing. Especially a kid. He'd much prefer to waste a little bit of time than come in too late.

A knock on the half-open door and the undeniable bulk of their commanding officer presented itself. Aspen Falls Chief of Police Cornelius Whitman.

"Please excuse my interruption of your meeting, Lieutenant," the chief said.

Butz looked like the kid caught spraying graffiti on the playground. Had Whit heard any of the exchange? Wouldn't matter. The chief knew all about the overweight, past-due-for-retirement Lieutenant Melvin Butz.

"I have some pertinent information for Detective Waters and I wanted to get it to him ASAP."

Butz nodded and squinted suspiciously at Chase. Chase bit back a laugh. He had absolutely no designs on Butz's job.

"The body of a young Hispanic female was discovered this afternoon. Could be your missing girl. There was no ID." Whit checked the paperwork he'd brought with him before handing it to Chase. "Her heart, both kidneys, and lungs had been removed."

The parent in Chase kicked into gear and he felt the horror, followed by anger and resolve. Then his professional self resurfaced. "Any connection to our other victim?"

"Other than being gutted like a fish and left somewhere to rot?" Whit asked.

"Yeah. Other than that."

Chapter Nine

Ute Indian Burial Ground
Thursday, September 20

The body had been found in the old Ute Burial Ground southwest of town. Chase parked his SUV on the shoulder by the other county cars, clicked off the ignition in the middle of a Coltrane riff, and hiked up the hill. Graves of Ute Indians, most still marked by piles of rocks, dotted the hillside.

He shook his head and tucked the half-eaten red licorice twist in his pocket. Wherever he worked a murder the space felt desecrated. *But here?* Something sour and burning worked its way up his throat into his mouth. The Ute had called this place the Shining Mountains. Both the land and the Indians had been here long before gold brought prospectors, civilization, and ski resorts.

And murder.

Crime scene tape surrounded a relatively small area, and Jax Taylor—the Medical Examiner—stood in the middle of it, alternately taking photos and diagramming the site. Chase watched her work. You do enough of these scenes and you learn to point and shoot with one hand.

When Dr. Taylor saw Chase coming toward her she let the camera fall against her chest and waited for him. Pulled down the mask covering her face.

"Detective."

"Hey, Doc."

She stepped to the side and allowed him to get his initial impressions. Some detectives liked the ME to tell them everything. Chase liked to see things for himself, and Jax Taylor knew the way he preferred to work.

He saw a young woman, her face chewed beyond recognition. From the look of her nude body, and judging mostly by her hands, which were smooth and unwrinkled, she was in her late teens to early twenties. He felt a flash of the horror she must have felt. The fear. He wondered if she'd been killed quickly or tortured.

Long black hair tangled and matted. Hispanic. Could she be Rachelle Benavides?

"Clothes or ID?"

"Not near the body."

He walked around to the other side of the dead girl. Squatted to get a closer look. It was like someone had done the autopsy already, but hadn't replaced the organs. A long, deep incision, from just below her neck to her abdomen gaped open. The exposed bones of the sternum reflected clean slices.

Shit. Chase closed off the part of his brain that wanted to cry out and rage against what this young woman had gone through. She would come to him in his dreams. She would be there when he woke in the mornings. But right now the best thing he could do for her was act as her advocate. Do his job.

He closed his eyes and heard the crackle and pop sounds of the masses of maggots who claimed their part of the body. Flies were all over the interior where once a heart pumped blood and lungs drew in oxygen. Chase waved away the flies and saw the empty spaces, the remaining internal organs almost unrecognizable. He saw bite marks around an area where flesh had been ripped away.

"Could wild animals have taken her heart and lungs?"

"Nope. They were surgically removed. Even with all of the decomp, the cuts are clean."

Chase examined the victim's face. It had been chewed to the point of obliteration but he couldn't see any obvious contusions on either her face or her head.

"Before you ask, other than the obvious, there are no other signs of trauma."

"You read my mind, Doc."

He observed the surroundings. No obvious blood pooled into the soil, no trampled ground to suggest a struggle. This was a dumpsite. Just like the other. Again, he didn't have the advantage a crime scene could give him.

Jax confirmed what he already knew. "Akila Copeland came to the scene but there was nothing much for her to find. She identified a few drag areas and that's all. What we have is a body without any other clues."

"How long ago, do you think?" Chase asked. The wind shifted and he pulled out his handkerchief and put it over his nose. The pungent vinegar smell burned his sinuses. Even trying to use his mouth to breathe couldn't keep the smell at bay. *Pretty fast decomposition if this was Rachelle Benavides.*

"Based on the deco juice and skin slip, I'd say she's been dead about a week. But with the missing organs and the fact that she wasn't sewn up afterward, it could be five days."

The Benavides girl had only been missing a day. This young woman was someone other than Rachelle Benavides. He now had three DBs, all Hispanic. *What the hell is going on?*

Chapter Ten

The Waters Home
Thursday, September 20

Bond put the finishing touches on the hurry-up dinner so Chase could get back to work. "It's a lousy time to catch a new case, that's all I'm saying."

"Like there's ever a good time?" Chase grabbed her and pulled her to him, then gently brushed her hair out of her face. When he nuzzled her neck in the way guaranteed to make her knees weak, she pressed against him. In their twenty-plus years, it had never failed to work.

"Funny." Bond pushed him away and pointed to the kitchen table. "Sit. Eat." She felt a warmth that stretched beyond her body's response.

"Girls!" She shouted up the stairs. "Come spend some time with your dad before he has to leave."

Seconds later Stephanie pounded down the stairs and flew past. Angela caught Bond looking in her direction and immediately slowed to a leisurely amble. Her oldest daughter looked like a younger version of Bond. Tall, long brown hair, wearing jeans and a t-shirt, she exuded all kinds of casual elegance. Stephanie had chopped her still white-blond hair off to a length which, with the right amount of goo, she could shape into spikes. Her personal expression of independence, she'd insisted on styling it all on her own. Clearly, the purple tights, lime green lederhosen, and hot pink and yellow striped blouse weren't enough. Not for the first time, Bond shuddered when she thought of the teenage years yet to come with this one.

She followed her daughters into the kitchen and wondered at the little-girl infatuation they both had with their dad. Were they ever that way with her? Chase's job seemed to leave her in the role of a single parent more often than not. Even though they tried to even things out, he got to be the hero while she played taskmaster and disciplinarian. Some days, it got to her more than others.

"Are we gonna do balloons tomorrow, Dad?" Angela asked.

Bond's throat tightened.

"Yeah, Daddy. Tomorrow is David's birthday. It's his party," Stephanie said.

Tears, rarely bidden except for when she needed release, filled Bond's eyes. *Damn.* Not the time. Her husband looked to her for some help, his own eyes pleading.

"Daddy has an important case he's working on and he might not be able to get away," Bond tried.

"What's more important than one of our birthdays?" Stephanie asked.

"Nothing," Chase said. "You tell me what time and I'll be here."

Stephanie's face clouded. "Daddy, does it matter that David never lived here with us?"

Chase pulled his youngest daughter's face up to see into her eyes. "We've talked about Santa, right? How he always knows where we are?"

He got a nod.

"Well, David knows the same way Santa does. He's connected to us. Forever." A catch in Chase's voice made that last word hard to hear.

"Forever, Daddy?"

Chase and Bond both spoke one word at the same time: "Forever."

Angela, quiet through this exchange, focused on her family. "Tomorrow would be a big one. Eighteen." She drilled in on her father. "It's an important birthday. We're home from school by three o'clock. Let's say four-thirty to release the balloons."

"You've got it, honey," Chase said. "Now I've got to head out."

He kissed Bond goodbye, and she double-checked his wallet to make sure he had enough cash for sustenance while he worked until who knows what time on this case. Chase had already called Butz to ask for the full squad on this and received a grudging okay. Bond wanted to kick ass when Chase told her about how his lieutenant responded to his request. A little bit of help would get him home sooner and maybe not dead on his feet.

Chase told her that Terri Johnson would join him and Daniel first thing tomorrow morning. Their caseload—her husband's own missing boy case, a bank embezzlement Daniel had all but wrapped up, and a dead-in-the-water attempted assault case of Terri's—would be handled by a couple of patrol officers who knew what they were doing. The three detectives would continue their involvement on their cases as needed while they focused on the murders and trying to find Rachelle Benavides.

Bond could be in for several evenings on her own. But Chase's job sure helped her keep her priorities straight. And highlighted the importance of giving her husband a soft place to land. Or crash-land as necessary.

"Tell Jax I said hi," Bond said as Chase walked to his SUV. "When this case gets settled, we should all get together for dinner."

Chase called over his shoulder. "When she's not working I'm not sure she comes up for air, even if Scott's with her."

Marriage to a man who'd used her hadn't soured Jax on love. After Jax's divorce, she and Scott Ortiz had begun seeing each other. They protected their fresh romance as if it were a soap bubble. After-hours belonged to the two of them.

"Fine," Bond laughed. "Tell her when this case gets settled, we should have a girlfriend lunch."

Her husband rewarded her with a chuckle as he swung his lanky frame into the SUV. He flashed the hand sign for "I love you" and drove away.

Bond spent the rest of the evening thinking about David and how badly she wanted to hold him again in her arms.

Chapter Eleven

Office of the Medical Examiner
Thursday, September 20

The Aspen Falls Medical Examiner's office boasted almost state-of-the-art equipment, especially impressive considering they were a small mountain community. Thankfully, the tax base of Aspen Falls was made up of wealthy residents and major year-round tourism, which allowed them to enjoy a more generous budget than other towns.

Every time Chase Waters walked into the autopsy room, the lack of holding drawers made him do a double-take. Modern ME offices stored their bodies on shelves. It might not be as dignified as one of those huge stainless steel vaults, but it sure utilized available space a lot more efficiently.

A visit he'd made to a morgue in Tucson was locked into his brain. Shelf after shelf filled with the bodies of loved ones who'd been so desperate for a better future they had risked their lives in the Sonoran Desert, and lost. Men, women and children who left mostly on foot to leave the poverty of Mexico behind them. Scores of hopefuls perished in the relentless heat.

He'd learned one more horrible fact on that visit to a Tucson morgue: before a medical examiner can be licensed, he or she must complete a certain number of autopsies. As hard as it would be to do in Aspen Falls, someplace like Tucson would have a lot more opportunity in a macabre kind of way. Offices along the Mexico-U.S. border had waiting lists for hopeful MEs. It was a horrible reflection on current conditions in that part of the country.

The windowless room in the Aspen Falls ME office had three autopsy tables. Each table was surrounded by negative pressure vents that looked like giant cheese graters. These vents were there to suck in smells and anything else that might be released into the air, to protect anyone in proximity from inhaling airborne contaminants. Based on the smell he'd encountered at the burial grounds, Chase figured whoever invented this contraption qualified as a hero to medical examiners and coroners everywhere.

The young body of the newest murder victim had been placed on one of the tables, with the other two empty. Chase didn't like autopsies but he attended them when he could, for two reasons. First, he wanted to see what the ME saw. There was always the chance they'd find the one 'thing' that might become significant later and wrap up the case. Second, as appropriately clinical as autopsies were—and this proved hard for him to explain to other detectives—he attended autopsies as a witness to a life. At least to the way a life ended. He always experienced a profound advocacy link simply by being present.

Chase listened to Jax as she rattled off her findings. The external examination provided no trace evidence that might be useful until the ME picked up her left arm.

"Well, I'll be. The left upper forearm indicates a recent needle puncture. My guess would be that some liquid agents were administered just prior to her death."

"Liquid agents?"

"An IV of some kind. We'll have to wait for the toxicology tests to know what drugs may have been used. All I can tell you is that it appears as if she was injected with something at this site—and probably not for too long."

Chase checked the other arm, then moved down to examine the skin between her toes. "No signs of extended drug use."

Jax placed the body on some blocks to make examination easier.

"You ready, Detective?"

"I'm guessing you're not going to start with the Y-incision?"

"Good guess." Jax caught his sarcastic reference. "If there's a problem with the embalming fluid later at the mortuary, let the record show we're in the clear."

He'd learned from an ME in Denver that it's important not to cut too far back on the shoulders when making the Y-incision because there's likely to be a problem with the embalming fluid: it can leak through the stitches if the incision is over the shoulders. Every step in this process worked to protect the dignity of the deceased.

"So, the skull is all that's left?" Chase asked.

"Pretty much."

Jax Taylor made a neat slice, ear-to-ear, over the top of the scalp and behind the ears. Chase waited to make sure there were no surprises with either the skull or the brain, nodded his thanks to Jax, and walked out of the room.

He stripped off his gear and considered what he needed to do next. When he arrived at the front desk he grabbed a phone book, found the number, and punched it into his cell phone. He shoved outside the building into a cool early evening, hoping he could get an appointment soon. The front door swung closed as the call went through.

"This is Chase Waters. I need to see you."

Chapter Twelve

Aspen Falls Police Department
Thursday, September 20

Back at the station, Chase checked his messages and then logged in to the departmental loop to check on any active cults in the area. This kind of mutilation was often connected with cults—for good reason. Cattle mutilations in Colorado went back for hundreds of years. Usually they were connected to kids practicing some kind of cult activity. Nothing showed up on the LEO site. He wasn't surprised. Maybe he could find something coming at it sideways. He turned to the internet. Google didn't exist simply for the idly curious. It had become a tool for law enforcement as well.

When he searched "cult," he got a whopping fourteen million hits. He revised his search to "cult mutilation." Twenty minutes later he'd printed out several documents related to cattle mutilation and a couple regarding something he hadn't thought of earlier. Covens.

Witches? Really? Chase made a call to the college. He learned about a registered coven on the campus, got the contact information, and made an appointment with their representative. What exactly made him think college

45

would be a good option for his daughters to continue their education?

Chase had to admit he got kind of a creepy feeling when the websites he'd pulled up had things like Satan worshippers as part of the FAQs. The normal-looking websites somehow gave credence to the whole concept and made him worry for the sake of the casual searcher. He made a mental note to block these from Angela and Stephanie's shared computer.

After he felt like he had a rudimentary knowledge, he decided to check the county law enforcement site for anything related to his cases.

He typed in "mutilation" and felt an electrical shock. Two cases popped up from the previous summer. Could this be right? Data errors happened in the best of circumstances—the output was only as accurate as the input—and he needed to confirm this information.

The cases were county, not city. Chase vaguely remembered hearing something about them last year, but he'd been working an exceptionally difficult case where one child had killed another child. At the time, he didn't have any room for a couple of county cases he couldn't possibly solve in his brain.

Chase had worked with the county sheriff's office more than once and he picked up his phone and called Jerry Coble. The sheriff had gone home for the day but the operator remained gracious and said she'd relay his name and contact information. Chase thanked her, reiterated the importance of the call, and assured her he would be available whenever Sheriff Coble had the time.

The autopsy reports from the two earlier DBs were laid open on Chase's desk. Information from his cult research lay next to them. It didn't feel right. He went back to the internet.

One posting caught his attention. Mutilated corpses were found in Mexico and determined to be ritualistic sacrifices to invoke blessings for a drug cartel. The religion of Santeria justified the carnage. All of his victims were Hispanic. Could there be a connection between them and a cartel?

The dark corners of the room seemed to grow darker, leeching the color from the rest of the space. Chase had dealt with the manifestation of evil often during his career. He could hope to do something about evil he could see and touch, but this unseen evil crawled up the scale to a hundred times worse. And he had no control over it.

He read a little more, then needed to stop. When he reached for some licorice the bag was empty.

Chase pressed a number on his phone and waited.

Bond's voice warmed his heart. "Hey, hon. What's up? You on your way home?"

He inhaled as if he could catch her familiar musky scent nearby. "Just needed to hear your voice. I'm going to be here another hour or so."

"You want me to let the kids wait up?"

He laughed. His wife knew that another hour or so could easily turn in to three or four or seven. "I'll be home by nine. Promise," he said. "Love you."

"I love you too."

Ready now to deal with more evil, Chase plugged Santeria into the search engine. There were a couple of postings associated with animal sacrifice and a lot of innuendo related to musicians and Hollywood celebrities. He clicked out of those sites. Innuendo would never count as evidence. Animal sacrifice did not connect beyond doubt to a mutilated human being.

The Mexican drug cartel angle had some possibilities, except for one thing. It did not match up at all with what he'd learned of Rachelle Benavides. It had been a long time since a civilian had been able to fool Chase. His gut told him that this young girl was not involved in drugs. For the moment at least, he'd give her the benefit of the doubt.

About to log out and head home for the night, his phone rang. What now?

"What the hell are you still doin' at work, Waters?" Sheriff Jerry Coble's voice forged a balm to his senses after dealing with cults and human sacrifice.

"Caught a case that's giving me fits, Sheriff. Not gonna sleep well until it's off the board."

He could almost see the man nod. "What do you need from the county?"

"Did you guys have a couple of incidents last summer of murders where the victims were mutilated?"

A brief silence on the line, then Coble cleared his throat. "Yep. We did."

"Did you solve them?"

"Nope, and my guess is you're not asking out of idle curiosity."

"I think we might have some connected cases in Aspen Falls."

"*Some*? As in, more than one?"

"Looks that way. What can you remember about them? Yours, I mean."

"Hell, Waters. I sent your lieutenant all of the particulars."

Chase decided the prudent course of action would be to avoid any discussion of Lieutenant Butz. "Were the victims Hispanic?"

"Yep. And missing what you might call vital parts."

"Did Dr. Taylor do the autopsies?" He couldn't imagine why she hadn't made a connection.

"Nope. Jax was off at some continuing ed classes or some conference or something," the sheriff said. "ME down in Denver took her place for about three weeks or so."

"Could you get me the paperwork?"

"I'll have it sent first thing when I get in the office tomorrow."

"Can you have it sent tonight?"

Chapter Thirteen

Aspen Falls Police Department
Friday, September 21

Chase strode into the meeting room with a half-dozen of The Coffee Pod's freshest muffins in one hand and three equally fresh coffees in the other. Daniel and Terri were already there.

The three of them worked well as a team. Someone had set up the whiteboards in front of the room, and Daniel stood in front of them, marker in hand. Chase smiled. Of the three detectives, Daniel had the most legible handwriting. Both Chase and Terri wrote so badly their notations were often difficult to read even when they knew what it was supposed to say.

"You look like hell." Terri leveled her gaze in his direction.

"Hey, I shaved." Chase peeled off a strip of tissue under his chin.

The notes he'd printed out before he went home last night sat on the table in front of the boards. They'd been read, and Daniel had already put up some column headers: DB #1 COUNTY, DB #2 COUNTY, DB #3

DUMPSTER, DB #4 HIKER, DB #5 BURIAL GROUNDS, MISSING: RACHELLE BENAVIDES, and MOTIVATION.

There were two solid vertical lines separating the missing girl from the others. Cops were among the most hopeful people Chase knew.

"Good job, Daniel," Chase said. "Except move #4 next to our missing. No mutilation like the others. May or may not be connected."

Daniel made the change, then began adding the detail from Chase's notes. Other than dates of discovery and autopsy results, there were precious few known facts. The hiker had the most. No ID, a wallet with seven dollars in cash and a photograph of a young woman. The back of the photograph had the name Maria, and the numbers 7/11. Presumably his wife, since the victim had also been wearing a cheap wedding band.

Chase told Daniel to add *Hispanic/Latino* under each name. Daniel added the word *illegal*.

"We don't know that they were here illegally, Daniel, and there's no doubt regarding the Benavides family's status," Chase said.

"I have a question," Terri said while Daniel corrected the board.

"Shoot."

"Why didn't we know about the two county homicides until now? It's not like Sheriff Coble to keep stuff to himself."

"Coble sent the information. It just didn't make it through the channels."

Daniel glanced up from his muffin, and arched an eyebrow. "Butz?"

"Yeah," Chase said.

Chase watched Daniel's lips compress into a hard line, but he didn't say a word about the ignorant racist attitudes of their lieutenant. Instead, the Hispanic detective reached for a marker and stood in front of the column titled MOTIVATION.

"Are you knuckle-draggers ready?" Daniel asked.

"We have shit for information," Terri said, staring at the board.

"Well then, we'll start with shit," Chase said.

The three detectives shot out a few possible ideas, then fell silent as they considered the list they'd come up with. The possibility of a serial killer seemed to top the list.

S/K WHO TARGETS HSPNC/LTNO S/K MEDICAL STUDENT W/A GRUDGE AGAINST HSPNC/LTNO ONE REAL MURDER BURIED BY KILLING OTHERS CULT

Whenever Chase read the shorthand for serial killer, "S/K" he always said "sicko" to himself. "We'll leave these up there for a while," Chase said, "but I don't think we're dealing with a textbook serial killer."

"Why not?" Terri asked.

"Couldn't tell you for sure, but it feels squirrely. For one, there's not enough time between some of the DBs. Most S/Ks have a little downtime before they need to kill again."

"But we've got a targeted group," Terri said.

"There could be a lot of explanations for why Hispanics seem to be the target." Chase thought about his visit with Ramona Benavides. "Illegals are not likely to go to the law—for any reason."

Terri's cell phone rang and she checked the Caller ID. "I've got to take this." She left the conference room and closed the door behind her.

Chase turned to Daniel. "Do you know what's going on with Terri?"

"Does anyone ever know what's going on with Terri?"

Chase shook his head. Terri Johnson won the prize for enigma in the department. A lot of cops had tried to date her. If she dated any of them—and Chase couldn't recall one name—they'd gotten to bat one time and not again. No one knew much of anything about her. She did her job and she did it well. You want more? Forget about it with Detective Johnson.

A new patrol officer walked into the meeting room. "We've got the witness—that homeless guy? Patrol found him about thirty minutes ago and brought him in. He's in the interview room."

Chase checked his watch. "Thanks. I'm on my way."

He turned to Daniel. "I'll follow up with the religion angle today. You and Terri go through Rachelle's cell phone records. Track down every number. We're looking for names that don't belong. Finish checking out her computer and copy as much of the profile pages as possible for all of her social network contacts. Call me if you find anything significant. Otherwise, we'll meet back here at five-fifteen."

Chapter Fourteen

Aspen Falls Police Department
Friday, September 21

Before walking in to the interview room, Chase took a look at his only witness through the open door. If these cases were connected, which his gut told him they were, then their best piece of evidence at this point rested on notoriously unreliable eyewitness testimony. Their conviction bank sank further by virtue of the condition of the twitching doper in the other room.

Chase glanced down at the paperwork from patrol. Stephen Hamilton, aka Skizzers, sat in the interview room. The scruffy man, dressed in filthy jeans and what looked like four sweatshirts, fidgeted. He picked at invisible bits on the table with his fingers, kicked his crossed legs and shook his long blond-gray hair away from his face. He bounced one shoulder and then the other into the air, all the while blinking nonstop and then staring at something only he could see in an upper corner of the room. All in the space of seven seconds.

Shit.

Chase entered the interview room and introduced himself, reaching out a hand to the homeless man.

Stephen "Skizzers" Hamilton froze, visibly processing what had happened and what an appropriate response might be. After some hesitation, he thrust out one of his thin hands. Pride infused his face at the accomplishment.

Shit.

Chase decided to begin with something simple. "Where were you last night, Skizzers? We looked for you and couldn't find you."

"Gandalf needed me."

"Excuse me?"

"Please, 'tective. You know, Gandalf. I consult with him from time to time."

Lord of the Rings. Shit.

"Plus, the vampires were looking for me. I needed to disappear."

Twenty minutes and a bowl of dry cornflakes later, Chase knew Skizzers' account would never in a million years hold up in court.

"Skizzers, think carefully. Did either of the two men you saw at the dumpster the night before last see you?" Their eyewitness, their one link to what happened the night before last, shook his head.

"Nope. They looked in my direction." A tiny grin played on his lips then disappeared. "Too bad for them. I had already cloaked myself."

Skizzers might be certain of his safety but the eyes of Stephen Hamilton were afraid.

Even though Skizzers' value to this investigation couldn't be lower, Chase refused to risk him getting killed. Technically, Chase wouldn't be questioned if he bounced Skizzers back to the streets and let him take his chances. Morally, Chase couldn't let that happen. "Is there someone you can stay with for a while? Some place outside of Aspen Falls?"

The homeless man sat in silence.

"Anyone?"

"I have a sister in Basalt."

"Do you have a number for her?" Just outside of Aspen, Basalt sounded perfect. In the event Chase needed to get to Skizzers, accessibility would not be prohibitive.

"Yeah, but I'll need a ride."

"No problem."

"Can I get a hamburger on the way?"

Chapter Fifteen

Aspen Falls Community Church
Friday, September 21

Chase had arranged to meet Ed Taylor at the church's outreach coffee shop. Pastor Taylor's hours were as bad as his and Chase was lucky to get an appointment this fast. Especially considering Chase hadn't been to church in months.

Chase's shoulders fell as he set the cup of coffee back down on the table. "You're telling me there are no cults in Aspen Falls." He'd really hoped for some bit of information that would lead him to the killer or killers—who didn't show any sign of stopping any time soon. He didn't like the idea of cults in Aspen Falls. He liked the idea of cults that killed even less. But even less than that? He hated not being able to pull this case together and bring the killers to justice.

"Not saying that at all. What I am saying is that unless cult activity is impacting someone who attends our church, I may not have any reason to know of their existence. And right now there is no one I know who is in that kind of trouble. That doesn't mean cults aren't out there. In fact, I'd be surprised to find out there aren't any."

"Why would that surprise you?"

"Do you believe in heaven?"

"From time to time."

Taylor laughed. "I hear what you're saying."

"What does that have to do with cults?"

"In heaven," Taylor said, "evil does not exist. It does not exist *at all*. But here on earth? It's a free-for-all for our souls, and to some, evil is an easier and more attractive way to walk. In the end those people will discover there's a price to pay. Only a fool would believe he lives in a world—or a country, or a neighborhood—without cults or other such things."

"Sounds like you're saying I should just look around, and my eyes will be opened."

"You're a detective. Your eyes have already been opened to a lot of terrible dark corners of this world and you've witnessed the physical results. What I'm saying is that just as there are wonderful things we can't see or touch while on this earth, there are evil things we can't see or touch. The cults are here, Chase. If you look for them you'll find them."

"Can you tell me where to begin?"

"Check out the college. Young people are often ill-prepared when they're away from home for the first time." Taylor looked thoughtful. "It's fertile ground."

"College kids and cults. Great. Something more for me to worry about with my own kids."

"Good luck to you, Chase."

When the two men shook hands, Chase felt the standard clasp morph into a grip. "Will I see you join Bond and your daughters at church this week? I think you'd find it helpful."

Not any time soon. "I'll have to see how this case goes."

Chase got back in the car, powered up his tablet, and found the contact information he'd noted for the witch's coven on campus. A place to start. He called the number and made an appointment with the High Priest.

Chapter Sixteen

Cobalt Mountain Drug Store
Friday, September 21

Stephanie sat in the car, mad. She felt her shoulders tense all up and pinch her neck. She didn't like all these changes. Not one bit. Just because Angela was older didn't make Angela right. And no one bothered to ask *her* how she felt about not having balloons anymore for David's birthday party.

Mommy had smiled real big when Angela said she thought the balloons might be bad for birds and things. Maybe even fish if a balloon got in the water. Like that could happen. Stephanie loved the bright balloons and she knew David did too.

When Mommy decided she wanted to open an antique store everything went poopy, and now Mommy didn't have time for her. Not for anything. If she could cuss without getting in trouble, she would. What was Mommy thinking?

And now this whole balloon thing.

We're supposed to write something personal to send to David? Burn the paper? Hel-loo. Isn't that gonna be bad for the air?

No one had bothered to ask her what she thought about all these changes.

In the store, Stephanie had decided to put her foot down like that lady duck did on the cartoon last Saturday. She stamped her foot. Again. Louder. "You guys are being pucky, and I don't want to do this anymore."

It didn't work. So Stephanie crossed her arms. In her head she asked them in a nice voice to stop but maybe outside of her head she yelled it a little. That's what she must have done. But if they'd been paying attention to her... if they had asked her what she thought about things... then she wouldn't have had to be so loud.

"Stephanie Marie Waters." Uh-oh. Her full name. Mom's mad voice.

Her mom handed her the car keys. "You march out to the car right this minute and think about your behavior."

Stephanie wanted to tell her mom her behavior was just fine. It was her mom's behavior that needed fixed. But she figured maybe she should save that for later.

She stared her mother in the eye, held her hands out, which were holding the special paper to write their special messages on, and opened her fingers wide. The paper plopped to the floor. Stephanie wished it would have hit louder and thought about picking it up to drop it again, but the look on her mom's face stopped her.

Fine. She was done with them. They were all just too stupid.

Three minutes later, sitting in the back seat of the car, Stephanie started feeling sorry about yelling in the middle of the store. Maybe she shouldn't have done that. Or dropped the paper for David's birthday on the floor. Now she felt bad. But not in the mad way, in the sad way. She decided to go say she was sorry. Get it over with.

Back inside the store Stephanie searched for her mom. As she looked around, she saw two men watching her mom and Angela like they knew them. Did they? One man held a phone to his ear and kept looking at the ground while he talked into it, then back up to her mom and her sister. The other one bounced on his feet like a cartoon person. Like someone who wanted to say something but couldn't. Maybe he had to pee.

Did her family know these men? Probably. Or else why would they be so interested?

Stephanie started walking toward them to say hi when she saw her mom grab a great big balloon that said "HAPPY BIRTHDAY" and move to the checkout lane.

Yes! A balloon!

Stephanie ran over to her mother and Angela, glad that she had felt bad before she saw the balloon. She didn't know why, but she knew that was better than not feeling bad about yelling and stuff and still getting a balloon.

"I'm sorry, Mommy."

"We'll talk a little more about your behavior when we get home."

She had apologized but sometimes her parents wanted to talk about things more. Fine with her. Especially since they had a balloon.

"We won't be releasing this balloon, Stephanie. But after the family celebration you can keep it in your room if you'd like."

"Really? Just for me? I mean—for David, then for me?"

"We're still going to talk when we get home."

"Okay. But I really am sorry."

Her mom paid for their purchases and they walked to the car. Stephanie carried the balloon very careful to protect it as she got in the back seat. Belted in, she looked toward the store and saw the two men again.

"Mommy, do those men know us?" Stephanie asked.

"What men, honey?"

Stephanie pointed while her mother started the car. From the tiny slice of her mommy she could see in the rearview mirror, she saw her mom stare. And she thought maybe her mommy's hands shook a little bit before they gripped the wheel.

Chapter Seventeen

Aspen Falls Mountain College
Friday, September 21

The warmer than usual day shocked Chase's system. He pulled his shirt away from his body, the idea of a shower sounding like a game plan. He looked up at the clear sky and hoped for a late afternoon rain. Unlikely. A group of racers zipped passed him on their bicycles, and he enjoyed the breeze they stirred up.

Chase hadn't found one thing in the last couple of hours that amounted to a hill of spent shells. Part of it might be the fact that some of the professors at Aspen Falls Mountain College were younger than he was. He not only stood out as a cop, he stood out as old. But this old cop knew elimination was part of the investigation process, and he really wanted to eliminate some possible scenarios this afternoon.

He had five minutes before his meeting at the Student Union with John Bohnert, High Priest for the coven on campus. It was easier to walk than drive and hunt up another parking spot, so Chase picked up his pace and hustled to the appointment.

Chase loved this campus. Students were casual and a lot more ethnically diverse than you'd expect at a remote mountain college in Colorado. As he hurried along, he watched as students gathered together, the sun dappled by shade from the mature trees on the campus. A few kids tossed a Frisbee around. The more things change, the more they stay the same.

He smelled fresh popcorn. The AFMC Union, a hundred and eighty degrees from the few tables and vending machines Chase remembered at his own alma mater, included a movie theater, bookstore, art gallery, two types of dining, a game room, study areas, and meeting rooms. New, modern, and filled with the chatter and laughter of young people, it sure didn't seem like a witch hangout. And that scared him.

Bohnert had suggested they meet in the art gallery on the second floor. Quiet, uncrowded, it was a place to size one another up without any prying eyes from Bohnert's rather private group. From there they could go to the retail dining area on the first floor.

Chase stepped onto the second floor and a rush of creativity assaulted him. Powerful artwork pulled him, demanded his attention. This quality from students? He meandered between mediums, enthralled at what he saw. Sculptures beyond his imagination, watercolors and oils, mixed media and even quilts. *Quilts*?

"Detective Waters?"

He spun. A regular-looking kid approached him. A kid who looked like any number of Angela's friends, only older. Clean-cut, a T-shirt emblazoned with the school mascot, and a backpack loaded with what Chase assumed were books. Nothing about this good-looking young man screamed *witch*. Did he have the right guy?

"John Bohnert?"

65

Bohnert nodded and lead the detective back to the staircase where he began the descent. "We quit wearing black pointy hats years ago. Funny thing, when we got rid of those, our warts magically disappeared."

Chase might not have liked the idea of witchcraft, and he might not have liked this guy's flip attitude, but he had a few questions he needed answers to. He'd play the humble role. "I'm sorry."

"Don't blame yourself, Detective. We deal with it all the time."

Settled in a somewhat private table in one of the restaurant areas with soft drinks and fries in front of them, the young man glared at Chase.

"I agreed to meet with you for one reason only. To impress upon you that covens are not cults. We don't hurt animals or people, and to be considered a cult is patently ridiculous, not to mention offensive."

"Fair enough." Chase took a sip of his drink. Not the time to discuss philosophical issues and what may or may not cause harm. He needed information. "Do you know of any cults on the campus that might harm animals or people?"

A group of kids walked passed them—a couple of them bounced off the edge of their table like pinballs—and Chase watched Bohnert for a reaction. He seemed to will himself to be calm. Closed eyes, a deep breath. Chase suspected anger management classes but said nothing.

Bohnert put his elbows on the table and laced his fingers. "Detective Waters, even a benign group such as a witches' coven must keep a low profile to keep our members safe. Not only from physical threat but from emotional and professional threat as well."

Chase figured that *parental threat* had to factor in there somewhere but he continued to hold his tongue.

"Can you imagine the lengths a group of people who actually caused harm to others would go to in order to remain private?"

"I admit, Mr. Bohnert, that I am ignorant of much of your practices and beliefs, and I appreciate the time you're taking to share some of it with me. However, you or your members are much more likely to have a fix on a possible cult than I am, wouldn't you agree?"

The self-assured college kid's right eye twitched and Chase saw a flicker of uncertainty shadow his face. "I suppose that might be true."

Chase handed him his card. "If you hear any whisper of cult activity, particularly if it involves any kind of sacrifice or mutilation, please contact me. Day or night."

He slipped Chase's card in a pocket without looking at it.

"May I ask another question?"

"I'm not stopping you," Bohnert said.

"Do your parents know what you're involved in?"

Bohnert went back to silent mode and Chase wondered if he'd lost him as a resource.

"My parents are dead.

Chapter Eighteen

The Waters Home
Friday, September 21

Chase took the piece of paper Bond handed him and glanced at the kitchen table where Angela and Stephanie were busy writing their private messages to David. Stephanie's apparently required crayons. He looked back at his wife.

Balloons were so much simpler.

"Have you written yours yet?" Chase asked. Maybe he could just sign his name to whatever Bond had come up with.

She nodded toward the countertop where Chase saw a sealed envelope. *Damn.*

"Why don't you go to your study and take a few minutes?"

Chase cleared his throat. "Uh... yeah, sounds good."

He felt as if he were walking through a dimly lit tunnel. His study loomed both familiar and foreign. On one hand Chase applauded his family's social conscience. On the other hand he wondered exactly how bad a few balloons could be.

He sat at his desk and waited. What the hell was he supposed to write on this piece of paper?

Images of his son floated into his mind. David calling him "Dada" for the first time and reaching chubby arms out to be held. First steps when he would fall into Bond's arms, and then fall into his—and oh, the laughter when he did. The night his normal spit-ups took on a wild element, he hit a raging fever, and they sat in the ER afraid they might lose him. T-ball and two-wheelers.

David. Working with him on the roadster. Listening to jazz together and beginning to talk about girls.

His son.

And all too soon, the day they lost him. Long QT Syndrome. A whacked-out electrical function in his heart. Inherited. A complete surprise to both of them. Chase would never forget that day. All the paperwork at the hospital. All the things he and Bond had to sign while their son lay dying. The consent forms for tests and more tests and finally to discontinue life support, when all he wanted to do was take his son and run. The terrible finality of their situation when they agreed to donate David's organs. He and Bond signing that last authorization.

Guilt and recrimination came later—blame too. And finally, after a long time, understanding and acceptance came because they had no other choice. If they were to survive intact as a family, they had to figure out a way to get through each day.

What could he write on this paper that would even come close to the loss? What would David want to hear? A tear fell on the paper before Chase even knew his eyes had filled.

He swiped the sheet and then his face. Picked up a pen and wrote three words:

I love you.

Chase folded the paper, but didn't move to rejoin the rest of his family. Suddenly he wanted to spend a little more time with David.

A few minutes later Chase heard a soft knock at his door.

"Are you ready?" Bond asked. "Do you need a little more time? The girls are getting anxious."

I'm never ready for this, Chase thought. How could a person ever be ready for this? Bond had tried so hard, come so far from those first dark days. He didn't want to say anything to drag her back down.

The four of them sat outside in front of the stone fire-pit, nobody saying anything. Each burned their message to David, beginning with Stephanie and ending with Chase. Stephanie read hers aloud, word by word. Angela, tears streaming down her face, choked out a happy birthday sentiment to her brother—one of the rare times their dramatic daughter didn't have a lot of words. Or drama.

Chase watched as his wife—the mother of his children—knelt before the fire pit. She closed her eyes, then focused her attention on each of them as she spoke.

"David Robert Waters, we love you. We mourn you. We mark you in our hearts today. You enriched our lives, and our love for you will keep you alive forever. Each of our lives will continue with grace and optimism, richer because you were, and are, a part of them. We will live strong and we will live fully, not only to honor our own lives, but to honor yours."

Chase moved to his wife, added his envelope to the fire, and held her close.

Later, as he got in his car to go back to the station, Bond stopped him.

"Something you should know."

He'd been married to a cop's wife long enough to know this could be important. He waited.

"I think someone was watching us when we were at the store," Bond said.

Chapter Nineteen

Aspen Falls Police Department
Friday, September 21

Daniel and Terri were already in the meeting room when Chase walked in later that afternoon, the murder board standing where they'd left it the last time they'd been together. Had it been only this morning?

"Sorry I'm late. What do you guys have?" Chase was frustrated beyond endurance by the amount of information he didn't have. Hopefully his team had experienced a better day.

"Not much on either her cell phone or her social network pages," Terri said. "But I did use them to reconstruct a calendar of sorts over the last thirty days."

"Good. We'll get to that," Chase said. "Daniel, were you able to get anything else off her computer?"

"She's so clean she's invisible. Other than her social network pages and sites related to either economics or social work, she only spent significant time on one of those ask-a-doctor sites."

"Was it before August fifteenth?" Terri asked.

Daniel checked his notes. "Nope. After. August twenty-ninth."

Terri shook her head. "That's weird. What I could piece together is that the last month has been completely normal except for a visit to Emergency on the fifteenth of August. She said she either had a cold or the flu."

"She went to Emergency for the flu?" Chase sipped some bitter coffee and made a face. "No wonder medical costs are so high."

"Uninsured people use the emergency rooms in hospitals like doctor's offices. They don't have a choice," Terri said.

"Some do and some don't," Daniel said. "Illegals are the real abusers of our system. They shouldn't even be here."

"Are you saying they have a choice?" Terri asked.

"Damn right. They chose to be here illegally. They can choose to go back where they came from. Leave our resources to people who have a right to them. To people who actually pay for them."

"Okay guys," Chase said. "We're getting off track. Can you tell us what pages she specifically went to on that ask-a-doctor site?"

"She searched all over the place but most of her time seemed to be spent on the pages for kidney function and vaginal infections," Daniel said. "Nothing useful." He looked at Chase. "What did you find?"

"Not as much as you did. I'm thinking cults are not the answer but if you want to join a coven, I have a contact."

All three detectives refocused on the murder board.

"I have an idea," Terri said.

"Go."

"If our victims aren't being eviscerated for a cult, there must be another reason."

Silence, then a trio of voices said, "Money."

"That has potential, Terri," Chase smiled. "It explains why the bodies were dumped."

Daniel nodded. "I'm supposed to be the money guy and it never occurred to me."

Chase looked at the board. "We need to make some connections between black market organs and the Hispanic community."

A knock at the door and Chief Whitman entered the room.

"We've found Rachelle Benavides." He didn't smile when he said it. "Actually, *we* didn't find her."

Chase's chest tightened. He swallowed.

"Elizabeth Benavides found the corpse of her mutilated sister fifteen minutes ago." The chief's voice came across tight and measured. His gaze pinned Chase. "Elizabeth Benavides is downstairs and wants to see you. See her and then fix this."

Damn! Chase wanted to get to the scene. See for himself. Check around for possible witnesses.

"Where did Elizabeth find her sister?" Chase asked.

"Inside an abandoned mine." The chief handed a slip of paper to him with directions.

Chase nodded toward Daniel and Terri. "You two head out now." Daniel reached for the paper. "Hold the scene for me. I'll be there as soon as I talk to Ms. Benavides."

Chapter Twenty

Aspen Falls Police Department
Friday, September 21

Chase prepared himself to handle whatever he found when he walked into the room. Family members—loved ones—could respond in bizarre ways under this kind of stress. His first impression was that Elizabeth Benavides's eyes were red and swollen, and her hair was disheveled. She looked small and sad. But when he walked toward her she stood, hands on hips, and watched him walk toward her. She looked like she was accusing him. Daring him.

"I'm sorry, Ms. Benavides. We'll do everything we can to find your sister's murderer."

"That's not good enough."

"I understand how you—"

"You understand nothing."

Chase pulled out his notebook. "I know you've already given your statement, but do you feel up to telling me what happened?"

"That's why I'm here, Detective."

Elizabeth Benavides sat down, back straight, hands folded in her lap. "I got a call on my cell phone. A man told me I could find my sister at the old abandoned silver mine on the west side of town. Actually, the asshole called it "Spic Town."

She fell silent and Chase gave her time to collect her thoughts. Elizabeth began to massage her thumbs, took a breath and continued, "When I arrived my cell phone rang again. Same guy. He said I would find myself in a similar position if I continued to talk to the police."

Elizabeth closed her eyes. "That's when I saw her, Detective. Rachelle . . . she was lying on her side, her back to me. She didn't move. The nude body of my sister. I ran to her to save her. To bring her back to me. But before I even got close I knew . . ." Tears ran unstopped down her face and fell into her lap. Elizabeth didn't seem to notice.

The young woman took a great breath. Exhaled. "And then I saw her. Oh, God. I saw the butchered body of my baby sister."

"I'm so sorry, Miss Benavides."

The young woman nodded, opened her eyes and slapped the tears off her face. "Someone murdered my sister. He thinks he can threaten me and scare me off. *Mierda!* He thinks he will control me as easily as he controls my neighbors. He is a *culero*. That asshole picked the wrong *chicana* to murder."

"You're very brave."

"I'm not brave. I'm *enojada*. An angry person doesn't need bravery."

"I promise I'll keep you updated during the investigation," Chase said.

"As I said before, that's not good enough."

Uh-oh. "What is it you would like me to do?"

"I want to be involved in the investigation."

"Ms. Benavides—"

"Elizabeth."

"This is not a game. There are dangers and we're equipped to deal with those dangers. You need to let us do our job."

"With your supervision or without it, I'm going after the son-of-a-bitch who killed my sister. I just thought maybe you could figure out a way to use me."

"Okay, I appreciate your position. I'll run your request by the chief of police. It will be up to him." Give her some space and maybe she would see reason. "Go home for now. I'm heading out to the scene and you don't need to be there again."

"Wrong. I'm coming. I figure you can either have a hope of controlling me or you can count on a rogue investigator out there who could potentially mess everything up for you."

"Messing things up for us messes them up for you as well."

"Not necessarily. I don't operate under your constraints."

Chase felt the familiar tension building in his neck and shoulders. There wasn't anything routine about the murder of Rachelle Benavides. And her sister had significantly upped the ante.

"Ms. Benavides—Elizabeth—you need to back off and let us do what we're trained to do."

"Detective, I'll back off and let you do what you're trained to do whenever I see you doing something I can't. But in the meantime, I can get information for you from my community you're unlikely to get from any other source. I can bring you things from Rachelle's experience. Do you get that? Without me you may as well send in RoboCop—one that only speaks Russian."

Chase's chest constricted. Punching someone in the face would help. *She's not even thirty. She makes a lot of good points, but hell. She's a civilian.* His instinct wanted him to tie her to the very chair she sat in and make her sit there until they solved this case. Somehow he knew—experience maybe?—attorneys would get involved and make a huge mess of his intentions. He had to kick his paternal attitude to the curb.

He didn't want her but he needed her. He considered his options and made a decision.

Chase walked to the door. "Well, come on then. I don't have all night."

At least this way he'd be in control.

Chapter Twenty-One

Sloan Enterprises
Friday, September 21

Edward Sloan sat at his desk. The elegant-looking man sitting across the expanse bothered him but he couldn't say why. Edward just knew he was disgusted by him. Repulsed.

In the long run though, it didn't matter. Edward cleared his throat. "Name your price."

Long, pale fingers steepled and paused, elbows resting on the arms of the chair. Edward could see the man's crossed knee, draped and situated so as not to create a wrinkle in his hand-tailored suit. Edward Sloan saw men every day who needed to make themselves appear better than the next man. One-upmanship. He had always refused to have any dealings with those men. It irked him that this time he didn't have a choice.

"We have already begun the process on your behalf. Up until now we've used our own resources, gratis. To continue could be quite expensive." The smooth delivery matched up well with the slippery shallowness Edward sensed in the man. Liquid. Like an oil slick on water.

"Name it." Anything to save his wife. Hell, saving Diana would save him. Two for the price of one.

"Mr. Sloan, you understand that this is somewhat beyond our normal scope of operation." The man brought his hands down and folded them in his lap. "That is not to say we don't have the means to accomplish the task. But there are additional risks involved."

Edward Sloan pulled himself tight against the desk and leaned forward. "I'm not in a position to negotiate. And *you* must understand, I will not be putting all of my faith in you. I will continue exploring the other areas available to me—and my money."

"I would do the same in your position. I assume that means you will continue seeking assistance overseas?"

"That, and within certain quasi-legal organizations in this country."

"You must love your wife very much."

Edward swallowed the bile in his throat. "That's the first thing you've said with which I don't have a problem."

The visitor pulled a card from his inside pocket. "These are the wiring instructions for my offshore account. I have noted the amount to be deposited. Once we have acquired the item you have stipulated, you will deposit a matching sum before we relinquish it." He handed the card to Edward.

"That's a lot of money."

"It is. But then I was under the impression that your wife's life was priceless."

Alone after his visitor left, Edward Sloan picked up the phone.

"Get my banker on the line."

Chapter Twenty-Two

Honey Silver Mine
Friday, September 21

Chase pulled up his SUV and turned off the ignition. Maintenance crews were setting up Klieg lights and hooking them up to a generator as the sun was about to set. Elizabeth Benavides sat in the passenger seat, not moving.

"You can wait here if you'd like." *Please wait here. Don't make me have to think of anything other than the scene.*

She shoved the door open and pulled herself from the vehicle. She turned to look him in the eyes, daring him to question her strength or purpose or right to be there.

"Fine. Then stay behind me. Don't move or do anything unless I tell you." He skewered her with a look. "Are we on the same page?"

Elizabeth nodded.

As Chase began to walk to where he could see Jax at work, Akila Copeland approached him.

"Hey, Chase. We've got to stop meeting like this."

"If only." He looked at the young CSI. "Leaving already?"

"This wasn't the crime scene. Not much for me to find. Next time can you get me an actual crime scene to investigate?

"I'll keep that in mind."

Chase strode to the taped-off area and walked through. Terri was the closest of his crew to the body, resting on her haunches and observing while Dr. Taylor checked various details and made notes, her camera clicking away at intervals.

Daniel was talking to a patrol officer, animated and pointing down the road. When Daniel saw Chase he signaled a stop with his hand, ended the conversation, and approached Chase.

The young detective shook his head. "The Daily is all over this one. I fielded one call and have let three others go to voicemail. We need to control the perimeter." The Aspen Falls Daily might be a small-town paper but they didn't miss much. Most of their staff, seasoned on larger city papers, chose to live in Aspen Falls because of the lifestyle. They could kick back when they wanted to, hit the slopes to catch the freshest powder, but could also exercise their olfactory muscles to sniff out prize-winning stories.

Chase called the patrol sergeant and requested two more uniforms even though this was obviously not the murder scene. Even if the press got every fact right, the rumors and speculation would fly, and their already difficult case would get that much harder. Information containment was as important as anything they'd done so far on this case. Which wasn't much. Time enough for press releases when they had something to say.

"What else do we have?"

Daniel hesitated, peering at the sullen young woman standing behind Chase.

Chase reminded Daniel who Elizabeth was with an abruptness that invited no questions. "Now, Detective. Tell me. What do we have?"

"Not the murder scene. Hispanic female, late teens or early twenties—"

"Seventeen," Elizabeth said. "Rachelle was seventeen."

Daniel turned to Chase, hesitating. The rest of what Daniel had to say would not be pretty, especially for a family member to hear. Chase nodded for him to continue.

"Her lungs, heart and both kidneys have been surgically removed."

Elizabeth sucked in a breath and grasped Chase's arm.

"Do we have a time of death?" Chase asked.

"Doc says it's been a day. No more than two. She said she'd have a better idea after she runs some more tests."

Elizabeth Benavides had shown up in his office on Wednesday. Probably about the same time her sister's body was being harvested for whatever could be sold on the black market.

Sometimes life sucked.

"I want you and Elizabeth to dig for some answers in the Hispanic community," Chase said. "That's where we'll begin to get a handle on what's going on in this town."

"Wait. She's a civilian—"

"That's right. She is. She's also a civilian who has access we don't." Chase watched Daniel. "And you'll be there to protect her."

"I don't know anything about that part of town."

"I know that, but you're the closest we've got. Use her connections, Daniel. Pretend you belong. Go tomorrow during the day. You should catch a lot of people home on a Saturday."

Chase walked over to where Terri was still taking notes with Dr. Taylor.

"Hey, Doc."

"Detective."

Chase stood over the lifeless body of Rachelle Benavides. The familiar twist in his gut made him remember the personal side of murder. The family's loss. The life cut short by violence. He'd never met Rachelle Benavides but he'd come to respect her in the few hours he'd spent on her case. He vowed to find her killer or killers.

He processed the nude body, caked blood on the café-au-lait skin—especially around the slice along her sternum—and the tiny diamond stud earrings in her ears. Seventeen. Not much older than Angela. *Damn it.*

"What's your initial impression?" Chase asked.

"This girl has had everything removed. All of the major organs. Heart, lungs, kidneys. All surgically excised." Jax Taylor paled. "If this is a doctor, I want his head on a platter. I want to be doing *his* autopsy."

"You don't think this could just be the work of a competent hunter? Someone used to dressing game?"

"No way. This person has been to medical school. I'm actually pretty in awe of his—or her—technique."

"I need the results as soon as you can get them. Call me if you find anything that might be important."

Terri Johnson stood up. "I think it's time we see what my contacts in the ER at Aspen Falls Memorial might be able to tell us."

"Funny you should mention that. I was thinking the same thing."

It was going to be a long night. Again.

Chapter Twenty-Three

Aspen Falls Memorial Hospital
Friday, September 21

The hospital emergency room seemed unnaturally quiet, but Chase bet it wouldn't be that way much longer. Friday night often brought out the worst in people who had worked hard all week and wanted to blow off steam. And for some reason the college kids seemed to prefer Aspen Falls Memorial to the campus infirmary.

Leslie James, the ER doctor on duty, looked up as they approached the desk. "Unless our communication system has crashed, you're not here on a new case." James moved around the desk to greet the detectives.

The ER doctor sported an easy-care haircut and what Chase thought Bond would call an adorable smile. Terri normally worked all of the sexual assault and rape cases, and Chase could tell the two women had developed a friendship over the years. A friendship forged no doubt by mutual respect for jobs where each woman saw a lot, one under street lights and the other under fluorescents.

Terri gave a nod toward Chase to include him in the conversation. "We're here more as students at the moment." She made the introductions. "What can you tell us about organ donation?"

Leslie James answered their questions at length. To her professional credit, she didn't ask them why they were standing in her ER, probing into a very specific area. Chase was especially impressed to discover that some things, like skin, could be stored for a period of time, but anything that required a beating heart and blood flow needed to be harvested and transplanted as soon as possible.

He pushed thoughts of his son away.

Chase was reminded that the process of pairing a donor to a recipient hinged on blood samples. Blood type matching, tissue matching and cross matching were all done via blood tests.

He thought of all of those painful legalities when David died—form upon form they had to sign. His memories shoved back. There was no pushing these thoughts away. He needed to acknowledge them and move on. Two years ago he had not wanted any more information than absolutely necessary for that moment. That moment—the pain—was big enough. It had taken over his world. He hadn't wanted to know the process.

And blood samples in a hospital would never raise a red flag. But maybe blood being drawn without a good purpose would. Chase didn't think his kids had ever had their blood drawn at the doctor's office when they'd gone in for colds or the flu. And Rachelle Benavides had complained about having flu symptoms on her social networking pages. Maybe the ER employed a different protocol.

"Is there any reason for a blood sample to be drawn when a patient comes in with cold or flu symptoms?" Chase asked.

"None," Leslie James said. "Viral illnesses would never require a blood test unless there were other indications, and most colds and flu are viral."

Terri flipped a page in her notebook. "Do you keep records of patients whose blood has been tested?"

"We do."

"Can you see if you did a blood test on one of them?"

"Terri, you know I can. But I can't give you that information without a warrant."

"And here I am, hoping for the entire list of names," Chase said. Chase glanced at the faces of the two women hoping they'd gotten his attempt at humor. He received confirmation in two identical rolls of eyes.

Terri looked at her friend. "She's dead."

"Doesn't matter. Still need a warrant. We have really picky attorneys."

Crap. Fatigue and frustration were wearing away Chase's patience. "Let's see what your attorneys think when the hospital is named as complicit in both previous and subsequent deaths related to our investigation," Chase said.

For the first time frigid air fogged the camaraderie. The humorous repartee was history.

"What are you saying, Detective?" Leslie James asked.

"I'm saying that someone should contact us first thing in the morning. We have a minimum of three deaths, possibly more, that could be linked to this hospital. I'm sure the public would appreciate a cooperative position as opposed to one that implies a cover-up."

"Detective Waters, I have no doubt you'll hear from someone tomorrow morning."

Out in the parking lot Terri squared her shoulders. "Did you have to be such a prick?"

"Look Terri, sometimes it takes a prick to shake up the waters, excuse the pun. The more the good guys know what we're looking for, the harder it is for the bad guys to hide."

"I just don't want my relationships jeopardized. I'll need them again, you know."

"I do know."

"You're planning on going public?"

"Not for as long as I can help it. Get a warrant. I want to see those records."

Chapter Twenty-Four

The Madrigal Home
Friday, September 21

Efraín set the book next to him on his bed. The shot the physician's assistant had given him yesterday at the hospital had worked wonders for his flu symptoms. He'd be able to work tomorrow and get back to his classes on Monday.

Efraín's parents were in the kitchen, and he could picture their ritual after-dinner coffee cups on the old scarred table. The dishes from his family's dinner would have been long since washed, dried and put away. The paper-thin walls of the small home made it seem as if Efraín sat at the table with them.

"*Dios!* How are we going to pay for the truck repairs, Armando?" His mother insisted they speak in English but she sometimes slipped into Spanish when something upset her. And money always upset her.

"We will find a way," his father said.

His father always said that. And somehow, for as long as Efraín could remember, they always had found a way. He had never been hungry. Never not had a roof over his head. That was way more than he could say for a lot of other people.

At sixteen he understood fully the things that separated him from everyone else in this small town, in this *country*, and the things that would forever make him different. It didn't matter that he placed in the top five percent of his class at Aspen Falls. It didn't matter that he had become a trusted and valued employee at Cobalt Mountain Books even though he had only worked part-time there for four months. It didn't matter that he had a dream—to be a writer. Nothing mattered in the end—except for where he came from.

His parents had tried desperately to get across the border from Mexico when his mother was pregnant with him. They'd been turned back—or scared back—three times before they finally found a way into the US. But they never made it to a hospital where he could get a legitimate birth certificate.

Efraín Tomás Hanks Madrigal met this world in a cattle shelter in the middle of nowhere. His parents told him he was a "legitimate American," but with no paper to prove it, he'd always been just another wetback from Mexico. His three siblings, two more boys and a girl to wrap things up, had all been born in Aspen Falls Memorial. *They were legal-legal.*

His name fit. The Spanish form of the Hebrew name Efrayim, Efraín meant "double-land" or "twin-land."

He didn't belong anywhere.

"Maybe we won't find a way this time, *mi esposo*." His mother's voice shook. "With your hours not being regular right now and my Aspen winter ladies still in their summer homes, we can barely pay our rent."

His mother's outlook relied on the practical while his father's leaned more to the spiritual.

"Confía en Dios." The soft words of his father, "Trust in God," both gratified and irked Efraín.

At some point didn't a man need to take control? Be responsible?

Chapter Twenty-Five

Aspen Falls Memorial Hospital, ICU
Friday, September 21

The woman had come to hate the soft lighting in her husband's hospital room, the jazz playing low because that's what he enjoyed, the still air that surrounded him. Rather than a kind of sexy background to their lives, these things signified sickness. Death. Helplessness. These things meant she waited for something that might never happen.

Waited for someone else to die.

They'd had no match through living donors and she hated this vulture she'd become. Listening to the police scanner for calls that might mean she and her husband would grow old together as they'd planned. A car accident. A fall. Even some kind of shoot-out. All they needed was one good kidney.

She had come to terms with the idea that violence might bring her peace. Even though she hated herself a little more every time she looked in a mirror, she had come to terms with being a scavenger. *You do what you have to do.*

She stood outside the door that would open to her own private hell and sucked in deep breaths. Somehow the pain-infused air of the hallway tasted better than the air in the room. The hallway held the pain of *other* people. The room held her own.

She shot up a prayer for strength and plastered on a smile because she loved him so much. She pulled open the door and walked in.

Chapter Twenty-Six

Aspen Falls' Hispanic Neighborhood
Saturday, September 22nd

Daniel Murillo just wanted this morning to be over. To get through the rest of the day, get out of this neighborhood, leave these people and their lives behind. It wasn't that he had abandoned his Hispanic heritage. Not at all. It was that he felt his Hispanic heritage had abandoned him.

Elizabeth Benavides walked at his side, more comfortable with these surroundings than he would ever be—or would ever want to be. He couldn't help but appreciate the beauty she wore like a casual pair of jeans. Most Hispanic women, in his experience, thought of themselves as goddesses. They moved and acted like they wore crowns—or at the very least, tiaras—and everyone around them should consider themselves a subject. Elizabeth Benavides moved with the grace of those women but without the superior attitude. She was relaxed and confident and eminently approachable, even when her eyes glazed over and her shoulders sagged for a moment. She was determined to find her sister's killer, and being a part of her community might be the key. The curves of her body and the curve of her lips warmed him. Maybe this enforced servitude in the Hispanic community wouldn't be as bad as he'd thought.

When they'd met a few minutes before ten, Elizabeth carried an insulated tote along with her purse. Daniel offered to carry the tote for her and she handed it over to him.

"Whoa. What do you have in here? Lead weights?"

"If you can't manage it, Detective, hand it back. I'm stronger than I look."

Daniel hefted the tote over his shoulder. "I've got it."

They'd been strolling up one block and down another for twenty minutes now. A lot of other people were enjoying the weather or they would have looked conspicuous.

Illegals frosted his butt. They were problems in more ways than one. Because of his appearance and his surname, Daniel Murillo had to prove his legitimacy and his potential every day of his life in the country he'd been born into as a fourth-generation citizen. Forget the military service he and his family had given. Forget the sacrifices they had made. Forget the fact that his brother lived in Boston, a respected neurosurgeon, and his sister was serving as a missionary in South America. Because some Mexicans had come north, not respecting the laws of this country, he had to pay.

It pissed him off.

And the beautiful young woman he stood with picked up on his attitude. "Let me do the talking. You open your mouth and you might as well open your wallet," Elizabeth Benavides said.

"My wallet?" Was she implying he'd have to pay for information?

"Isn't that where you keep your Tea Party card?"

"Hey—"

"Just be quiet and look pretty while I ask the questions."

Daniel conceded she might have a point. For the moment anyway, he agreed to walk along beside her, silent, on this warm Saturday morning.

He gazed down one street and saw four guys working on a low rider. The purple paint sparkled rich and luxuriant in the sunshine. Three young girls in tight jeans and midriff blouses stood near, pretending not to notice the glances thrown in their direction from the young men in between paying attention to the inner workings of the motor and wiping fingerprints off the surface of the car.

A group of grade-school children rushed passed them. The youngsters spoke Spanglish, a colorful combination of Spanish and English, while they kicked a battered—almost flat—basketball between them. Not far behind them two mothers walked, engrossed in conversation. One of them pushed an ancient, heavy stroller and the other one moved forward hand-in-hand with a toddler.

He and Elizabeth kept walking. He knew she had extended some kind of sensor. She didn't talk, and he had stubbornly decided to be quiet and "look pretty," regardless of what happened around them.

In the next block aromas cascaded over him. Scents he hadn't smelled in such a direct way in decades. They passed by a house with the unmistakable smell of fresh tortillas, a hint of tamales just coming together. Homemade chorizo overpowered him a few steps later, and he fought the impulse to lick his lips.

Daniel had never been so aware of a neighborhood. Still, he wanted out of this place. He wanted to exist in a place less *specific*. Less ethnic. Less asking to be condemned. Less condemning of him. Wherever that nebulous place existed, it wasn't here. This place, where the sound of Spanish fractured the air, heavy with the scent of grease and beans, made him angry. These people made his life more difficult simply because of their existence. They embarrassed him. Their struggles south of the border impacted his struggle north of the border. He was legal while they were not.

But few seemed able to tell the difference.

They walked and walked, sometimes talking, mostly not. Any talking that was done was between Elizabeth and the locals. The park was packed with families—kids, parents, grandparents. Daniel hadn't known there were so many Hispanics in Aspen Falls. About one-thirty, Elizabeth pointed to a picnic table in a small park. A family packing away the remains of their picnic lunch waved Elizabeth and Daniel over. "We're finished. You're welcome to our table."

"Thank you."

Elizabeth motioned for Daniel to hand her the insulated tote and she opened it on the table. Elizabeth Benavides, whose murdered sister's body she had found the day before, had packed a lunch for two. She pulled out an embroidered table cloth, two large cloth napkins, real plates—not paper—and utensils, followed by homemade tamales, a garden salad, and two cold beers.

"This way we don't really have to stop for lunch. We can stay in the neighborhood and see if we can learn something."

"We're not learning anything fast, in case you haven't noticed."

"You give up too easy," Elizabeth said.

They ate their lunch in silence, except for when Elizabeth spoke to other young women as they walked passed. Mostly in English, but occasionally in Spanish. Daniel pretended not to notice the curious glances the passersby slid in his direction as they hugged Elizabeth and expressed their condolences, promising to let her know if they heard anything that might help.

Afterward, Elizabeth repacked the tote, and Daniel hoisted it on his shoulder once again—noticeably lighter—and the pair began their slow tour of the community. Whether it was the beer or the woman—he couldn't tell which—Daniel also felt lighter. More relaxed. Well, more relaxed than he imagined he would ever feel in this part of Aspen Falls.

Daniel marveled at the casual way Elizabeth meandered down the streets, speaking to this person and nodding at that one. Saying just the right thing and gesturing in exactly the right way.

She belonged.

Daniel, aware that men and women who lived in this neighborhood watched him and inspected him, grew more uncomfortable. These people held him in suspicion, and he bristled. He'd felt these prying eyes before—from the world he had worked so hard to be a part of.

And he knew he belonged in neither.

He waited on a corner while Elizabeth walked a short distance down a side street to where a group of women stood and chatted. It would be untrue to say that he felt embarrassed by his Mexican heritage. Far from it. He considered himself a proud American with the strong and uplifting background of a Mexican family who had found a huge amount of success in overcoming loss. What embarrassed him was the attitude—and the brass balls—this current generation of Mexicans had in assuming that the border didn't exist. That his country defaulted to them and could be taken. That the laws of his country were just so much shit.

It pissed him off that he had to pay the price for their arrogance. Every single day.

"I may have found something," Elizabeth said. "Well, some*one* really."

A young woman stood a few steps behind Elizabeth. Shy. Pretty.

The girl in the photograph found in the wallet of a dead man discovered on a hiking trail.

Chapter Twenty-Seven

Aspen Falls Police Department
Saturday, September 22

Chase tipped his coffee cup to his mouth and got nothing but air. *Dang.* He pushed his chair back and stood to get more caffeine. Bad caffeine. Publicly funded, station-house caffeine. But still, caffeine. He didn't want to take the time to go get some good stuff from The Coffee Pod.

The quiet station allowed him to get a lot of work done. Transplant and organ donation research both inspired and depressed him. So much need and too few options. He poured the gray-hued liquid into his favorite cup. Bond had gotten it for him when he made Senior Detective a couple years ago. On the side of the cup people could see, it said HEAD DICK, and on the side that faced him when he drank, it said DICK HEAD. It kept him humble.

"Hey, Waters, dump that sludge. I've got a couple of things you want." Terri stepped into the room, the exact right color of coffee cups in her hands, and some bagels in a bag.

All right! Chase poured the liquid in a nearby plant that continued to thrive despite its deprived and depraved environment.

"Your timing is perfect," he said. "Get that warrant?"

"Better. Got the warrant last night and just spent the last hour in the ER while they printed out their records. They gave us the last ten months. More than that and they'll need to go into their archives."

"You are truly an angel of mercy, Terri."

"It's what they pay me for."

Terri pulled out hundreds of pages of hospital records and his good mood slipped a notch—or ten.

He leafed through them. "These are just orders for blood tests?"

"Yep."

"There must be five thousand names here."

"Six thousand three hundred and thirty-one. Dates, names, reason for visit, and findings."

Chase took the pile, divided it into two equal stacks and said, "Call The Pod. See if they'll make a delivery in about an hour."

"What exactly are we looking for?" Terri asked.

"Wish I could tell you. Look for anything odd. Something that jumps out at you," Chase said. "Look for a pattern."

Chapter Twenty-Eight

Possible site for Cobalt Mountain Antiques
Saturday, September 22

The GPS took Bond into an area just outside of downtown Aspen Falls. Beautiful, but way outside of the busy commercial area she had in mind. There would be no walk-in traffic here. Which meant it would take that much longer for her business to get in the black. A giant waste of time.

She passed by something called the Preston Clinic, surrounded by a long stone wall. The impressive masonry was about six feet high and had continued for at least the last half mile as she'd driven past. Bond had never heard of the place. Must be some kind of rehab for the rich and famous. Somehow she didn't think they'd be in the market for antiques.

"Are we there yet?" What parent hadn't heard this refrain from their offspring? An image flashed in Bond's mind of a family in a covered wagon with a child in the rear asking the same question.

"Lizzie says less than two minutes." Lizzie was the name the family had given the GPS in her Navigator.

Chase's had been christened Waldo, as in "Where's
Waldo?" She had no clue why Lizzie had received her
moniker. But Lizzie she was.

Angela piped up. "Can we go to Goodfellows for
lunch?" Both girls loved making their own pizzas at the
restaurant in Snowmass Village.

"I'll think about it. In the meantime, best behavior,
okay?"

Bond pulled the Navigator up in front of one of the
cutest Victorians she'd seen in Aspen Falls. Three different
colors displayed in perfect harmony. But here? How in the
world could she make a go of a new business here?

Less than a minute later her Realtor, Blake Adams,
pulled her Beamer X5 to a stop. Nothing but top-of-the-
line for Blake.

"Hey, Bond." The Realtor nodded in an abstract way
toward Angela and Stephanie. "Easy to find, right?"

"With the help of my GPS."

"What do you think of the neighborhood?"

"It's gorgeous and upscale and who wouldn't like
this?" Bond asked. "But where am I going to get any walk-
in traffic way out here? Other than Hollywood rehabbers
from the clinic?"

"I'd love to be able to tell you they were all rehabbers
there—you could make a fortune. But the truth is, you
won't find many Hollywood elite hanging out at the
Preston Clinic."

"Well, who then?"

"All I can tell you is that whoever uses that clinic, for
whatever reasons, must have more money and pull than
anyone I've ever heard of."

"Wow. Not even you, Realtor to the Stars, have the
scoop?"

"All I know is we're talking serious money. Sure, some of our normal Hollywood crowd probably goes there, but this clinic goes beyond that money."

Bond turned to her girls. "If you want to check this out with me, come now. Otherwise stay put until I get back." Each girl pushed her door open.

"Fine. Stay close and be ready to go the minute I call you." Bond had no illusion they'd be interested in seeing the layout of the house. She barely registered a black Mustang heading down the street. It didn't slow down so she brushed any uneasiness aside.

Blake adjusted her jeans inside her Sorrell boots before starting for the door. "You are about to see all of the reasons why this place can kick butt. Being out of the way will make it that much more desirable to people with big bank accounts."

Chapter Twenty-Nine

Aspen Falls Police Department
Saturday, September 22

Chase and Terri had been sitting at the table going over records from Aspen Falls Memorial's Emergency Room for hours. They'd raced down one blind alley after another, still no closer to finding a pattern.

The names and dates on the hospital records had become blurred. Who knew there were this many sick people in such a small community?

Chase stretched his neck, rolled his shoulders, and arched his back. Detective work often bordered on the mundane. Of course they never showed this part of the job on television.

Chase had sent Terri out a few minutes ago for fresh air—and more coffee. If they didn't catch a break in a couple of hours—

Wait. Chase looked again at the page in front of him. Flipped back a few more. Then a few more. *Bingo.* He grabbed a fresh legal pad and began to write, faster and faster. He stood up with the pages and paced the room, back to the table to write again.

"Yes!"

Terri walked in, tired and sagging with the weight of tall cups of coffee.

"Terri, order some pizza, then help me go through this list from the beginning. We've found a crack and it could be a very, very important crack. As in cracking this case."

"From the beginning? Chase, are you—"

"Not kidding. Remember when we found a few patients here and there who came in with flu symptoms and blood tests were ordered? We thought we had something then but it went nowhere. Mistakes happen. That's what we thought. Now, we're going to go through each name again and check for all of the uninsured Hispanic patients, regardless of why they were in the ER. Make a note on each one whether or not blood tests were ordered. My bet is they were—almost every single time."

Terri handed him his coffee and went back to her stack of records. She set her cup down and grabbed her pile. Squinted at Chase.

"And that tells us what exactly?"

"Think about it. If the killings are to harvest organs for the black market, what group could be targeted without risk that police would be called in right away?"

Terri's tired face remained blank. They were all tired.

Chase tried again. "What group is among the least likely to report missing persons?"

Terri's face split into a grin. "Illegal immigrants."

"Exactly." Chase tossed her a fresh legal pad. "We'll compile a new list and go from there. Not all of the people on the list will be illegal, but my bet is a majority of them will fall into that group."

"This feels a little like racial profiling."

"I call it solving murders."

Chapter Thirty

Aspen Falls' Hispanic Neighborhood
Saturday, September 22

Elizabeth made the introductions and Daniel knew she'd found someone connected to the case. It turned out the casual conversations Elizabeth had engaged in earlier in the day had actually led her to where she might find the woman in the photograph of the unidentified man in the morgue. Daniel's estimation of Elizabeth continued to climb.

"Maria Sanchez may have information useful in the investigation of not only my sister's murder, but her husband's disappearance. She has agreed to talk with you, and only you, as long as I am also present."

In Spanish, Daniel said, "I appreciate your willingness to talk with us, Mrs. Sanchez. My car is about four blocks from here and we can be at the station in about twenty minutes."

Daniel watched as panic seized the young woman. She backed up, eyes wide, her head shook from side to side. "No!"

Rapid Spanish followed between the two women and Daniel had a hard time following the conversation. Elizabeth turned to him, a hand on Sanchez's shoulder.

"We need to talk somewhere less official. She will not go to the police station."

"Ask her to wait a moment while I make a call. Tell her it's okay. We'll figure something out."

Daniel walked away and punched Chase's number into his cell. "Hey, it's Daniel. We found the woman in the photograph the dead hiker had in his wallet. She won't come in. Probably an illegal. What do you want me to do?"

Chase answered, "We're on to something from the records and I don't want to leave. Plus, I would need you there anyway to help translate. You handle this. Get her to agree to have it recorded. You've got your recorder, right?"

Daniel ended the call.

"Is there a café near here?"

"There's a bar but it doesn't open for another hour or two."

"See if she'll go with us to The Coffee Pod. It should be quiet there." Daniel would present the recorder when they were seated somewhere. *One step at a time.*

Elizabeth spoke softly to Maria Sanchez. At first she shook her head and tried to pull away but Elizabeth held her firm. They exchanged a few more words, then Maria's shoulders caved in and she nodded. Elizabeth loosened her grip and turned to Daniel.

"She'll come with us. She wants to find out what happened to her husband."

They walked to Daniel's car, the two women a few steps behind him. He hoped they wouldn't decide to take off. Chase would be less than pleased.

Three people rode in silence to The Coffee Pod, but the energy inside the closed doors of the car buzzed with the thoughts and fears and determination of at least two strong personalities. Daniel, outgunned, needed to take control to assure that if this case ever went to court, they had all the bases covered.

"Ms. Benavides, I will be handling the questions for Mrs. Sanchez once we get to The Coffee Pod. I expect you to remain quiet unless I ask you to say something. Do you understand?"

"*Ms. Benavides*? After spending an entire day together, it's *Ms. Benavides*? You need to get a handle on what it means to have a partner, because I—"

"Whoa. Let's get this straight. You and I are not partners. At the most, you're assisting this investigation. At the least, you're a loose cannon who could bring everything down unless someone babysits you."

"*Babysit*? You are acting like a *culo*, Great Detective Murillo. If I didn't need the information, if I could trust you for one moment to find my sister's murderer, I would tell you to let me out now. And you know exactly how far you would get with our new friend."

Elizabeth Benavides's face glowed a deep umber. Her eyes flashed between him and Maria Sanchez. When they landed back on Daniel he could not meet her hostile glare. He worked a swallow down his throat while he eased into a parking space in front of the coffee shop.

"Please, Ms. Benavides... Elizabeth. I appreciate everything you bring to this interview. I apologize for being so abrupt. But my job is to make sure the right questions get asked in the right way in the event we end up in court, and to ask the questions that will most likely lead us to whoever murdered your sister, and possibly Maria Sanchez's husband."

She gave a slight jerk of her head but seemed to calm down a little. Daniel sighed.

Settled in a private corner of the coffee shop with two Cuban coffees and a French roast, Daniel began by asking

Maria about her husband. His name, where they lived, all the details they didn't have. He asked if she had a picture of José, and she removed one from a well-worn billfold. A young man smiled into the camera. Daniel turned it over. *7/11*. They didn't need much more confirmation. He slid the photograph across the table to Maria.

"I'm so sorry," Daniel said.

Tears filled the young woman's eyes and spilled down her cheeks. She wiped them away and sat silently for a moment. A small nod of her head.

In Spanish she said, "I knew my José would not leave me. I knew it. You will find his murderer, yes?"

Chapter Thirty-One

Aspen Falls Police Department
Sunday, September 23

The next morning, Chase felt an almost palpable current run through the meeting room. The murder board finally reflected a few more answers than questions.

He shared what he and Terri had found, a distinct pattern of uninsured Hispanic patients in the ER receiving unnecessary blood tests, including Rachelle Benavides. He'd also scheduled an interview with the transplant coordinator at Memorial for Monday.

Daniel told them about Maria and José Sanchez. His hand flew over the murder board while he spoke.

"Two men offered Sanchez two thousand dollars for one of his kidneys about two months ago. Maria Sanchez never met them but she saw them talking to her husband once. She's meeting with Dobson this afternoon to try and come up with a couple of sketches."

Chase took a sip of coffee. "Can't we get Carol Myers? She builds a much stronger bond with people than Dobson. We get better sketches."

"Carol is on assignment in Colorado Springs until next week. I didn't think you'd want to wait."

"You're right. I don't."

"How did you get to Maria again?" Terri asked.

Daniel blushed. "Elizabeth Benavides introduced us."

Terri smiled.

"Anyway, when Sanchez balked at giving up one of his kidneys they sweetened the pot. Said they had a source to get them legal papers. Not just Sanchez, but his wife as well. For a price."

"Let me guess," Chase said. "Two thousand dollars."

"That's right. And Maria Sanchez said they added another little threat to the mix."

Chase and Terri waited.

Daniel quit writing on the whiteboard and turned to look directly at them. Put his hands on the table and leaned down. "Maria Sanchez said the two men made it clear that if her husband didn't accept their generous offer, they would still get what they needed from him."

Chase pushed back from the table and paced the room. "So they went along with the plan and Sanchez sold a kidney for two grand. Did he try and buy some papers?"

"Maria says yes. Of course they never saw anything."

"We should get his autopsy results back tomorrow. We know he had a nephrectomy but we don't know if that had anything to do with why he died."

"His wife said he hadn't been feeling well. Thought a walk would help. Guess the guy liked to hike in the hills." Daniel finished changing the header for DB #4 to read José Sanchez.

"Terri, you go back to your contact at the ER," Chase said. "What's her name again?"

"Leslie James."

"Yeah. Can you trust her?"

"She's never given me any reason not to."

"Someone in the ER has either been poorly trained or else that individual is involved in this somehow. The ER is a link, and I think James is more likely to talk to you than me."

"You got that right, after the way you threatened her the first time you met."

"What's that?" Daniel asked, a smile tugging at his face.

"Never mind." Chase checked out the board. "Is there any way you and Elizabeth can find out the name of the guy they found in the dumpster? See if there's any kind of connection to her sister?"

Terri's cell phone rang and she dug it out of a pocket. Without a word to either Chase or Daniel she stepped out of the room. Both detectives opted to pretend they'd seen nothing.

Daniel tossed the marker on the table. "I'll call Elizabeth and set something up." He shook his head. "She's kind of hard to control."

"She might be hard to control but at least we can keep her safe. And her contacts within the Hispanic community have already proven invaluable to us. Without her we may never have heard from Maria Sanchez."

Daniel didn't say anything.

"Am I right?"

Daniel took a deep breath. When he exhaled, Chase heard a "Yeah," but would have sworn there were some other words included.

Chapter Thirty-Two

Aspen Falls Memorial Hospital
Monday, September 24

Chase was standing in the drab waiting room for the administrative wing of the hospital when a strange woman seemed to come out of nowhere. He extended his hand, fighting the sudden surrealism she stirred up.

"Thanks for meeting with me on such short notice, uh"—Chase glanced at the business card in his hand and took special care to pronounce the name—"Ms. Berdichevsky."

"Call me Birdie." The woman smiled and bounced on her feet while she shook his hand. Short and dressed in green from head to toe, she made him think of the forest fairies in his kids' story books. She could as easily have her free arm crooked around a tree trunk as the bunch of manila folders she carried. Birdie's reddish-brown hair reminded Chase of one of those weed and stick arrangements Bond kept experimenting with in their foyer. He guessed the green scarf clamped around the odd woman's head served a greater purpose than accessorizing her outfit. A musky, spicy scent filled the air around her, as if set off by undulating exotic plants. He thought it smelled interesting and was grateful it didn't make him sneeze.

Birdie worked as the organ procurement liaison with the hospital. She'd agreed to give Chase a crash course in the business side of organ donation if he would agree to actually meet a few of the people behind the statistics. He made it clear that while he wanted to get as much background information as possible, he didn't have the luxury of spending hours in the hospital. Without divulging any connection to a current case, he let her know time was of the essence.

Chase did his best to keep up with her bounce-hop gait as they moved down the brightly lit corridor.

Birdie waved him on. "Leslie James tells me you need some more information on transplanted people." Her English was heavily accented. She twisted toward him and he half expected her to leap in the air. This woman broadcast an undeniable high level of energy. Exhausting almost. She grinned. "I am your girl and I will have you out of here in less than an hour with your questions filled."

Chase always tried to build a broad spectrum of knowledge related to his cases. Little pieces of information had helped close more than one in the past. Ever since David's death, he'd wanted to understand more about organ donation. The visit to this particular floor of Aspen Falls Memorial made all kinds of sense—both personal and professional. He had asked Leslie James not to tell anyone the reason for his visit. As far as anyone else was to know, he was there for a quick VIP tour.

They stopped in front of a bank of elevators. Three other people joined them while they waited. Conversation stilled but Birdie kept up a steady pulse with her feet— heels and toes, heels and toes.

115

Polite elevator conversation ended when they exited on the fifth floor. And Birdie's high energy gave way to quiet dedication. If Chase hadn't seen it for himself, he wouldn't have believed the transformation. The woman who almost drove him to distraction in less than three minutes paused, took a deep breath, and gazed into his eyes. "I am going to show you a few people who are waiting for miracles. If they say no to talking to you, it's no all the way."

Her manner calm and focused, even as her English proved more of a grasp and a grin, she opened the first folder and glanced quickly at its contents. File closed, she glided in slow motion ahead of Chase, but just beneath the surface he could sense a tiger continued to pace. And bounce.

They entered a lobby area void of people. An older woman sat behind the nurse's station with a phone pressed against her ear. She waved distractedly at Birdie and motioned toward a set of automatic doors. They walked through them in silence.

This room had several people in it. Most sat in comfortable chairs reading books and magazines. One gentleman lay on a bed, eyes closed. Every one of them in their own world and every one of them hooked up to a machine.

Birdie turned to him. "This is one of the more or minus twenty dialysis centers in Colorado and the only local to give a patient the choice between home and a center for life needs." She spoke in the low voice of an art museum docent. "Each one of these people breathes because they go through this workout several times a week. Each one of them will die sooner than they were made for if they do not get a kidney. Each one of them is on the waiting list. Each one of them hopes to be transplanted."

Birdie angled across the room toward a middle-aged man who sat in a reading chair, soft light spilling over his head and broad shoulders. Chase saw the book cover. A Harry Potter but he wasn't sure which one. By the size of the tome, he guessed it was one of the earlier ones.

As they neared, the man looked up and a smile split his face. "Bir-die." His voice resonated a deep bass as he spun her name like a song. Warm and welcoming, he radiated hospitality. "What a pleasure to see you."

"Mitchell, I'd like you to meet Chase Waters Detective. I am giving him a bit of a trip this morning and you are one of the spotlights."

Mitchell laughed, deep and sonorous, and Chase knew he'd like to spend more time in this man's company. A sense of humor when his life depended on a machine? When his days no longer belonged to him but to this room? He must be an amazing person.

"Well, Chase Waters Detective, if Birdie vouches for you, then I'm at your disposal." His eyes shone with an inner light.

They spent the next ten minutes talking. And to Chase's surprise—laughing. Mitchell, or Mitch, had just celebrated his sixty-second birthday. Traveling had once been high on his agenda and he hoped it would be again. He and his wife had set foot in many countries, and most continents.

A father of two and grandfather to one, Mitchell loved to play golf, the saxophone, and cards—particularly whist—in that order.

Chase and Mitch shared some musical favorites—from Sarah Vaughn to Charlie Parker—and their conversation never lulled. And yes, with that voice of his, he'd been a professional announcer—on both radio and television. But kidney failure had forced him into early retirement. He missed his life but determined to make the most of each day where he focused on his friends and whatever small joys he could find.

Chase found himself wishing for a little more time with Mitchell, and at his new friend's invitation, planned to have some follow-up visits where they could talk some more.

"You two hit each other off. I knew this." Birdie seemed pleased but subdued.

Her flip-side persona still rattled him, yet somehow it worked. Her intense animation transformed into huge compassion when dealing with people whose lives had been stolen, and her hard edges smoothed out when she sucked some of their tragedy into her own body by being near them. Like some weird reactive chameleon, she had an innate sense of the best way to approach people without being phony.

"So, what's the story? When will Mitchell get his kidney?"

She nodded. Swallowed. Started walking down the hallway. Without looking in his direction she said, "Twenty people die today in this great country waiting to be transplanted. *Twenty.* Today twenty and tomorrow twenty. And most of those twenty wait for kidney kind of miracle." She stopped and stared at Chase dead-on. "Mitchell will never have old life. He here to live two more years. Bottoms."

"But surely in two years—"

"There are larger people up the waiting list than Mitch. People who might die tomorrow. And then there is the problem to match. It happens, but most days for most people it does not. People are more than one hundred fifteen thousand on the waiting list right now. Facebook helped but not enough. New adds to be transplanted rise twice faster than what people choose to give. Mitch does not look good to live."

Chase wondered what he'd do in Mitch's place. He thought about the dark pit he'd fallen into after David's death. About the rubble and destruction he'd carefully walked around—in an attempt to avoid dealing with any feelings. There were differences between what he'd gone through and Mitch's situation, sure. An uncomfortable awareness settled over him as suspicion grew about where his attitude would fall. He knew he'd be back to visit Mitch at his earliest opportunity—after this case wrapped up. He had a lot to learn.

Birdie took Chase to visit two more people in the hospital. On the way, she filled him in on statistics, ins-and-outs, and details of organ donation, including ethical conflicts that exist even in legitimate operations. All of it in her off-key, but sometimes better than good, English.

Chase watched her, looking for a sign that she might be involved with illegal organ procurement. She certainly had the knowledge and background, but did she have the callousness required? Maybe she was inadvertently assisting somehow.

The next patient they saw, a middle-aged man named Simon, was waiting for a lung. Simon seemed bitter, and although he acknowledged Birdie and forced a kind of politeness at Chase, he didn't go out of his way to welcome them the way Mitchell had.

While Mitch's days held soft slow dances, Simon's were all sharp battles. Chase hated how easily he identified with the surly man. Simon's angry eyes indicated he had given his life over to energy-draining, negative poisons. Chase saw an image in his mind, of Simon feasting on a venomous plague. The man devoured it. Chase thanked God he'd found his way out of that hopeless realm, but he knew in his heart how quickly he could find himself there again.

Simon would change places with him in an instant—with no regret. Chase understood Simon's hardened heart, and that scared him more than any article on Santeria ever would.

His cell phone rang. *Terri.* "What's up?" He listened for a minute. "Okay, go ahead. Do what you've gotta do. An hour isn't gonna kill us. I'll contact you if something important comes up." *Terri's involved in something. So far, not a problem. So far.*

The last patient, Juliette, they didn't talk to. She resembled his Stephanie as she slept. Nine years old. Chase looked at the small form under the covers in her hospital bed and trapped a groan. Juliette needed a heart. She ranked very near the top of the infamous, magical list. Simplifying it a great deal, if a heart became available, and it wasn't a match for one of the two people higher on the list than Juliette but *did* match her, she'd automatically move to first place for that organ. A woman slept in a cot next to her bed. Her disheveled appearance marked her as the mother. A plate of picked-over food sat on a tray next to the cot. Hopelessness permeated the air, fused with brutal anger around its edges.

Balloons, wall posters and stuffed animals did little to disguise the institutional purpose of the room. Soft yellows and pink attempted to counter the stainless gray and beige without success. The end result sent the message of a little girl trapped in a nightmare.

Chase felt his own heart quake at the memory of David and all they had lost. He wondered what he would have done if they'd known David needed a new heart, with none readily available. Would he have turned to the black market? Would he have hocked everything to save his son's life? Even if it meant some stranger—someone he didn't know or love—might have needlessly died? Been murdered? Chase felt spiders crawl over his conscience and forced the thoughts aside.

He and Birdie moved on to the elevator in silence. When they arrived at the ground floor, Birdie moved as if to slough off a cloak. She waved her arms, still carrying the folders in one, and shook her head, twig-stick hair flapping. A couple of quick kicks with her legs and the energetic, exhausting Birdie re-emerged. Watching her, Chase stalled somewhere between alarm and relief.

"They are all my people, you know. My family. I laugh with them, cry with them, fold my hands to God with them, and sometimes I hold them while they die. It is not easy, but it is my happiness. My gift."

Chase wondered who had it hardest—Birdie or her "people."

"Tell me about your experience, Birdie, if it's not too personal."

"It is all personal. If not personal, it would not matter." She peeled off with her skip-step down a hallway leading to the hospital cafeteria. "Do not you worry. We are not eating here—I need to put my eye on a lady for a slice."

He waited while she veered behind the counter almost bowling over an elderly woman who checked food trays and took the money of hospital diners. Birdie flung the files down by the cash register and wrapped her skinny arms around the woman who did a good job of covering up her surprise—and her smile.

"What in the world?" The old woman's accent filled the air as she swatted Birdie's arms away. "Can not you let me do my job the way it is supposed to be done?"

Swinging around, one arm gently guiding her victim, Birdie faced Chase. "Irina, I'd like you to meet Chase Waters Detective. I am gifting him my people today. Chase, this is the amazing woman, Mrs. Irina Kostakov."

121

The woman's eyes flicked to meet his for a moment, then fell away. Chase nodded in acknowledgement as a faint blush stained her wrinkled cheeks. "I'm pleased to meet you, Mrs. Kostakov.

Birdie released her arm and planted a kiss on Irina's cheek. The wrinkled woman reached up and cupped Birdie's face in her hands, murmuring something to her in Russian. Eyes welling, Birdie gave one last hug and began flip-flopping back the way they'd come before Chase could react. A smile and another nod toward Mrs. Kostakov, then he hurried to catch up to the dashing woman. He decided Birdie was aptly named—always taking off in flight.

"Irina had a son. I am transplanted because of his bone. He and friends fly into Aspen to play golf and crash plane into Aspen Mountain. Irina live in state of New Jersey, but push herself here to be to the end place her son breathed." Birdie did a hop-dance and turned to face him. "And be near me, I think. I am filled with life and alive and sticking my feet down today because of her Alexi."

Stunned, Chase asked, "How did you find out the name of your donor?" Had they missed something when David died? There were so many forms.

"Both the transplanted people must agree to have their name said. Or, in the case of Alexi, his next of line. She did, I did, so we did."

Chase looked at his watch. He'd been here almost thirty minutes, and although he'd become aware of the life-or-death urgency for organ donations, he had a couple more questions. "Are all of the transplant surgeries done here at Memorial?"

"For regular money people."

"What do you mean?"

"People who are transplanted by insurance visit Memorial."

"Where else is there?"

"High money people go to here or the clinic."

"A clinic?"

"Private. Preston Clinic."

"Birdie, I want to thank you for taking the time to introduce me to these people who mean so much to you, and giving me a primer in transplants. May I call you if I have any more questions?"

"My phone is always in my ear."

Chase took that as a yes.

Chapter Thirty-Three

The Preston Clinic
Monday, September 24

Bobby Carlisle pushed his sunglasses up on his head and ushered the young man into the clinic through a side entrance. "Wait over there. Someone will come and get you in a minute."

"When do I get my money?"

"After the operation."

"But you said—"

"*After* the operation."

"I think maybe this is a mistake. I think I have changed my mind." The kid, barely seventeen, moved to leave.

Carlisle blocked the door. He shoved his coat to the side to reveal a gun strapped to his chest. "Leaving would be a mistake. A bad one. The last one you would ever make. We have an agreement and I expect you to honor it. You know about honor?"

The kid looked at the floor. "I know honor."

"Good. Then wait over there. It will be over sooner than you can say Immigration and Customs Enforcement."

These lowlife criminals with accents pissed him off more and more every time. Idiots. The scum from Mexico were useful but he hated the need to interact with them.

He pulled out his cell and punched in a number. "I've got a possible rabbit so I need you to get the cash." He gave the 'eyes on you' signal to the kid then turned his back on him. "Eight hundred." He spun back around. "Good. See you soon."

Pablo, or whatever his name was, had agreed on three hundred dollars for one of his kidneys. Carlisle's "commissions" were building a nice little nest egg for his future. He had amassed a tidy sum over the years. In addition, he'd made some particularly good investments. Soon it would be time to cut and run. He hadn't decided whether or not to share the money with his brother. Probably not. Sammy was slow and bound to lose it. Then he'd be needing a place to live. Better keep complete control and give his brother an allowance. Pay him for protection or something.

* * *

He stretched his patience for the benefit of the two men sitting across the rather broad expanse of his desk. He handled the gold letter opener in his hand like a weapon— a long thin finger tested the point. To keep his operation small meant he had to deal with the flunkies. Part of him hated this—the part where he had to have patience—but part of him loved to dip his manicured fingers in the street-smart portion of his business. It reminded him of his youth when he had survived from day to day by his wits.

"You need to do two things if you are to remain on my payroll. First, you need to try and find a brain between you and figure out what to do with the product suppliers when we're finished with them. You've gotten lazy. Too many are being discovered, and eventually that will spell disaster for our work here. Second, you need to fine-tune your information related to the routine of the next heart donor. You must be prepared to bring her here on a moment's notice."

He scowled at the brothers. "Did you have something you wanted to say?"

Bobby looked up. "I have a question."

When the man said nothing, Bobby plunged ahead. "Why did you have us tell the bitch where to find her sister's body if we're so concerned about discovery?"

"Never, ever use that kind of language in front of me again. Do you understand?"

Bobby shifted in his seat. "Yes. Sir."

"The older sister had already gone to the police. She's pushy and mouthy. We need her to shut up."

The man sat back in his chair, fingered the letter opener one more time, then skewered his gaze on the two unfortunate men sitting in front of him. "Are you prepared to do the job? If you have some concerns about my requirements or your ability to meet them, I need to know. Now."

"No, sir. We're good." The more diminutive of the two spoke. Maybe he knew about what happened to former employees who knew too much. Or maybe he really thought he had a handle on things. It didn't matter. Not the time to make a change. Too much depended on information they'd already accumulated about the heart donor.

"Don't disappoint me." He pulled a small sheet of paper from a notebook and handed it to the small man. He smiled at the hesitancy and slight tremble before the paper was accepted. *Power. Gotta love it.* "This is a minor supply situation that's in addition to your main project, but we've made a commitment to produce the product. You have one week to gain consent from the kid for one of his kidneys, otherwise, we will need to gain access with a less secure outcome. And you will need to have determined a preferred disposal method."

The man pulled a file open and began to finger the pages. "We're done here."

* * *

"I got it, Bonehead. Quit bugging me."

Sammy wiped his hands on his pants for the five hundredth time. "But Bobby, we got to get this right. There's so much we gotta do, it's confusing."

"That's why you've got me. First thing is the disposal, right? We do the same thing we did a year ago. Look for some mutilation group to hide our toss. We'll head over to the campus and poke around. Bound to be some group of assholes there."

"Good. That's good. Give u s a place to dump the leftovers."

"And we've been following little heart girl for a few days. We'll have the details down soon. Could be a hard snatch because she's never by herself, but she's just a kid. Surprise will be in our favor."

Bobby waited a minute for Sammy to process his words. When he saw his partner, actually his older brother, blink a couple of times he figured everything had finally sunk in.

"So you're with me then?"

"I'm always with you, Bobby. You should know that by now. You might have the brains but there's no way you can take care of yourself in a fight."

"You got that right. I need you."

"Who's our next supplier?"

Bobby unfolded the paper, laughed, then handed it over to his brother to read.

He watched as Sammy read the top line that said the best place for contact was Cobalt Mountain Books, and then moved on to the contact name. His brother looked up, eyes wide. "Really? Tom Hanks?"

"Efraín Tomás Hanks Madrigal. Kid with a name like that is gonna be an easy sell."

Chapter Thirty-Four

Aspen Falls' Hispanic Neighborhood
Monday, September 24

Daniel and Elizabeth walked the neighborhood much like they had on Saturday, but today they were bundled against the cold. A high country storm teased the mountain town with the promise of winter and the white powder their ski slopes were known for.

"We want to try and identify another body, Elizabeth." Daniel watched her reaction before making the decision to say more. Satisfied by what he saw he continued, "We're not certain of a tie-in but there's a chance it's connected. Maybe part of a pattern. And the young man we're trying to put a name to may have a family here who is looking for some answers." He didn't need to add the fact that she searched for her own answers. "Are you comfortable with this?"

"Detective Murillo—"

"Daniel, please."

She nodded. "I am doing this—helping you—for one reason only. To find whoever is responsible for my sister's murder. It sounds like you think I might be of some help in finding someone to identify this body. Fine. I'll do whatever I can. As long as it leads to my sister's murderer. Am I making myself clear?"

"Your neighbors may not like the idea of your working with the police, regardless of the reason. And you know someone is very unhappy with the fact that you are talking to us. You've already been warned."

"Are you trying to scare me away, Daniel?"

He hesitated. His name on her lips threw him off track. "I just want to make sure you know the downside. The risk. And I need to know you're with us. With me."

"As long as I'm comfortable with our direction—to find out why my sister died and who is responsible—I'm with you every step."

A small dog barked and bolted in front of the two of them, then stopped to lift his leg on a tree. When he finished taking care of business he raised his head to Elizabeth who quickly knelt to pet him before he darted away.

Surprised and a little alarmed at her willingness to reach out to a strange dog, Daniel reached to pull her back to him. "You shouldn't have done that. He could have bitten you."

Elizabeth laughed. "That was Pedro. He's a neighborhood dog."

"Neighborhood dog?"

"He lives with everyone. And no one." She looked pointedly at Daniel. "Besides, I'm pretty good at knowing how far to go without being bitten."

"Good. Glad to hear it. Now let's go talk to people who are here illegally. Especially if they have a loved one who is missing. Young. Male. Anyone."

"Leave it to me."

Elizabeth led him down a dirt alley behind businesses housed in clapboard buildings with peeling paint. Abandoned vans and rusty, dented pickup trucks filled much of the land between the buildings and the alley. Dust covered everything. Daniel knew this part of town from his days on patrol. There wasn't a lot of crime in this area—more drunk and disorderly arrests than anything else—but still it wasn't his favorite part of town.

At the end of the alley Elizabeth turned right and they moved into a group of men standing around on the corner, some smoking, others with their fists stuck deep in coat pockets. Daniel knew these men had missed their chance at day-laborer jobs but had nowhere else to go. Besides, it wouldn't be the first time an employer came around looking for a few more hands about midday.

Elizabeth approached one man, Daniel at her side, and spoke quietly. Wearing clean but worn jeans, even more worn boots, a t-shirt and light jacket, the man turned a sun-wrinkled, tobacco-dried face to Daniel before glancing quickly away. Daniel was pretty sure the man was a lot younger than he looked. He peered at Daniel again and tossed a cigarette butt to the ground. While his boot ground the filter longer than necessary, he shrugged and gestured down the street.

Daniel began walking in the direction the man had suggested even before Elizabeth finished her conversation with him. He had no idea where they were going but he didn't want to waste any more time at this day-laborer pickup spot. He could taste the air. There's a fine line between lack of hope and despair—and more than one person had crossed that line while standing on this corner.

Elizabeth pumped up next to him. "Why are you in such a hurry?"

"Aren't you?"

"There is such a thing as courtesy. You might learn something if you gave it a try."

"Sorry."

131

"You wish these people would just go back where they came from, don't you?"

Daniel didn't respond.

It took a moment for Daniel to realize he'd lost his walking partner. He twisted around and saw Elizabeth, her hands on her hips with her feet firmly planted. His mama had taught him that when he saw a woman in this stance he needed to do something. Quickly. "My experience tells me that might be the best alternative for those people."

She stood there not moving. Then her right foot began to tap.

"I have issues."

"No shit, Sherlock."

Daniel stopped before he said something he couldn't take back. He dug a little deeper into his memory tapes looking for the sound of his mother's voice teaching him about courtesy. He had some manners in there somewhere, he knew. Finally he heard his mother talking to him while he watched this beautiful, smart-mouthed woman on display.

"Maybe you can help me with them." He only half kidded.

He watched as Elizabeth snatched a smile back before it caught. *Aha!* His charm succeeded even when his personal hang-ups got in the way.

"By the way, where are we going?" Daniel asked.

"We're going to Juan's."

"Who's Juan?"

Elizabeth pointed. Dirt almost obscured a neon Corona sign in the barred window. A heavy metal door, scratched and dented, marked the entry, and a battered and flaking sign indicated they'd arrived at their destination. The name Juan's Place probably started out as a good truth-avoidance mechanism when errant husbands were met at their doors by angry wives. Somehow being at Juan's sounded a lot better than getting drunk at the local dive. Daniel imagined that for a little while anyway, Juan took the blame.

"You should wait here. I'm not comfortable with you going in there."

She shook her head and set her jaw. Damn, he thought. What did he do wrong now?

"Daniel, you won't get any answers without me. So tough shit. Park your gallantry at the curb." She opened the door and walked in.

Chapter Thirty-Five

Juan's Place
Monday, September 24

Daniel waited for his eyes to adjust to the darkness inside the bar. Conversation that he'd heard on the other side of the door stopped while the patrons checked out the newcomers. A few whispers and low murmurs provided a decidedly different backdrop than the one prior to their entrance. The tenor of the place had changed. Tension made the air thick.

Beneath the quiet, Daniel was aware that men's hands had slipped to their pockets—one or two to their waistbands. Daniel cursed under his breath. If they got out of here without any bloodshed it would be a miracle.

He looked around the bar. It was larger than it looked from the outside and the word "old" came to mind. Clean, but old. Not antique-treasure-old, used-old. Serviceable. He remembered something his mother used to say, "If it isn't broke, keep using it until it is." Apparently nothing had broken in Juan's Place for the last fifty or sixty years.

Elizabeth crossed the expanse, weaving between a few empty tables. She approached the bartender while Daniel hurried to catch up. "I'm looking for the man who knows about the missings. Where is he?" Three men, silent and hunched over their drinks, watched Elizabeth out of the corners of their eyes without lifting their heads. The bulky man behind the bar hesitated and pretended not to hear her request, but Daniel saw him take a surreptitious glance to his right. Even deeper shadows pooled beyond the bar. Daniel could make out a row of booths along the wall, all empty except for one. A man sat alone, facing them. He gave a slight nod. The bartender then turned his full attention on Elizabeth who had repeated her request, this time a little louder, her body leaning over the bar. He pointed a beefy finger and Elizabeth didn't hesitate.

The acceptance of them by the man in the shadows relaxed the atmosphere in the gloom, but somehow Daniel liked this even less. He touched his secured weapon with his elbow, then trailed Elizabeth.

Continuing to use Spanish, Elizabeth addressed the quiet stranger. She didn't leave the man an inch to move and Daniel worried. Back an animal into a corner and he is likely to attack.

"My sister has been murdered and I am looking for her killer. You and I have both heard about 'the missings' in our community, and I'm told you know something about them. There's a good chance whoever is responsible for their disappearance is also responsible for my sister's death. Will you talk to us?"

The entire time Elizabeth spoke, the man's eyes remained fixed on Daniel. Those eyes, surprisingly light in a dark Chicano face, were hot with reined-in anger. His body signaled casual, easy: the kind of end-of-the-day posture all workingmen get, whether they've spent hours in the sweat of manual labor or sitting behind a desk. Forget that the clock said noon, his demeanor said relaxed. But his eyes told a different story. Intense. Unrelenting.

Elizabeth paused for a moment, waiting for an answer. The man's attention never left Daniel.

"Do you always," he enunciated in slow, precise Spanish, "let women do your talking?" The man did not so much as twitch. His voice remained low. Calm. "Did you leave your balls behind with your Mexican heritage?"

Daniel took a step closer. Pulled Elizabeth out of the way. Leaned in.

"My balls," he replied in Spanish, "are where they've always been. Do you want to see who has the bigger pair?"

The man smiled. Then he laughed. Harder. So loud the rest of the bar once again grew silent. "I won't work with someone who clearly denies who he is. You won't get anything from me regardless of the beauty of the women you send ahead." He cocked his head. "However, I've heard good things about someone in your department. Tell Detective Waters I will come to see him this afternoon. Tell him it's time for me to find someone I can trust and that it isn't you."

Daniel sensed someone behind him. He looked over his shoulder. Five men stood ready to protect the man sitting in front of him. They were ready to put their lives and futures on the line for this arrogant bully. "Who can I tell Detective Waters to expect?

"Tell him to expect Mex." A low flick of his right hand and his defenders went back to their tables, but Daniel knew that one miscue and things could change in a very bad way.

Not all of the men had retreated. Daniel felt the heat and energy emanating from someone who remained behind him and he reached inside his jacket.

The man called Mex spoke again. "Let these two go. They are not here to harm anyone."

Daniel heard the slick suck of metal, a blade called home. The man who held the knife walked around to look

Daniel in the face, then spit on his shoes. A defiant glare made it clear that Daniel, the enemy, had best keep an eye out. And he would not be welcome at Juan's Place any time soon.

Chapter Thirty-Six

Aspen Falls Municipal Library
Monday, September 24

Bond pulled her SUV into a parking space at the library and turned off the ignition, then transferred her cell phone from her left ear to her right. "Daddy, I've been worried about you." She pushed out of the vehicle and walked to the entrance. The two benches placed outside the library, flanked by planters that in the summertime overflowed with flowers and greenery, were empty. Bond brushed off a spot and sat down, then turned her face to the sun. Clouds formed then scattered. Bright enough to keep her sunglasses on.

"I'm fine, sugar. Why were you worried?" The resonant voice immediately shot her through with a calm and steady force. She would always be Daddy's Little Girl.

"Mother called incessantly the other day and then seemed obtuse and deliberately vague when I wanted to know why. She knew I'd seen every attempt on my Caller ID."

"Well, sugar, you talked to her and she told you not to worry about me. You shouldn't have had to worry at all."

"You know Mother." A cloud pushed itself over the sun and she dipped her chin.

Her father laughed. A rich laughter from deep in his chest that she loved. It held a promise to her. A promise of protection. Security. "That I do, baby girl. That I do."

Bond pulled her sweater a little tighter around her. "So nothing's going on?"

"The only thing that's going on in my life is that I'm missing my daughter. My daughter and my son-in-law and those amazing grandkids you've given me."

"You're sure?"

"Positive, sugar."

"Why would Mother be so persistent? That's not like her."

"I have a feeling I might know why. She has been known to take a kernel of gossip and blow it out of all kinds of proportion."

"Such as?"

"How much time do you have?" He chuckled, then cleared his throat and fell silent. Softer, he said, "Except maybe this is one rumor she hasn't blown out of proportion. I've been beside myself with frustration over the whole thing. I'm not used to being powerless in any situation."

"What is it?" Bond hated to think of her dad upset about anything.

"You may not even remember him. You've only met Judge Atkins a few times."

Bond felt pieces of her mind freeze. A low roar began to flood her ears and built to a bellow. She wanted to scream but she couldn't catch her breath. She swallowed. *Breathe. Just breathe.* Bond forced herself to focus, her left arm hugged around her waist while she pressed the phone tight to her ear. The roar slipped to a rumble.

"I remember him," Bond said.

"Did your mother tell you what he's been up against?"

"She hasn't mentioned him." Not in almost thirty years, Bond thought.

"Some woman is saying that he molested... God, I hate saying that word... that this great man actually molested her some twenty years ago."

Bond couldn't push a sound out—even if she could have formed a coherent thought—but her father didn't seem to notice.

"And someone else came out with the same bale of lies. This is against a man who has contributed millions of dollars to Chicago charities over the years. I've been upset about all the insinuations since they first surfaced. Maybe that's what your mother wanted to talk to you about. But Sugar, your old man is fine. Hale and hearty, as they say."

Bond found her voice. "I'm glad, Daddy."

"Don't you worry about me. I'll be pushing folks around for quite a while longer. But I am glad you called. It's always good to hear your voice."

"Yours too, Daddy."

Bond clicked off her phone and her torso caved into itself, shoulders and arms listless. Dead weights. A huge black hole beckoned in her mind. One she didn't want to enter. One she'd have to deal with. *Later*.

Not now. Now she needed to read to a kindergarten class—her second one for the week. She needed to take this cold—this clammy—feeling and put it away until she had a chance to be alone and decide what to do. Instinct told her that this time the memories these feelings evoked probably weren't going to just disappear. She had managed her life with this in the background for thirty years and she could manage a little while longer. *Later. I'll deal with this later.*

Bond pulled her shoulders back. Swallowed. Took one breath. Two. She stepped into the library and walked to the noon-time reading area.

The young teacher got the youngsters settled and quiet. Bond walked through the cross-legged audience and settled into a rocking chair that was positioned like a throne before the queen's subjects. She held up the colorful picture book they were going to read today. After the kids oohed and aahed over the cover and the first two pages, she pulled the book toward her and began to read.

"The elephant was big and blue and carried a bright yellow umbrella in his trunk. Amanda could see for miles and miles from her special red chair with gold trim that sat on top of the elephant." Bond read and turned the page.

Powerful aftershave. Hard muscles. It didn't feel right. He made her feel uncomfortable. But he was the adult. A friend of her family. An Important Man.

He called her into his study to show her a book he had about all kinds of horses. He had her sit on a sofa in front of a fireplace while he searched the shelves. Pulled one down and handed it to her. She didn't notice when he closed and locked the door to the room.

That aftershave. The weight of him.

"Mrs. Waters! Mrs. Waters! Can you hear me? Are you okay?" Bond opened her eyes to see the worried stares of both the children's librarian and the kindergarten teacher. Relief washed over their faces as she moved to sit up.

When she did she saw the scared expressions from the young class. She made an effort to smile and wave away their concerns. Their fear.

"I'm fine. Really. I guess this is what happens when I don't get enough sleep at night. Do you think?" She winked at the children who rewarded her effort with immediate acceptance and laughter.

141

Bond looked at the teacher and handed her the story book. "Miss Anderson is going to finish reading your story today, children. I think I need a nap."

Two minutes later she sat in her car. She knew now why her mother had been calling. Her mother wanted to know if she'd heard the news about Judge Atkins. Her mother wanted to remind her of the promise she'd made almost thirty years ago—the promise to never say another word about what had happened that day when her mother found her in tears.

A promise she had kept.

Chapter Thirty-Seven

The Preston Clinic
Monday, September 24

Chase pulled into the unmarked drive and wondered why he'd never heard of this place. How could a business—any business—exist so far under the radar that a detective on the Aspen Falls Police Department had never heard of it? Maybe money could buy anything. Apparently it could buy anonymity.

Approximately a quarter of a mile off the main road and around a curve, a huge iron gate barred further progress. Chase noted both the intercom and the cameras. He pulled his car up, opened his window, and sat waiting for someone to contact him via the speaker. When they didn't, he reached out and pushed the red call button. Still nothing.

As he was about to push the button again, the device crackled to life. "Detective Waters, you are cleared to enter. You are asked to stay on the primary road. When you arrive at the main building, please park your vehicle under the portico and give your keys to the attendant."

What the hell?

The double iron gates slid apart. As he passed through, a flash indicated a photograph and he wondered if the quality would match that of the traffic control cameras set up around town. Somehow he knew there would be no comparison. *Shoot. This camera probably could read the time on his watch and tell whether or not he needed a shave.*

Not surprisingly, the second he had cleared the opening the gates closed behind him. Money had its privileges. And its paranoia.

How did they know his name? Obviously they had some way of checking via his license plates. How could a non-law-enforcement entity gain access to that kind of information?

Even as the surprise visit fell apart before his eyes, his cop intuition zinged. This kind of power—this kind of money—hid all kinds of secrets. His challenge would be to figure out whether any of the secrets it hid mattered to him or his investigation.

The paved road—how much did this cost to maintain?—wound through pine trees and aspen groves. Chase spotted a few unobtrusive cameras and then the road began to climb. Sunlight slipped through the dense growth of pines and glittered like airborne diamonds. Scanning the trees he saw more partially hidden video equipment and realized the average visitor would never know it was there. This operation might be paranoid but they knew how to keep their paranoia a secret.

At the top of the hill, on a prime piece of real estate, the Preston Clinic came into view. It looked like a country mansion. Stone and windows and balconies lifted above grounds that would easily require a crew of twenty to maintain. A lot of the residents in Aspen Falls had money, but this trumped anything he'd seen in the area.

He slowed and made note of the surroundings. A stable to the north, individual cottages meandering along a creek bed to the south. The Preston Clinic screamed resort rather than hospital.

A young man in full livery, standing at the doors of the clinic, watched his SUV approach. Chase wished he'd hit the car wash before he made the trip. Not even to the target and he was already one down. The uniformed valet did not move to open his door, but instead waited while Chase walked up to the entrance, then ceremoniously pulled open one of the enormous carved barriers at the last moment.

Inside, Chase found himself in a lobby area filled with light and flowers and comfortable-looking chairs. A fireplace, six times the size of any fireplace he'd ever seen, boasted a full blaze. How many cords of wood did they go through in a month?

An attractive blonde dressed in a conservative, but short business suit approached him and held out her hand. "Detective Waters. Welcome to the Preston Clinic. How may we help you today?"

"I'm sorry. You seem to have the advantage. I didn't catch your name."

"That would be because I didn't throw it to you." Her laugh was throaty and suggestive. "Here it comes, are you ready?"

Was she flirting with him?

"My name is Cassandra. Cassandra Lindgren. That would be with a 'C'. Are you better prepared now to let me assist you?"

From "we" to "me." Flirting. Definitely flirting.

"How long has the Preston Clinic been here?"

"We've been open almost two years, but as you probably know we're very low-key. It took us over a year to build the clinic to our specifications."

"Two years?"

"I'm gratified by your surprise. Part of what we promise our clients—for an enormous amount of money, by the way—is privacy. It appears we are meeting that commitment. We might even include this exchange in our next brochure—that is if we had brochures."

The muted sound of a phone rang once then stopped. Either it had been answered on the first ring, or the system had been set up to only allow one audible intrusion into the idyllic setting.

"Would you like a tour, Detective?"

"Wouldn't that be against your policy?"

"You got me. The tour would not include any contact with our clientele. You would spend time here without actually getting any information regarding those we are currently serving. If that's what you're after, you are out of luck."

"Can you at least tell me what services you perform for your clientele?"

"Of course. The Preston Clinic's clients include people who want to have a nip and a tuck without their public knowing, or their board of directors. Youth is a sign of power in our society, as you may or may not be aware." She looked pointedly at his graying hair and crow's feet. "We also have enormous success in combating addictions—from cocaine to oxy to sex. We can handle it all. But the primary purpose for this location—oh, did you know this was one of several?—is to facilitate life-or-death situations. We are known, in those certain circles that are aware of our existence, for our ability to successfully extend life through the skill of our surgical staff. We have a ninety-eight percent survival rate for our transplant clients, all of them—not just kidney—after three years. That's practically unheard of."

Chase thought about Mitchell. And the fact that in all likelihood he would never have the opportunity to even get a chance at achieving a survival rate statistic.

"How do you obtain your organs, Ms. Lindgren?"

Her flirtatious smile vanished, replaced with a sour expression. A wall had gone up. Solid. Tall. "Detective, many of our organs come through the normal channels. Occasionally we have live donors—a kidney donor for example—and in other instances we are able to obtain suitable organs outside of the United States and fly them in. I assure you we are in compliance with the laws of all of the countries with whom we deal and where we operate."

"I assume you keep records of all of your organ and tissue acquisitions? Whether they are through normal channels or otherwise?"

Cassandra with a "C" bristled. "Of course, Detective. If there is ever a problem, we want to protect both our patients and the clinic. We always know our sources."

She anticipated his next question. "However, we believe deeply in our patient-doctor confidentiality. Even if you obtain a warrant, you should expect the matter to end up in court. We have never divulged any information willingly. And you should know that our legal team is very well paid."

Chase wondered why an ethically run clinic would require a well-paid legal team.

"Thank you, Ms. Lindgren. You've been very helpful." As Chase turned to leave, he could sense the stutter-step of the point person for the Preston Clinic. She hadn't expected him to leave so quickly. He wished he could be a fly on the wall to hear her phone call the minute his car left the drive.

On his way back to the station, Chase decided they needed to put the clinic under a microscope. The people associated with the private enterprise had money. And money is what was driving these murders.

Money, and the fear of death.

Chapter Thirty-Eight

Aspen Falls Police Department
Monday, September 24

Chase hung up the phone. John Bohnert, the high priest of the witches' coven on campus, had called him with a name and contact information for a Santeria follower willing to meet with him. However, Bohnert cautioned that Raul Ramirez considered the entire situation an intrusion into his life, and Ramirez's anger at the events that forced him to surface—even for a moment—might make him less than cooperative.

Although tempted to forget the cult angle and move on, Chase's training wouldn't let him drop a possible lead without investigating it to the end. He called Ramirez and set up a time to meet. The telephone conversation didn't last long and Chase did most of the talking. The Santeria practitioner refused to come to the station and refused the first three alternative places Chase suggested. They finally agreed to meet at the north end of the City Market parking lot at four o'clock. Chase knew Ramirez would never have come forward on his own and their meeting would likely be tense.

Chase did a computer search for Raul Ramirez and got well over a million hits. But when he added Santeria to the mix it looked like there might be some connections to a drug cartel in Mexico. Chase would make sure someone knew of his plans to meet with this guy.

"Hey lawman, looking for these?" Bond walked up to his desk and held out an unopened bag of Twizzlers. He'd left them on the kitchen counter.

His heart welled at her thoughtfulness. The surprise of seeing his wife while he was at work never failed to delight him. "Thanks for bringing these." He didn't tell her he'd stopped at the store earlier and bought another bag.

"My contribution to the case."

Chase laughed, then noticed the dark circles under her eyes. She looked exhausted. Sick even. "Come with me."

He grabbed her hand and took her to a small conference room. Once inside he closed the door, pulled her into his arms and kissed her on her forehead. "What's wrong?"

Bond's eyes veiled and she pretended to pick some lint off her jacket. "Oh, you know. I'm worried about investing so much money in the store, and I keep seeing that black Mustang around town. But my worry about money is natural and it's a small town, so seeing the same car isn't all that strange. I'm just being silly."

"We haven't invested a dime yet so there's still plenty of time to reconsider, although I know you'll make whatever you do a success. And you're right. In Aspen Falls we're likely to see the same car over and over again but I'll keep an eye out. If you see it again, get a plate number."

Bond nodded.

"What else?" Chase asked.

"Nothing."

Chase wanted to hold her and protect her and fix whatever had caused those dark circles. She seemed suddenly fragile—not the strong, confident woman he knew and loved. But if he pushed her now she'd either fall apart or withdraw completely.

"How about I make sure I'm home for dinner with the girls tonight, then you and I can have a little time to talk about this 'nothing'?"

Bond would not meet his gaze but she gave a jerky little nod.

Someone knocked on the conference room door.

"There you are. Sorry to interrupt." The desk sergeant, who was anything but sorry, stuck his head in the room. "Some guy named Mex says you're expecting him. You weren't at your desk. Couldn't find you."

Chase bit back a sarcastic comment about the detection skills of the deskman. The snarky words he'd almost uttered were because he was worried about Bond.

"Tell him I'll be right out."

"Guy looks like he isn't the waiting around kind," the sergeant said. He stood there as if he was looking for some reaction from Chase.

"That's okay," Bond said. "I'm leaving." She moved to the door.

"Bond, wait."

She turned her eyes to him. The confusion and pleading he saw in them made him want to seriously hurt whoever or whatever plagued his wife. But he would not force her to tell him about it now.

"Thanks for the Twizzlers. I'll see you later."

* * *

Clean pressed jeans. A starched, white, collared shirt with pearl snap buttons. Polished, dark cowboy boots. A black

151

Stetson held casually. Fresh haircut. Mex didn't look like an immigrant—legal or illegal—let alone like someone who hangs out in a seedy bar.

Chase put out his hand. "Chase Waters."

The man put his free hand in Chase's and looked him in the eye. "Mex."

Chase threw him a questioning glance. "Mex? Is that a nickname?"

"You could call me Carlos Alberto Basilio Teodoro Duque de Estrada Anderson."

Chase arched an eyebrow. "Mex it is. But where did the Anderson come from?"

"A wayward American fell in love with a Mexican beauty and never looked back."

Chase found himself liking this man right away. His instincts, rarely wrong, told him Mex Anderson was a complicated man with an uncomplicated moral compass. But it bothered Chase the man had refused to talk to Daniel.

He led Mex back to the same conference room he'd been in with Bond. On the table sat a notepad and a pen. The remote for the DVD recorder sat within easy reach. Two glasses and a pitcher of water signaled a friendly meeting, not adversarial.

"Tell me a little about yourself," Chase said.

"Just a guy from Mexico trying to keep his head above water."

"You have no discernible accent."

"You can attribute that to whatever you want but I did spend four years at San Diego State University."

"What did you study?"

"I majored in Criminal Justice with a minor in Chicano Studies."

"I'm impressed."

"Don't be. I didn't write the courses. I just took 'em. Then I moved back to Mexico."

"Why?"

"Why not? That's where my family lived. I had dual citizenship. I had choices others didn't. I chose Mexico."

"What did you do there?"

Mex fell silent.

"Well?"

Mex wrapped his knuckles on the table twice as if he'd come to a decision. "Law enforcement."

Chase knew Mex had a story to tell and one day they'd sit down over some brews and talk. But right now he had a case to solve.

"What can you tell me about my John and Jane Doe DBs?"

"How many?"

"Three recent but one has been identified—José Sanchez. They're my cases. I'm also aware of two more a year ago this summer that are County. And I have one that was never a DB—Rachelle Benavides."

"You're not aware of them all."

That was exactly what Chase didn't want to hear.

"In the last eighteen months I know of eleven people in my community who have disappeared."

Bile burned up Chase's throat. "Eleven?" He fought the word.

"Actually more than eleven—eleven are connected to your case. I found out what happened to the others. Most of them went back to Mexico. A couple were arrested for crimes in Denver and deported. One simply had enough of a haranguing bitch of a wife and decided to try his luck elsewhere."

"How do you know all of this?" Chase felt at a disadvantage.

"Technically, these people aren't here. They are illegal. So when they have a problem they come to me. Mostly I resolve simple disputes. But occasionally I need to get involved in more complex issues. Over the last year or so I've been searching for a way to connect with local law enforcement to form an alliance of sorts."

"Why do undocumented people trust you? You have a law enforcement background."

"Ah... they don't know under what circumstances I left Mexico, and the stories that have filled the void of information are wild. They also don't know I'm a citizen here. I've kept those secrets so they are comfortable coming to me—someone they think is in the same legal position as them."

"Okay. Can you help me not only identify the two victims I have in the morgue, but also help me tie these murders together?"

"Detective, I will help you identify your victims if I can. Beyond that we will need to see how our mutual trust level develops. I also have a request."

"Yes?"

"From time to time it would help if I had access to your resources."

"Such as?"

"Motor vehicle records, your lab or the ME's, search dogs. That kind of thing. But it would need to be off the record."

"The only one of those I can promise you off the record contact would be the search dogs. Jamie Taylor is the best handler in the area and she does it on a volunteer basis."

Mex glanced away. "That's a start, I guess."

"You have more information."

Mex didn't take the bait. "Tell me something. Have you ever been in a position where you would do anything—*anything*—to help a loved one? Even break the law?"

Chapter Thirty-Nine

The Sloan Residence
Monday, September 24

Maggie was taking tea and toast to Mrs. Sloan on a silver serving tray when the door opened and her employer walked in. "Why Mr. Sloan, you're home early." Maggie smiled up at him. "Diana will be delighted."

Edward Sloan leaned over to smell the flowers arranged in a tiny vase on the tray. "Maggie, how long have you worked here? Lived with us?"

"Thirty-three years, Mr. Sloan."

"And how often have I asked you to call me Edward?"

"Nearly every day, Mr. Sloan."

"And yet you call me Mr. Sloan, and my wife by her given name. Why is that?"

"I *like* her name, Mr. Sloan."

She enjoyed their running joke. Maggie Sinclair considered herself as much a part of their family as any of the Sloan children. Yes, they paid her. But it wasn't unlike the money they made available to Eleanor and Eddie whenever they required it. Edward and Diana Sloan were friends she could count on. Indeed, she had turned to their friendship more than once over the years.

"Did Dr. Jackson have anything new to report from his last visit?"

Maggie shook her head. "I'm afraid it's just more of the same. She's slipping away from us and there's naught we can do."

"Thank you, Maggie. I'll go change out of this suit and be in to see her in a few minutes so we can get caught up on our days."

"Dinner at your usual time?"

"You're a lifesaver. Would you have it sent to my room? It's been a long day."

Maggie nodded. "Dr. Jackson said he'd be by later to check on his patient."

Her heart wept as Edward Sloan tried to give her his old reassuring smile. He didn't quite pull it off. For the last few weeks two private nurses hadn't been enough to assure Dr. Jackson that Diana Sloan was receiving all the care and attention she needed. He'd increased his personal calls to three a day.

The truth was Edward Sloan's wife needed far more than even twenty visits a day could provide.

Maggie balanced the tray while she twisted the handle and pushed open the door.

"Hello, Diana. I've brought your afternoon tea."

She placed the tray on a beautiful side table and bent to raise the woman who had become her friend. While Diana slumped forward like a little girl's forgotten doll on a shelf, Maggie fluffed the pile of scented pillows. With arms of steel and hands of butterfly wings, she guided Diana onto her feathered throne. Maggie then popped the legs open on the serving tray and placed it gently on the bed in front of Diana.

"Mags, you have gentrified us over the years. I feel part English." Diana tried to lift the spoon to stir some sugar and cream into her cup but her hand clattered the silver against the delicate china.

Maggie perched on the side of the bed and readied the cuppa. She held it gently up to Diana's mouth for her to take a sip.

"Thank you. That's wonderful." Diana's head fell back on the pillows. "Did I hear Edward a minute ago?"

"You did. He's home early and will be in to share some private time with you as soon as he gets out of his work clothes."

The smallest of chuckles popped from Diana's mouth. "You make it sound like he wears overalls."

Maggie smiled as she pictured the suit that easily cost as much as she made in two months. "He just wants to be fresh for you."

"Do I look okay?" Diana raised a hand to pat her hair.

Maggie's eyes teared up with the effort she saw that tiny movement take. "You are as lovely as ever."

There was a gentle knocking on the door and Edward Sloan entered. His presence filled the room but he had eyes only for his wife.

Maggie knew what he saw when he looked at Diana. He saw the woman he loved, just as Maggie saw her best friend. They each tried to see behind Diana's listless eyes in search of the strong woman, the loving woman, the compassionate woman they'd each fallen in love with in their own way.

So Diana's eyes were where the two people who loved her most chose to focus.

Maggie gave her friend a hug. The bones she touched were those of a small bird. "I'll see you later, love."

She needed to leave quickly now. Today her strength seemed to have taken a blow and she felt on the verge of tears. She didn't want Diana to see her crying. She laid a hand on Edward's arm as she exited the room.

He would do anything for the woman who held his heart.

Anything.

Chapter Forty

Aspen Falls Memorial Hospital
Monday, September 24

Detective Terri Johnson walked up to the doors of the Emergency Room at Memorial. She ran through her memories of Memorial's ER doctor, Leslie James. Had everything she'd done been on the up and up? Could she be trusted?

Terri remembered an occasion that troubled her. She had been in the ER on an assault case when another woman, battered and bloody, staggered in. Terri pegged the woman without question as a local prostitute. Leslie took one look at the stumbling woman and ushered her into an exam area. Fifteen minutes later Leslie James returned to the victim Terri was working with and didn't say a word. When Terri questioned her about the walk-in patient, Leslie had shaken her head and said, "Who are you talking about?"

Where did Leslie James's priorities stack up? If she fudged a little on one end of the scale, where she treated patients without reporting anything, maybe she fudged a little on the other end of the scale. Would a financial benefit lure her to do other things like run blood tests that weren't necessary so needed organs could be obtained by rich people?

Terri decided to approach her interview with Leslie James from the side rather than dead on. She needed to be sure she could trust her. Too many lives, too many answers, depended on it.

Inside the ER there were two groups of people waiting. Since she didn't see any blood and no one looked like they were about to puke she figured them for family or friends. They had that strange combined look of worry and boredom people get when they hang out in hospital waiting rooms.

The receptionist recognized her and waved her back to the secure area. It didn't take long for Terri to find Leslie James. She stood over an older man pressing on his abdomen. Terri caught Leslie's eye.

"When you're finished here I need a moment."

Leslie nodded and continued her examination.

Ten minutes later Leslie James found Terri at the nurse's station.

"What's up?"

"How many people come through the ER without formal admission?" Even though she asked a direct question it didn't have anything to do with what she really wanted to know. Sideways. First she would make sure her trust in Leslie James could stand up.

James hesitated. "What do you mean?"

"You treated a woman here one night who'd been beaten and you didn't raise an eyebrow or fill out a form. Why not?"

Leslie James took a deep breath. "Why should I tell you anything?"

"Because it's the right thing to do?"

A gurney carrying another ER patient passed them and a nurse huffed loud enough to make sure the two women knew the injured person required Leslie's attention.

"I'll be right there," Leslie called after the nurse. "Look, Terri. There are some people who come here when they need help because they know I won't ask any questions. If I got all formal and legal they wouldn't trust me. Sometimes they need someone they can trust."

"You know that's illegal."

"If I ever thought you needed to be called in on an incident I wouldn't hesitate. But usually it's something that would just take up your time without changing anything. Do you understand?"

"You and I are gonna need to sit down and talk about this. We need to find a way to work together," Terri said.

"I know. I figured we'd be at this point sooner or later. Just thought our later would be much, much later."

Terri let the choices of the ER doctor go for the moment. She had more important things to discuss. "What I need to know tonight is how blood tests are ordered from the ER and who can order them."

"That's easy."

"Go."

"Blood tests are ordered by a doctor, period."

Terri weighed what Leslie said. She didn't think Leslie James had anything to do with her current cases. "How are they ordered?"

"By computer. Like everything else these days."

"Can any doctor order the tests?"

"Of course, as long as they have a password to access our system."

Time to rethink the possibilities. It could still be an ER employee but it could also be any doctor in the Memorial system. They needed to take a look at all of the local doctors. Local doctors who had privileges at the hospital with access to the hospital's computer. As the search narrowed it also expanded.

Great.

"I need a list of all of your ER employees and any doctor who may have access to your system. Do I need another warrant?"

"Probably, yes." Leslie obviously considered the past, present and future of the ER. "However, given the current set of circumstances and the implications—I mean, how often do I get served a warrant for a patient list—I think I could argue my case to the hospital board should it come to that. I'll get you those names."

Chapter Forty-One

City Market Parking Lot
Monday, September 24

Chase would not admit it to anybody, but meeting with this Santeria guy made him nervous. No doubt about it. From everything he'd read on the internet about this religion, it had some history and some pretty big power. He found himself wishing he'd talked to God a little more regularly, or at least gone to church. His corner felt a little empty.

Clouds formed overhead. This time of year they could bring either rain or snow—or both. The temperatures had been warm so he figured if they got any precipitation it would be rain. But in the high country anything could happen.

Chase parked and debated what to do while he waited for four o'clock to roll around. He decided to go into the grocery store and pick up a couple of things. More Twizzlers wouldn't hurt, and he'd noticed they were running low on French roast at home. He stepped outside of his vehicle. An icy wind made the thermometer a liar and he cursed his decision not to wear a coat. He hadn't bothered with any weather forecasts for the last couple of days—he had his own storms to worry about. He pictured his fleece jacket hooked on a peg in his locker.

Purchases made, Chase walked back to his car. As he unlocked the back door to stow the grocery bag another car pulled up, stopped about twenty yards away, then crept closer. Chase expected fog to suddenly fall and swirl like in horror movies. Maybe those clouds would pull together for a lightning show—some sign to warn him about the man about to walk into his life. The severed heads he'd seen online rolled into his thoughts.

Chase tossed the bag inside and closed the door. Turned to face the approaching car—the slithering car—as it came to a stop. He determined to look both calm and warm and leaned against the side of his car. The cold cut through his clothes. *Shit*. But he didn't move.

The Toyota Camry sat for a good thirty seconds. Finally the driver cut the engine. Another interminable passage of time, then Chase heard a click.

One dirty Nike and then a second one hit the pavement, followed by a rather small, jean-clad wiry man wearing a faded Miami Dolphins T-shirt beneath his unzipped navy jacket. He observed long and wind-blown black hair, a scrunched face and—even from this distance—angry dark eyes. Even with those eyes, he was just a guy. Nothing he couldn't handle. He hoped. Chase's tension lifted.

Ramirez stood three feet away. His stance said he hated being in this position.

"I'm investigating some murders," Chase opened the conversation. "The bodies have been mutilated, organs removed. Do you or anyone in your group know anything about these killings?"

"Group?"

"Sect? Congregation? Help me out here."

165

"If my group, sect or congregation did have any knowledge of these acts, do you think I'd be meeting you here in the first place? Do you think I'd be dying to confide and confess to a cop?"

"Knowledge does not mean involvement. And I'm not casting any kind of blame."

"What you're casting is disruption. If these mutilations had stayed under whatever kind of control they required, my life would be uninterrupted. Instead I find myself outed in a most disagreeable manner." Ramirez's formal speech pattern was at odds with his straggly appearance. Chase noted the clenched fists. "I'm angry. And in my own way, I have as much of an interest in finding the killers as you."

"You don't need the heat."

"They don't pay you the big bucks for nothing, *amigo.*"

Chase hated the term *amigo* applied to him by this man. "Will you let me know if you hear of anything that will help us?"

"You now know my identity. You now know of the existence of Santeria practitioners in Aspen Falls. The only reason I would have for getting further involved would be retribution."

"And?"

"*Yo no sé.* I couldn't say, Detective. This exposure is filled with reasons to retaliate. But trust me, *if* something should happen to your suspects you will never know for certain Santeria had anything to do with it. I do not expect to ever have to meet with the likes of you again."

Ramirez moved back to his car and hesitated before getting in. "Detective?"

"Yes?"

"Leave me out of this from now on. I have nothing more to say to you. But I promise, if you don't take care of Presley Adams and his clinic, I will."

Chapter Forty-Two

Near Aspen Falls Middle School
Monday, September 24

Bobby Carlisle pointed. "There she is." They'd been sitting out in front of this goddamned school for the last twenty minutes. About time she showed.

"Which one?"

"Sammy, open your eyes, man. We've only been following her for... how long?" If they were ever caught, it would be his older brother who would bring them down. Sammy had the attention span of a gnat and his IQ was slightly less. But he did have some muscles.

"You know how long. It's just that she changes."

"Changes what?"

"Clothes and shit."

Bobby squeezed his lips as tight as he could. They'd figured out pretty fast that this teenage bimbo usually had family around her. Friends. She was rarely alone.

Except for when she wanted a late night out with those friends. Then, for at least a little while, she was alone. They'd seen her sneak out three times in the last two weeks. She was good, but they were better.

Timing was everything. Sneaking in and out was a little iffy. If she was gonna get caught by her parents, it would be either as she left the house or when she came home. If for some reason the adults heard her while she was trying to get away from the house and they were doing the job, things could get bad fast. Their safest grab would be when she was coming home before she had a chance to do something stupid. Or leaving wherever it was she'd gone to party.

He wasn't really worried. Teenagers could be counted on to make stupid decisions. They had enough information on her and when she made a wrong move they'd be there.

Chapter Forty-Three

The Greene Home
Monday, September 24

Detective Terri Johnson sat in her car in front of the home of Carol Greene and her eight year-old granddaughter, Lily. She fiddled with her radio, then checked her vanity mirror. She rarely wore lipstick but this was a special occasion.

She was fifteen minutes early. If Terri sat here much longer, one of the neighbors would probably call the police to report a suspicious vehicle. A stalker. It would be a problem. She put her foot on the brake and began to push the button for the keyless ignition. She'd drive around town for a bit. Should've thought of that first. Nerves had gummed up her thinking.

The door of the home opened and Carol Greene waved her in. *Crap. Caught.*

Chest tight and heart thrumming Terri waved back, grabbed her purse and took a moment to breathe. This visit was as important to the two people who lived in that house as it was to her. At least the three of them wouldn't be alone.

Thank God they wouldn't be alone.

Terri set her phone to vibrate and made sure her weapon remained well concealed under her jacket as she exited her car. She pinned a smile to her face and hoped it didn't come across like a grimace. Terri felt like she had slipped under water and desperately needed to come up for air. She put one foot in front of the other until she got to the door.

"Detective Johnson, thank you for coming." The older woman pressed her hands against her thighs and gave them a wipe.

Carol Greene's body language bounced into Terri's consciousness, penetrated the insecurity that surrounded her like a veil of water and released her, throwing her to the surface where she could breathe again. "Please call me Terri."

The woman relaxed and took a deep breath of her own. "Terri. Thank you."

Mrs. Greene held the door open and stepped aside while Terri entered the living room. The floorboards of the house, a small Victorian like ninety percent of the houses in Aspen Falls of a certain age, creaked under her weight. The home had been lovingly maintained for decades, but time had begun to show through the patches. Carol Greene had raised both a daughter and a granddaughter on her own before her illness. Cancer didn't leave much time for carpentry.

"You know Krysta Corinn, our attorney. And you also know Myrna Kittredge with Child Services." Even though the introductions were unnecessary, Terri appreciated the slow dance toward the reason for her visit. Everyone sat around the dining room table, coffee cups in front of them. A delicate plate in the middle of the table held a carefully displayed pile of untouched cookies.

Terri glanced around and Myrna Kittredge anticipated her question. "Lily is playing outside with one of our caregivers to give us a few minutes."

Krysta Corinn cleared her throat. "Terri, we're here to make sure we're all on the same page regarding Lily's future, and if we're in accordance, to allow you and the girl to begin to get to know each other. You were instrumental in assuring Lily's mother a safe place to stay and raise her child when her ex-husband became volatile, a fact important both to Lily's mother, her grandmother," she nodded toward Carol, "and to Lily herself. When Carol learned through Ms. Kittredge that you had been trying to adopt a child she contacted me."

Terri looked at Carol Greene. "I was so sorry to hear of your illness."

The grandmother nodded.

"Mrs. Greene, I cannot begin to tell you how honored I am that you would consider allowing me to finish raising your granddaughter. When I worked your daughter's case I found her to be a woman of exceptional strength when it came to Lily." She struggled to find the right words. "Your daughter had so much courage. She brought honor to both you and her daughter. Like too many other women she fell in love with a man not worthy of her, and when she discovered her mistake she tried to correct it. She made a decision that cost her life. In many ways I feel like I failed her. Somehow I should have been there. But in my heart of hearts, even with the way things turned out, I know she made the right decision."

"Detective Johnson—Terri—I was never more proud of Deirdre than when she made the decision to leave her husband. There's no way you could have prevented her murder. He would have gotten to her sooner or later. Because of you she at least had a few months of freedom. You helped her realize her value as a daughter, a mother

and a woman. She respected you. She would want Lily to have a role model like you. Even if I didn't have this, this...
" her hand fluttered in front of her chest, "I would want you in Lily's life."

"Does Lily know you're ill?" Terri asked.

Carol Greene's eyes filled with tears, and she nodded. "She's a smart little girl. She knew something was going on and I've never lied to her."

A door slammed shut. "Is this her?" All of the adults sitting at the table turned to look at the source of the question.

Terri saw a girl, tall for eight years old, standing in the doorway, arms crossed. Her chin lifted a fraction at the sudden attention—or it could be Terri had a lot to learn about the stances of little girls.

Terri tried to swallow—to say something—but her mouth had gone dry.

173

Chapter Forty-Four

The Benavides Home
Monday, September 24

Chase was updating the file. He hated paperwork, even if it was at the computer. He thought maybe he'd be able to get home for a few minutes and grab an early dinner with his family before returning to work.

Whit knocked on his door and came in. "We've got a situation you should be aware of."

This can't be good. "What?"

"There's been a fire at the Benavides home."

Shit.

Chase threw his car into park and pushed open the door, searching for any member of the Benavides family. Acrid smoke continued to billow from hot spots around the home. The tidy yard in the front, the part that had not been consumed by fire, had been trampled by those fighting to save the structure.

He saw Mrs. Benavides sitting off by herself on a lawn chair in the front yard. The tiny woman was bundled into a thick down coat with at least three scarves wrapped around her neck and head. Relief washed over him. He rushed toward her and dropped to his knees.

"You!" She spat in his face.

Chase carefully removed his handkerchief, grateful one more time that his wife made him carry them every single day. He backed away from the woman he'd been so concerned about and wiped his face.

"This all your fault. My daughter dead and now we lose in fire." The woman sat up straighter. "All you. First Rachelle, and now... this *your* fire."

Chase watched her mouth work, seeking enough saliva for another attack. Before she could work up another round he asked her, "Where's Elizabeth?"

"She come home from her walk with Daniel." The older woman softened. Apparently she liked the detective who had been escorting her daughter the last couple of days. "Then she go to the market for dinner." The older woman paused and her voice changed. "I need go out to garden to get fresh herbs. Killing frost any day now. We need use." Ramona Benavidez's eyes teared as she looked at her home.

Chase remembered his grandmother. Even in the midst of tragedy, the practical needs of feeding and clothing her family drew her attention. He looked at the smoldering ruin of a kitchen. Using the last of the summer herbs was the last thing she should have been concerned about. No kitchen remained in which herbs could be put to any use. At least she and her daughter were safe.

Chase excused himself and walked up to the FD captain. "Hey, Pat. What's your take on this fire?

"Funny you should ask. No doubt about it, this fire started because someone wanted the house to burn."

"How can you know so soon?"

"You mean other than how fast the flames engulfed the entire structure? Or the heat? And the warning sign on the garage? Walk around to the back and take a look."

Chase moved through a group of firefighters. Behind the house, spray-painted on the wall of the detached garage, he read the words "QUIT TALKING BITCH." Not especially unique but they'd gotten their point across.

Elizabeth was out of this investigation even if he had to put her in protective custody.

He went back to talk to the captain.

"It's not a total loss, Chase. A small burn area in the front, which we were able to control quickly. Another flash point in the back got most of the kitchen, but the rest of the house probably didn't even have much smoke damage. Winds don't usually help us but this time they did."

"Other than the graffiti on the garage, can you prove arson?"

"No doubt. But arson just enough to make a point." The captain stopped and sniffed. "You know someone who would want to make a point to this family, Detective? Do you know who wrote the message on the garage wall?"

"We're working on it."

"Work faster. A warning is one thing. Next time I don't think they'll be so particular about what burns."

Elizabeth Benavides blasted up next to him, her anger and fear melding into a formidable female ready to do her own kind of battle. "What the hell happened? Mamá said I should ask you."

"Elizabeth, I appreciate your desire to help. And you have. But that's over now."

"That's not what I asked you." She set her jaw. "What are you talking about?"

Chase read people well. And he knew Elizabeth Benavides knew exactly what he was talking about. "This fire could have killed someone—you know it and I know it.

This one? Another warning. A strong one and probably the last. The next time something happens it won't be a warning. I don't want that kind of responsibility. Do you?"

Elizabeth's face hardened and her eyes squinted into steel. A tear worked its way out of her right eye and crawled down her face.

"I know this is hard," Chase said.

"How could you know? Don't tell me you know." Elizabeth choked the words out. "Have you ever lost somebody you loved before you should have?"

The sun slipped behind the western edge of Cobalt Mountain and they went from dusk to night in the blink of an eye. Chase felt the familiar bruise in his chest.

The scene was now lit by the numerous headlights of response vehicles and curious bystanders. Chase cleared his throat. "Yes, Miss Benavides, as a matter of fact I have."

They stood in silence while the firefighters packed up their gear and prepared to depart. The captain walked up to Elizabeth. "Do you have someplace your family can stay while you make the repairs to your home?"

"Don't worry about us. Our neighbors will help."

The firefighter touched his hat in a salute and walked away.

Elizabeth's father had joined her mother. The couple stood as close together as they could without quite touching. Heads bowed close together for a moment, then turned toward their home, and finally toward their daughter.

"You might be willing to risk your life, Elizabeth. But are you willing to risk theirs?"

She brought a fist up and hit him in the chest. Hard. Chase remained still and she hit him again. This time without the force. Without the anger.

177

"I will keep you informed every step of the way. But your involvement in this investigation is over. Agreed?"

An older couple approached Elizabeth's parents. Pulled them away from their home and began walking across the street. Mrs. Benavides stumbled and supporting arms reached out to steady her.

"I need you to find my sister's murderers. I need them to pay."

"We will."

Elizabeth hesitated. "We are having a service Wednesday morning. You should come."

"I will."

Chase turned to leave, checking traffic before he crossed to his car. Light from a streetlight spilled over a dark, possibly black, Mustang. He hesitated then changed course. Four strides in the direction of the parked car, it pulled out, did a three-point maneuver and left the scene.

Chapter Forty-Five

Aspen Falls Police Department
Monday, September 24

Chase hurried into the meeting room and surveyed the other two detectives. Terri appeared fresh but Daniel sagged in the chair and his normally crisp clothes melted into wrinkles.

"You okay?"

No response.

"Daniel, you okay?"

"What did I miss?" The detective focused mournful eyes on Chase. "Tell me what I did wrong that ended up with Elizabeth's house burning to the ground."

"Her house didn't burn to the ground and no one got hurt. And you did nothing wrong."

Daniel fell silent.

"I need you both on top of this with me. We have a new number of victims. Twelve."

Both detectives sat straighter in their chairs. "Twelve?" In stereo.

"Thanks to Daniel and Elizabeth, I met with a contact—credible—who knows of eleven missing people from the Hispanic community. With Rachelle Benavides we have twelve."

"Names?" Terri asked.

"Not yet but he'll get them to us." Chase tossed his folder on the table. "There's another thing. I want to know if either of you turn up a connection to a black Mustang."

"What's the connection?" Daniel asked.

"One direct—a black Mustang was parked on the street across from the Benavides home. When I approached, it took off."

"Plates?" Terri wanted to know.

"Didn't get a chance to see the license plates. But I did note two occupants. Both white, both male, thirties."

"And the indirect?" Daniel asked.

"Skizzers talked about the Batmobile the night we found the body in the dumpster. Wasn't the Batmobile black? Could be a Mustang. And someone in a black Mustang has been shadowing my family. May or may not have anything to do with our case. But the coincidence bothers me."

"Following your family?" Terri pressed.

"A black Mustang has shown up often enough that Bond noticed. I don't know if one thing is connected to the other. Just call me if you see one." Chase looked at Terri. "What did you get from the ER?"

"Another list of names, but not quite as many. Orders for blood tests are computerized, and supposedly only the doctors have access, but we all know computers can be hacked, passwords can be discovered, and security can pretty well suck when there's a computer involved."

Daniel laughed. "Almost as bad as when it's person-to-person."

"Touché." Terri winked at Chase. She'd egged Daniel on with her computer comment and it worked. Daniel Murillo hadn't worked fraud cases for years without coming away with a healthy respect for the fact that more fraud occurs in person than via technology. He had a hard time trying to convince his fellow detectives, but when a waitress gave Terri back the wrong credit card and then tried to deny it Daniel had new believers.

"At any rate," Terri continued, "I have a list of all ER employees, including docs, who have access to the system. They're required to change passwords every month but we should be able to find our hacker pretty fast. The doctors get a printout every week with their test requests on it. Some are better record keepers than others, but we should be able to find a pattern and someone responsible."

"Assuming it's someone in the ER," Daniel added.

"Who else would it be?"

"Just keeping an open mind."

"You wanna help with the list?"

"Sure."

"Here are copies of the sketches Dobson did on the two men Maria Sanchez saw." Chase handed out the pictures. "Show them around and see if anyone recognizes either man."

The detectives studied the drawings. Terri spoke first. "Wish we could've gotten Carol, but we'll work with what we've got."

"We also received the preliminary autopsy results back on Sanchez. Looks like he died of sepsis from the nephrectomy," Chase said.

Daniel looked thoughtful. "He died from bacteria. Because he sold a kidney to buy papers for himself and his wife."

"Have either of you heard of the Preston Clinic?" Chase asked.

Blank stares and headshakes answered his question.

"It's a private hospital for the wealthy. Just west of town. They do transplants, among other things."

181

"How come we don't know about it?" Terri asked.

"I asked myself the same thing. We've all lived here long enough to know that money can buy just about anything—and that apparently includes everything from publicity to secrecy. The Preston Clinic falls on the secrecy side of things. Only they call it 'privacy.' We need to see what private secrets we can uncover." Chase pulled out a Twizzler and bit off the end. "We're working with an entity that has been able to operate on the down-low for a long time. I'm getting the decided impression that there are some very deep secrets in the very deep pockets of the Preston Clinic."

"I'll see what Leslie James knows about them."

Chief Whitman walked into the room. "Sorry to interrupt."

"No problem, Chief. What can we do for you?" Whit would not interrupt a meeting without a good reason.

"I got a call from the sheriff. Said you didn't get some information he'd sent along several months ago."

"Yeah, true. But we have it now." Whit had to have a different reason for being here.

"And I got another call. From someone named Cassandra Lindgren at the Preston Clinic. She doesn't want to deal with you in the future. If they're to be bothered, they're to be bothered by me."

Okay, a little better reason, but Chase knew there had to be more.

"And as busy as my day has been fielding calls related to you and this case, I received yet one more call."

Chase could tell he should pay close attention now.

"A friend of mine who's fighting the good fight in Mexico called to put in a positive word for someone you met with earlier today. Does the name Mex Anderson ring a bell?"

"Kind of hard to forget a name like that isn't it? Mr. Anderson and I did meet. He alluded to some additional information but so far he's only upped our probable body count."

"Well, he's in my office now and ready to talk a little more."

Chapter Forty-Six

Aspen Falls Police Department
Monday, September 24

Chase followed Whit into the chief's office. Mex Anderson stood, cowboy hat in hand, inspecting Whit's wall of photos. They weren't the usual, and Chase had always sensed some pride in Whit because of that fact. No glad-handing politicians or framed awards. No pictures of Whit in full dress uniform, not even a photograph of the current president. And Chase was pretty sure the man had gotten Whit's vote.

Chief Cornelius Whitman's wall of photos consisted of birds. Most of them colored shots, all of them framed, and every one of them a photo taken by the chief.

Without acknowledging Whit and Chase, Mex spoke. "You have an impressive collection, Chief Whitman. A wide variety of Colorado birds—but one doesn't belong."

"Yes?" Whit watched his visitor.

"*Toxostoma curvirostre.* Curve-billed Thrashers are common in Mexico. I never knew them to go farther north than Arizona and New Mexico."

"Are you a birder, Mr. Anderson?"

"I've always appreciated the freedom, tenacity and spiritual quality of birds. A single feather is a miraculous feat of engineering."

Chase intervened. "Chief Whitman says you're ready to give us some more information."

"I'm ready for more than that, Detective Waters. But I'll be taking things one step at a time."

"As long as the step you're taking now helps us solve these murders, I'm good," Chase said.

"It's information. What you do with it is up to you."

"Good. Go." Chase quelled his need to push. People were falling dead all around him. When he did catch a few minutes of sleep his dreams crawled through his gut and fed his guilt in gory detail. His team's responsibility increased for every new death, and with each bit of information they dug up, his personal responsibility tripled.

Mex gestured toward the chairs. "Please, we need to sit."

Chase took another look at Mex. He had a scar along his hairline, his knuckles looked like they'd been through a meat grinder more than once, and yet he wanted them to sit. Fine, they'd sit. *If the man has viable information and wants tea and cookies, I will find some damned tea and cookies in this building.*

Whit walked around his desk and left the two chairs in front open. Chase sat first, then Mex joined them.

"Thank you," Mex said. "In my experience I have found that often friends will sit—while enemies stand." Chase met his gaze and noted that Mex waited until Whit did as well. "Doesn't mean shit, of course. But it makes me feel better."

"Mr. Anderson, I don't want to jeopardize any information you may be willing to share to further this investigation, but I am under intense pressure to provide some answers," Chase said. "If you have something to tell me, now would be good."

"I've told you about the eleven missing people within the Hispanic community. I suspect they are all dead. I suspect they all died in either the same way Rachelle Benavides died or the way José Sanchez died."

"Wait," Chase said. "How do you know how José Sanchez died? Or Rachelle Benavides, for that matter? We didn't get the autopsy results back on Sanchez until this afternoon."

"It's a small community, Detective. And I'm pretty much at the center of it when it comes to things like this."

Chase decided to wait to push the issue until he heard what Mex Anderson had to say. He signaled for Mex to continue.

"For the last year or so, people have been routinely approached with a proposal to sell an organ. For example, one of their kidneys. People believe they have found the poor man's answer to cash for gold. Most have survived, but others, who I suspect turned down the initial offer, donated more than they ever bargained for. Especially those whose blood type is on the rare side."

Chase leaned forward. "Do you know who is behind these offers?"

Chapter Forty-Seven

Aspen Falls Police Department
Monday, September 24

Chase's normal cop suspicion kicked in and he watched for any sign of subterfuge from Mex. He saw none. "Do you? Do you know who's behind these murders?"

"If I did, believe me, I wouldn't be here now." Mex looked at Whit who sat quietly behind his desk, hands steepled in front of him. "Do you have anything to drink?"

Whit got up and walked over to a dark walnut wall unit where he pulled out three glasses and a bottle of amber liquid. He leaned over and opened another door that housed a refrigerator/freezer combo. "Rocks?"

"Neat," Chase and Mex said in unison.

Whit closed the door and poured two fingers in each tumbler.

"How much money is being offered?" Chase asked.

"I've heard amounts from three hundred dollars to well over two thousand."

"How many people are you talking about?"

"More than twenty that I know of."

"Does that include the eleven who are missing?"

"Nope. The twenty, twenty-five I'm talking about are walking around, as far as I know."

"Are they still in Aspen Falls?"

"Not many. Most have moved on."

"Would any of the people who are still in town be willing to talk to me?"

Mex shook his head. "Maybe not even me, once they hear I've met with you."

Chase wanted to hit something. *So close.* He could flex some legal muscle and force them to come in, but in the end he knew he'd get nothing. And he'd have a public relations nightmare. "Do you know whether or not any of them have been to the emergency room at Memorial?"

"Odds are most of them have been there at some point. It's the only place people without insurance can get medical attention without having to pay up front."

"Aren't there free clinics?" Whit asked.

"They're around. They tend to ask more questions than some people are comfortable answering. And they tend to be understaffed and closed more often than they're open."

Memorial jumped up the line of important elements in this investigation. But Chase knew that until they had some solid facts, he would not be taking on the hospital that meant so much to the community. After tourism and the college, Aspen Falls Memorial ranked third for economic importance. He'd pushed his luck with the local politicos more than once. This time he would walk into that arena fully armored and with weapons to spare.

"Do you know of anyone who's been approached recently?"

"Nope. But I think they're out there."

"Can you put the word out for information?" Chase worked to keep a lid on his frustration. He felt like they were so close to breaking this thing. "I mean, if there's someone out there right now with this kind of an offer, could you find out?"

"Maybe from someone who knows me. Speaking with you—and the word will get out that I'm speaking with you—isn't going to help. I can only try."

Mex was willing to risk his own reputation with his people in order to help them. Chase's respect for Mex Anderson only continued to rise.

"Can I count on you?"

"I don't recommend it."

Chapter Forty-Eight

The Sloan Residence
Monday, September 24

That evening, Edward Sloan wept behind the closed doors of his study. Tears spilled from his eyes but he didn't have the desire or the energy to wipe them away.

Things weren't supposed to happen this way. All of his life Edward had made plans. Long, detailed, perfect plans. And for the most part the things he planned had become reality.

Diana dying was not any part of Edward Sloan's great plans.

He stood and pushed his feet through the thick carpet to the sink. He washed his face, feeling every one of his sixty-seven years.

Martin Jackson had just left. The doctor's compassion warmed Edward even as his practicality chilled him. The time had come to move Diana to a hospital room.

If a donor became available she would be that much more accessible for immediate surgery. If a donor didn't become available...

Palliative care. He hated those godforsaken words. They meant failure. They meant loss.

He smoothed the wrinkles from his casual slacks and tugged his lightweight sweater into place. Even though the study's en suite had a full set of brushes, he chose to run his fingers through his hair instead. If he looked too fresh Diana would know something had upset him.

Back at his desk he picked up the phone and asked Maggie to bring some tea to his wife's room. He wasn't sure he could swallow a thing but he needed a prop.

Edward walked over to his liquor cabinet, uncorked some Blanton's, and poured a generous amount into a snifter. Yep. He could swallow. He just couldn't taste anything.

His private line rang.

"Sloan."

"Good afternoon, Mr. Sloan."

Edward set the drink on his desk not bothering with a coaster. Not bothering with a response.

"We are very close to procuring the item you require."

"When?"

"Soon. Quite soon."

"And?"

"I understand the time has come to make different arrangements for your wife's care."

"How do you—"

"It doesn't matter. But I hope you will consider the private clinic we are associated with just outside of Aspen Falls."

Edward's research had been top-notch. He knew about the clinic. "Why?"

"No hospital suite, or staff, can compare to our quality. We offer the highest level of care, luxury—and perhaps most importantly—privacy, available in the world."

"We're very happy with Dr. Jackson, and privacy is not among our concerns at this time."

"I assure you that even though Dr. Jackson is not a part of our staff, he would be able to continue to be in charge of your wife's treatment. My suggestion is made simply as an offer for your consideration. In the event we are able to find the appropriate item, it would be more convenient to have her at a facility where we can coordinate everything with efficiency."

"And if I find it somewhere else?"

"Dr. Jackson will confirm our surgeons rank among the highest anywhere. But of course you would always have the option of moving her to another location."

"I'll talk to Dr. Jackson and let you know."

"We can have a room ready for her in twenty minutes. You have my word the transfer will be seamless."

Edward Sloan severed the connection.

Chapter Forty-nine

The Waters Home
Monday, September 24

Chase walked through the door and called out. "Bond, I'm so sorry." No response. "Bond?"

He walked through the dimly lit kitchen, all cleaned and cleared from dinner. *Damn.* He could hear the television in the family room and headed in that direction. He stopped in the doorway to watch his family.

Bond sat on the sofa, an afghan wrapped around her shoulders, feet tucked under her legs, a book held listlessly in her hands. Angela multi-tasked between watching TV, listening to her iPod and working her Sudoku game, while Stephanie lay in front of the fire, her head propped up on a pillow while she watched TV. McKenzie was curled up next to his youngest daughter, one open eye assuring the tiny guard dog that the intruder belonged.

Chase glanced at the television screen. Bond had popped in one of their daughters' favorites. Something about a lost dog and fighting parents who come back together when their son and daughter take off to find the pup. Chase couldn't remember the title. A half-eaten bowl of microwave popcorn from last night sat in the center of the coffee table within easy reach of the girls.

Stephanie looked up and called to him. "Daddy!" She jumped to her feet and ran into his arms. He loved coming home even if he had to turn around and leave again.

Bond glanced at him, smiled, then paused the movie. She didn't turn the television off—just paused the movie. The wife of a cop. A cop who had a murder case. She knew he wouldn't be staying. Chase smiled back at her.

"Dad, there's a party I want to go to Friday night. Mom said I needed to ask you." Angela got to the point.

"Don't you want to soften me up first?"

Angela blushed and rolled her eyes at the same time. *Ah, the teenage years.* But she stood up and walked up to him, wrapped her arms around him and said, "I love you, Daddy."

"Am I the world's best daddy?"

"Nope."

"No?"

"You're the universe's best daddy."

He decided not to question the technical differences between 'world' and 'universe' and to take what he could get.

"Does your mom have the details about the party?"

A nod answered his question and the slightly pouty lips told him Bond had a problem with those details. "Your mom and I will talk about it, okay? We'll make a decision together and let you know."

An image of a black Mustang flashed in his mind. He pushed it away.

"Let me know when exactly?"

"Once we've decided, you'll be the first to know."

"Kids are gonna ask me tomorrow."

"Well then, if you need to have an answer right now to give your friends tomorrow, the answer is no."

"I'll wait."

"Good move."

Chase noticed Bond's pallor. "Girls, Mom and I need to talk about something before I go back to work. Would you mind—?"

"We figured." Stephanie tilted her face up for a kiss as the two sisters left the room. "Mommy has been real quiet tonight."

After his daughters were gone, Chase sat down at the end of the couch and pulled Bond's feet toward him. He began a gentle massage of one foot and then the other. "Are you ready to talk?"

Bond closed her eyes, a single tear tracking down her cheek. Either the flames from the fireplace or the light from the television played off the liquid. Whichever, it seared his soul.

* * *

Bond felt numb. For all these years she'd kept a lid on this part of her life. The horror of the moment and all of the lies that followed had been sealed away. Covered. In some way, every day since that one day had held a lie. Including every day she spent with her husband.

She'd never told Chase. She'd never told anyone. Her promise to her mother had held her—bound her—and become so steeped in her psyche that nothing—no memory—had ever tugged at her. Nothing had ever bubbled up intent on release.

Until now.

"Damn you," she breathed the words.

Chase quit massaging her feet. "Excuse me?"

She pulled her feet back toward her. "You heard me."

"Barely." Chase clasped his hands in front of him. "Are you saying that whatever is wrong with you is my fault? That I did something to hurt you?"

Oh God, how had she gotten in this mess? What would he say when she finally told him? Because she knew now she would tell him. Would he hate her? Not for what had happened but for what happened afterward? Would he see her as weak?

She *had* been weak. Stupid. A girl. But even a girl should have been bolder than she had been. She had listened to the half plea and half command of her mother.

Bond thought of Angela and Stephanie and prayed first of all that they'd never find themselves in that situation, and second of all that they'd raise holy hell if they did.

Not like her.

She found her voice. "Damn you, Chase Waters. I know you're working on a murder investigation. Your focus is on the job. Don't ask me to talk about this now when I know you need to leave soon. Don't ask me to be so damned selfish that I would interfere with that. Damn you." She threw off the afghan and reached for the remote to turn off the television.

"And don't ask me," she continued, "to be so insignificant that you can squeeze me in. I'm more than that. What I have to tell you is more than that."

She felt the tears flowing freely and made no move to wipe them away but she would need a tissue if she wanted to breathe through her nose. Chase stood and walked to the powder room across the hall, coming back with a box of tissues. *Damn.* She loved this man even though he could aggravate her easier than anyone else.

"I'm not going anywhere. Not before you tell me what's going on with you."

"Fine. Make it my fault if someone else gets murdered because you were waiting for me to talk to you. Perfect. Just perfect."

"If that's how you really feel, you might want to start talking now because I'm not going anywhere until you tell me whatever it is you need to tell me." He reached for her. "I'm not leaving you, Bond."

They'd been through so much—dealt with the worst thing parents could ever deal with—and managed in the end to come out stronger as a couple. Their love, and their commitment to that love and one another, made them unique among their friends. When she looked into his eyes, Bond saw the depth of her husband's love for her. She saw him work to hold on to that love, wondering what she had to tell him.

But if what Bond had to say could alter their future in a negative way, they really didn't have much of a future anyway.

She found a place where she could turn on her voice and produce her words and hold her emotions in abeyance.

She told him everything.

* * *

After a superhuman effort to control his rage, Chase fully processed what Bond told him. She needed him to be there and not be crazed. She needed to know he loved her. She needed to say the words out loud for only the second time in her life.

Why the hell had she never told him? What kind of mother would make a child promise to keep her molestation a secret? Scratch that. He knew exactly what kind of a mother would do that to a child. His mother-in-law.

Chase wrapped his arms around the woman he loved. She cried until she couldn't cry any more, her used tissues scattered all around the sofa. McKenzie, for once not interested in the tasty treats, sat pushed up against Bond. The little bichon waited, as Chase did, for Bond to cry herself out. For the person they both loved to come back to herself and to them.

The fire, embers now, lay quiet. The peaceful silence came with a little chill to the room. Chase kissed Bond's forehead and put his hands up to cradle her face. "You are a remarkable woman. I am more in love with you this minute than I have ever been. I have some questions but they can wait for another time."

She gasped in some air. "You need to leave."

"I *need* to make sure you're okay." He ran his thumb along her jaw line and waited for her to look him in the eye. "As okay as you can be."

"Go." She pushed him away. "Please. I have enough guilt."

"You're joking, right?" Chase reached for one of her hands. "Nothing that happened to you, not even keeping the secret you promised to keep, is your fault. None of it is worthy of an ounce of guilt from you."

"But you said you have some questions. You doubt me?"

"Not for a minute. Not ever."

She sighed. Breathed a little easier. Fell deep into the sofa, pulling the afghan up to her neck. "Thank you."

Chase's cellphone rang. He looked at the caller ID and then to Bond. He had to take it. His wife smiled and quirked her head.

"What's up, Daniel?"

"I think I may have found that black Mustang."

He put his hand over the phone and told Bond the news.

"How?" Chase asked.

"The old-fashioned way. I went looking for it."

His eyes searched Bond's for understanding. She nodded.

"I'm on my way."

"Will you be okay until we can talk some more?" Chase asked.

"You know I will be. That's who I am. Go. Work. Make the world a better place." She attempted a smile then reached out and touched his hand. "Just one thing."

"What's that?" *Anything, Bond. Anything that's within my power is yours.*

"Find out who owns that black Mustang."

Chapter Fifty

Aspen Falls Police Department
Monday, September 24

Chase didn't remember the drive between his house and the station. His anger at his mother-in-law blocked his mental awareness. Somehow he managed to arrive in the parking lot without killing anyone. Though that's exactly what he'd been thinking about doing.

He opened the glove compartment and pulled out a handful of Twizzlers, then stuffed all but one of them in his coat pocket. The one he stuck in his mouth was stiff from the cold and he welcomed the additional pressure. Better than grinding his molars into powder.

Bond had assured him she felt better—relieved, even—and would take a sleeping pill and go to bed. Before he left he'd kissed both of his daughters good night and hugged his wife one last time. She had looked less tense. Tired but not anxious. The brittleness had left her, but an exhausted fragility remained. She'd kissed him, assured him again she was okay, but what he saw was the sadness in her eyes.

It was almost eleven thirty in Chicago. He wanted to call his father-in-law and get him out here on the first plane smokin'. But if his mother-in-law answered the phone, he didn't trust himself to talk to her without ripping her a new one. He'd wait until the morning to call Stuart Wentworth at his office. Chase would make the man promise to say nothing to Celeste. Bond didn't need the stress a call from her mother would produce.

His cell phone rang. He didn't recognize the number.

"Waters."

"It's Mex. I may have some information for you. Come by my house tomorrow morning."

Chase took down the address. Nice part of town. He wondered how that went over with the people at Juan's Place.

"Why can't you tell me now?" Chase paused. "Mex?" The man had hung up. Call over.

Chapter Fifty-One

Aspen Falls Memorial Hospital
Monday, September 24

When Terri returned to Memorial Hospital to ask Leslie James some questions about the Preston Clinic, she was busy with a patient. A quick trip to the hospital cafeteria and Terri returned to the front desk carrying two cups of hot coffee and two bowls of what looked like brownies à la mode.

The doctor didn't miss a keystroke as she entered data into a computer. "Back so soon, Detective?"

"Do you have time for a break?"

"I'm not getting you any more lists of names today. You've met your quota, don't you think?" With a click of the mouse the computer went back to the login screen.

Terri smiled. "Yeah, thanks for that. But this is something else."

Leslie checked the status board and nodded. "Melanie, mark me out for fifteen but page me if the patient in three becomes a problem. He's stabilized and asleep right now. We're working on getting him admitted."

The doctor checked out the gifts Terri still held in her hand. "I could use some caffeine and sugar. Nice bribe."

Settled into a quiet corner of the doctor's lounge, Terri felt her tension build while Leslie James's appeared to slip away.

Terri left her food untouched and waited while the doctor took both a sip of coffee and a bite of brownie. Leslie closed her eyes in total food rapture.

Terri took a breath and jumped in. "Have you heard of the Preston Clinic?"

Leslie opened her eyes. "Sure. The private clinic just outside of town."

"What do you know about it?"

"Well, it isn't for the rich. It's for the filthy rich. The one percenters. And apparently there's plenty of money in the world. In addition to the clinic here, the same owners have clinics in Zurich, Caracas, and Rio de Janeiro. There's a rumor they're opening one in Los Cabos."

"Are they regular hospitals?"

"Yes and no. I'm sure they have plenty of patients who are there for the same reasons you or I would be admitted to a hospital. But these clinics have specialties. Plastic surgery, rehab, fertility... all the things that if you're a private person, or a very, very public person, you'd prefer to keep secret."

"What's the specialty for the one here?"

"They perform the same things their other clinics do, but the one in Aspen Falls has become known—as much as a secretive clinic can become known—for transplants."

That matched what Chase had been told.

Terri took a sip of coffee. Lukewarm. Scanned the room for a microwave and saw one about twenty feet away. "I need to warm this up. How about you?"

"I'm an emergency room doc. Cold coffee is the norm for me. I'm not sure if my body would know how to process hot caffeine."

Terri warmed up her coffee. When the microwave signaled she pulled out her cup and turned back to Leslie.

"Are there any rumors surrounding the clinic?" she asked the doctor.

Leslie sniffed and turned her head away from Terri.

Bull's-eye.

Terri slid onto her chair. "C'mon, Leslie. This is important. It might help take some of the heat off Memorial."

"What heat?"

"The heat that's likely to come. We don't have enough information yet, and in any event, we're still investigating. But you might be able to help us cast a wider net."

Another doctor came in and pulled open the refrigerator. Slammed it shut.

"Fuck. Someone ate my goddamned pizza. Why the hell can't the assholes around here buy their own shit?" He stormed back out.

"Embarrassing," Leslie said.

"Cops aren't anywhere near that bad."

"Please believe me, he's an exception."

"Is his bedside manner as colorful?"

"From what I've seen, he reserves his best for those he works with."

"What's his name?"

"Armand Fyfe. I think he had to fight the Barney Fyfe thing too much as a kid and sort of went over the top."

"Sort of?"

"Anyway, you asked if I've heard any rumors about the Preston Clinic." Leslie James squished her fork against the brownie dish to get up the last bit of chocolate. "In the interest of spreading the net you're about to throw over us, I think I'll share a couple."

"There's another brownie in it for you if one of those rumors includes something about a celebrity." Aspen always got the Hollywood gossip and now it looked like maybe Aspen Falls might have something of their own. Terri's movie-goer ears perked up, even as her professional senses amped into high gear.

Leslie told her the hot new "It" couple had supposedly checked in together. One for a little nip and tuck, one for some rehab.

"Both of them? At the same time?"

"Yep."

"What did she have done?"

Leslie grinned. "Detective, you know better than to jump to those kind of conclusions. *She* was in for rehab. *He* went under the knife."

"I'll bring your brownie with me the next time I come by."

"Promises, promises."

"What about any rumors related to our investigation?"

Leslie seemed to consider. "We all work through UNOS to coordinate ninety-nine percent of our transplanted organs."

"UNOS?"

"United Network for Organ Sharing. What's that big network law enforcement uses?"

"NCIC? National Crime Information Center?"

"Yeah. UNOS is the NCIC for organ donors and recipients."

"Okay, so...?"

"The list of people who need a new organ is huge. Right now there are about a hundred and fifteen thousand people waiting, ranked by need."

"Okay, so...?"

"Either all of the wealthy patients at the Preston Clinic are right at the top of the list, or they have another source for viable organs and tissue."

"Why do you say that?"

"Rumor has it, that tiny little clinic on the outskirts of this tiny mountain town performs three times as many transplants as Johns-Hopkins—and Johns-Hopkins is the big house on the block."

Chapter Fifty-Two

Aspen Falls Police Department
Monday, September 24

Chase, energized with the idea of new information, worried about Bond, pissed off at both her parents, and frustrated with Mex, marched into the space he shared with Daniel and Terri. Daniel sat at his desk, fingers flying over his keyboard.

Without missing a beat Daniel said, "The car is registered to Robert W. Carlisle, aged thirty-nine. LKA is 271 Spruce, apartment 312."

"Checked for priors?"

"Coming up any minute."

"How did you find the car? Are you sure it's the right one?"

"I felt guilty and angry about the fire at Elizabeth's and decided to go find the black Mustang. How many black Mustangs have you seen in Aspen Falls? I'm pretty sure this is the right one, all right. We'll get a better idea if he has a sheet. And we know a black Mustang seems to be involved, at least in a witness capacity, with at least one murder and an arson. I just started my own grid search, beginning on the west side. The apartment complex where

I located the Mustang only has carports, no individual garages. In Aspen Falls, can you imagine?"

Daniel was hyped.

"The guy's car payment must be twice what he pays for rent." He shook his head. "I almost missed it. I had about tossed in the towel and given up for the night. The parking lot wasn't well lit, the cars were difficult to make out in the carports, and I didn't want to put the spotlight on all of them."

The detective finally glanced up at Chase. "You didn't happen to bring any coffee, did you?"

On cue, Terri walked in bearing not only caffeine but also brownies.

"Terri, you're an angel," Daniel said.

"Not really. An angel would do things like this even if she didn't get quantity discounts."

"One of you can have my brownie," Chase said. He pulled out his Twizzlers. "I'm glad we're all here. You guys up for a quick team meeting before we call it a night? We could each use some rest." Chase looked at the other two. Both of them bursting with pieces of information to add to their developing pile. Chase only hoped the pieces fit. And that they weren't too tired to see it if they did.

Daniel walked up to the white murder board and picked up a marker. "Go," he said.

"There's someone approaching people in the Hispanic community, offering them money if they agree to sell one of their dispensable organs." Chase updated them on the numbers of people Mex personally knew about who had sold something—usually bone marrow or a kidney. "Most seem to have lived to tell about it, but there are quite a few who have simply gone missing."

"That might tie in with the rumors about the Preston Clinic." Terri gave her report. "They're anecdotal at best but it sure does make that place look sketchy."

"Good work. Since we're dealing with some political heat from the clinic, I'd better bring the chief in on this before we push them more." Chase made a note to call Whit in the morning. He also made a note to get Mex some copies of the drawings the sketch artist had made of the people José Sanchez's wife had seen with her husband.

"By the way, I'm meeting with Mex Anderson in the morning. He says he might have something for us," Chase informed the others.

"He didn't say what?" Terri glanced at Daniel.

"He hung up before I could press him."

"The man has issues," Terri said. Daniel had fallen silent.

"Tell me about it," Chase said. "Daniel, bring Terri up to date on the black Mustang."

Daniel told Terri how he'd found the car and Terri took notes regarding the driver's name, address and license plates. "We're not sure there's any direct involvement, but it's interesting." He nodded at Chase. "I got the guy's sheet. Mostly simple assault, a couple of felony menacing. A brother was mentioned. Samuel. His LKA is in the same building. I'm guessing since brother Bobby has a few priors, Sammy does as well."

"If you find any kind of connection to our cases, let me know. I don't care what time it is. I'm heading home." Chase rubbed his forehead, then reached for some more red licorice.

Chapter Fifty-Three

The Waters Home
Monday, September 24

Angela tied her shoelaces, then moved to her bedroom door. The snick of the latch sounded like a gunshot and she froze. Listened. Inched the door open and peeked out. The silence and darkness told her what she wanted to know.

Her parents were asleep. They'd told her she couldn't go to the party, but she didn't want to miss out. And a lot of her other friends would be getting there the same way— by sneaking out.

Stealth-like, she moved down the stairs and toward the front entry. There she entered the code to disable their home security system, checked to make sure she had her house key, and eased out the door. Angela whispered a quick thanks that the beep tones for the alarm keypad had been disabled because of her dad's hours. She made a mental note to remember to reset the alarm when she got home. The last time she'd forgotten and her mom had noticed the next morning.

Once she hit the driveway she broke into a jog, exhilaration bubbling out of her in bursts of giggles.

Angela rounded the bottom curve of the drive and saw Heather's silver Jetta. The car actually belonged to Heather's older sister, who let her borrow it once in a while for a fee. At fifteen, Heather only had her learner's permit. Well, almost.

Angela hopped into the car and she and Heather both broke into hysterical laughter.

When the headlights from a car parked facing the other direction cut through the night, the girls stopped laughing. Had they been caught? Then Heather giggled. "You'd think they could have found a better place to make out."

The car pulled out and drove away, leaving Angela wondering why it had been sitting at the bottom of her drive. Had she seen that black Mustang before?

Chapter Fifty-Four

The Waters Home
Tuesday, September 25

The next morning, Chase sat in his quiet den, the door closed, his family preparing for their individual days. He needed some seclusion for a few minutes.

He steeled himself, then picked up the phone to make the call he dreaded. The private line in Chicago rang. Twice. Three times. Stuart Wentworth worked long hours and Chase felt certain he'd be in his office before eight.

"Bond, is everything all right?" The caller ID made Chase feel bad. Clearly he didn't call his father-in-law often enough.

"It's me, Stuart. I don't want to alarm you. Your daughter is physically fine but she needs you right now. Can you catch a flight out this morning?"

"What's happened?"

"She needs to be the one to tell you, not me."

"Well put her on, dammit."

"No. I will not put her on. She needs you to be here."

"Have you called Celeste? Is she packing?"

"Stuart, you have to trust me on this one. Not only do you need to come by yourself, Celeste can't know the reason. I don't want her calling Bond. I don't want Bond speaking to her mother until the two of you have had a chance to talk."

"What the hell is this all about, Chase?"

"Trust me. It's for Bond's benefit."

"Hold on." Concern made Stuart's voice gruff. Chase heard a click followed by the sound of a Beethoven bagatelle through his phone. *Für Elise*, one of his favorites. When the song ended Chase experienced a ghost of a smile to hear Dave Brubeck's *Take Five*. The last time he'd been with his father-in-law he'd introduced the man to jazz in a way the wealthy businessman had never taken the time to experience. Up close, relaxed and personal. The music stopped abruptly.

"My personal plane is being readied. I'll tell Celeste I have an emergency in the Denver office but don't expect to have to stay the night. That way she won't want to come since she wouldn't have time to get to Aspen Falls."

"Thank you, Stuart."

"I'll call you before we land in Aspen."

"Someone will be there to meet you."

"It had better be you."

Chase hung up the phone and hoped he'd made the right decision. Stuart Wentworth might never forgive him if he made the trip and it didn't help. Even more important, Bond might never forgive him.

Chapter Fifty-Five

Mex Anderson's Home
Tuesday, September 25

Chase pulled up the long circular drive to the front of the gray stone house and parked behind a lime-green VW bug. A three-car garage could be seen in the back of the house—someone else must be visiting. People in this part of town didn't leave their vehicles out.

Smaller than any of its ostentatious neighbors, the home exuded charm and refinement. Hardy fall blooms filled a berm where the trees and large rocks left room. Sunlight glinted off windows and Chase heard the sound of a waterfall.

It looked as if Mex Anderson had a few more secrets.

A stone bridge connected the drive to the entrance. Part of the water sound became obvious as a man-made stream rushed from somewhere in the back of the property. Chase noted deep hollows where fish would be able to winter. It wouldn't surprise him if a heater kept the water flowing year-round.

He tried the knocker first. An enormous double door made with eight-inch hand-hewn planks bore one of the largest cast-iron knockers he'd ever seen. A few seconds later he pushed the doorbell. Impatient, he pulled his cell and began a search for the number Mex had called from last night. Before he finished, a beautiful woman with the same eyes as Mex answered the door.

"May I help you?" she asked in unaccented English.

Chase's quick glimpse of the interior behind her gave him the impression of leather, fine rugs and light. He focused on the Mex-replica who stood in front of him.

"My name is Chase Waters. I'm a detective with the Aspen Falls Police Department. Mex asked me to drop by this morning to see him."

A strange look passed over her face.

"Do I have the right house?" Chase asked. "Does Mex Anderson live here?"

"Excuse me. One minute please." She closed the door.

Chase paced. He inspected the grout holding the stone together at the entry; then the perfect exterior lighting that complemented the high-country elegance the rest of the house displayed. He saw those things and then he paced some more.

His gut told him that unless they stopped this killer now they'd have at least one more victim by the end of the week. Time was not on their side. There were a lot of pieces that needed to come together and a lot of secrets that needed to be revealed. Fear had a way of masking things beyond recognition, and it was the people who were living with fear that were the most vulnerable. He heard the sound of a waterfall, but rather than relaxing him as the sound usually did, it seemed to underscore the situation. He was anxious to get whatever information Mex had for him and then put it to use. He waited for the woman to come back. Or Mex. Preferably Mex.

Damn, I'm going in. He reached for the handle.

The door swung open. The woman held his card in her hands and wore one of the saddest expressions he'd ever seen.

"I'm sorry, Detective Waters. My brother is not available this morning."

"And you are?"

"Sedona will do for me as well as Mex does for my brother."

"Sedona, did you ask him? He told me this morning would be a good time to see him."

The gorgeous woman's shoulders raised and held tight for a moment. When they fell, air escaped her lungs. She inspected him for a moment. She held the door wide inviting him in.

In addition to Chase's initial impression, he added fine works of art, slate and hardwood floors, and a view out the backstretch of windows that would make Midas envious. The mountains appeared like they were literally in the backyard.

"Please wait here, Detective. My brother is ill but I will ask him one more time if he can speak with you."

Ill? Mex had sounded fine last night. Abrupt maybe but that could be his style. If there had been any sign of illness Chase had missed it completely.

A few minutes later and Sedona returned. "I'm sorry. Today isn't good. My brother will contact you when he's feeling better."

Regardless of the intriguing Mex Anderson mystery the morning had opened, Chase saw it as a monumental waste of his time. He nodded to the woman and turned toward the door. "Tell your brother not to bother unless he has something that will actually help. And he can come to me next time. I don't have time for this."

Chase walked across the bridge to his car. Sitting behind the wheel, he took a minute to check his messages.

His father-in-law had texted him earlier to tell him he'd arrive at the Aspen airport at about eleven-thirty. Whit had requested a face-to-face when he got in, and Samuel Carlisle's sheet was in and matched his brother's and then some for priors.

He twisted the key in the ignition, then glanced back at the beautiful wood door. Open. A figure in front.

Chase had to look twice to recognize Mex Anderson. He looked ten years older. Faded. Worn. Wrinkled.

He turned the engine off and opened the car door, then stepped out and turned to face the specter.

Chase pushed the door closed with a gentle shove. He didn't want to make the apparition in front of him vanish.

"You wanted to see me?" Chase asked.

"Might have something."

"Okay." Don't waste my time, he wanted to say. Mex looked a little like every user Chase had ever seen, regardless of the digs they lived in. But something was different. Off. Desperate in a different kind of lost way.

"Look, today isn't good," Mex said.

"I can see that. But you called me, remember?"

Mex disappeared back inside the shadows of the house, but left the door open.

Pissed *and* curious. One or the other usually got Chase's attention. Both at once? No way could he drive away now. Instead he walked back across the wooden bridge.

217

Chapter Fifty-Six

Mex Anderson's Home
Tuesday, September 25

Chase entered a living room that blended the best of Mexican and mountain in a refined—expensive looking—kind of way. Who did Mex's decorating? Maybe his sister? Did Mex have a wife?

Who is this guy?

Chase turned to his right. It seemed as good of a direction as any to head off in to look for his host.

"Please, Detective Waters. A minute?" Sedona called from behind him. "Please? Follow me." She spoke over her shoulder, long hair slipping around her waist. "There are things you need to know and Mex has allowed me to tell you."

The woman led him to a kitchen that Bond... hell *he*... would consider killing for. More than the slab granite, phenomenal cooktop, wine keeper, walk-in pantry with crackled glass doors and other appointments; more than the designer lighting and hardwood floors and damned good use of space... more than any of that was the view. The windows were floor to ceiling, wall to wall. What appeared to be a seamless piece of glass, curved around three walls, actually had some kind of grout that was almost as clear and transparent as the glass it supported.

Cobalt Mountain was the most prominent but at the right angle, Chase thought he picked up part of Burnt Mountain near Snowmass. And below those timeless mountains of stone, almost breathing with life, Chase could see the valley with a river flowing not far away. The source of the water sound in the back was real, not manmade. Chase looked around the space to see if he could squeeze in a john, a shower and a flat screen. He would never want to leave this room.

"It's beautiful, isn't it?"

Chase could only nod.

"When my brother built this house he knew where he would spend his time and he knew it needed to be spectacular." Sedona moved to a built-in Keurig system and pulled a cup from the nearby cabinet. "Coffee?"

"Sounds good."

"What kind would you like?" Sedona pulled out the kind of wooden box teas are kept in and opened it for Chase.

He thumbed through the options for his cup of coffee. "Promise me," he selected some kind of double shot Hazelnut espresso hoping he looked like he did this all the time, "Promise me you will never show this machine or these options to my detectives. Unless you're prepared to donate one to our squad room—and keep it supplied."

Sedona almost smiled and Chase watched the action take incredible physical features and make them radiant. She came closer to Bond's beauty than any other woman Chase had ever met, but something seemed a little strained. "You remind me a little of my wife."

A russet blush perfumed her cheeks and she turned away. Chase had the good sense to shut up.

After a moment of silence while the coffee maker pressed the rich aromas into his cup, she gestured to the table that sat in an optimal position to enjoy the view. "Please sit. I'll bring your coffee to you."

Chase chose a chair and spent the next few seconds breathing in the color and sense of drama the panorama provided. The coffee, whatever he'd chosen, would be like icing on the cake.

Sedona set his coffee in front of him. In addition she'd plated a selection of warm muffins. Chase had no idea where they'd come from or how they'd gotten warm. The pull from the window didn't allow for trivial things.

"You know Mex was a chief of police in Mexico, right?"

Well, if the vague statement that he'd been in law enforcement meant he'd been a chief, yeah. Chase nodded and took a sip of coffee. Rich.

"I'm going to go out on a limb and guess he hasn't told you anything more. Am I right?"

"You are."

Sedona nodded, as if she placed a finger on the page that told her that this was where she needed to pick up the story.

"Mex, Francesca—his wife—and their two children were living the perfect life in the country he loved. Mexico. Francesca had told him that afternoon that they would soon grow their family from four to five. Mex called me with the news. His heart sang louder than his words."

The woman pushed unseen crumbs from the table into her palm and rose to walk to the sink. Brushed her hands. She turned her face to the amazing landscape but Chase knew she didn't see it. Mex's sister stood silent. Not moving. Remembering the details of whatever came next.

"When my brother called me again I couldn't understand him. He didn't make any sense. He told me his family—his entire family—had been murdered. Tortured for hours then killed. He said he'd refused to sell out to the drug cartel. The destruction of his life, of everything he loved, had been the price. In one afternoon my brother went from being on top of the world to being buried somewhere deep beneath it."

Chase's internal note-taker dropped his pen, his notepad—everything—as he envisioned the horror.

"They also killed our parents."

"Everyone?"

"No one in my brother's family lived. Except for the two of us. Why they let me live I'll never know."

Chase thought he knew. To hold her over him at a later point if they wanted. Now Mex knew what horror they could wreak. Leverage.

"What did your brother do?"

"He hunted them for as long as he could follow a trail. The cartel was one thing... and logically beyond one man's reach. But the doers? Those he felt he could deal with? They became his target."

Two deer meandered into the view close to the house. Calm and deliberate, they foraged on the natural grasses seemingly oblivious to danger. Chase knew better. One quick move on the inside of this window and they would take off.

"Mex followed the men directly responsible for the murders first into southern Mexico, then to Texas, then Venezuela and finally to Honduras. That's where he lost them. That's where he also lost his spirit. He believes the men were killed by their own organization. Mex came home broken—a heavy depression settled onto his soul."

"Depression?"

"My brother suffers from situational depression. Something triggers it, and for a short period of time his

221

strongest instinct is to withdraw. It all relates to the murders."

"How does he come out of it?"

"Meds. They help him get back in control. Back to himself. He's learned it's nothing to be ashamed of. It just is."

A thought slashed through Chase. *David*. The son he'd lost. The guilt and shame that had hounded him ever since the day David died. The guilt and shame that landed him frequently in a place where he wanted to withdraw from the world. Withdraw from life and from everyone he loved. Withdraw into a sort of temporary death of his own.

A movement caught Chase's attention and he turned.

Chapter Fifty-Seven

Mex Anderson's Home
Tuesday, September 25

"You need to do something today," Mex said from the entrance to the kitchen. He still looked disheveled. Not quite the put-together man with creased jeans Chase had only recently met.

The detective watched the man about whom he'd just learned something significant. Something personal and painful. The loss Chase had experienced, as horrible as it was, couldn't compare to the loss this man had endured.

"I have some names for you."

"Names?"

Mex walked into the kitchen and stood in front of the refrigerator. "The boy in the dumpster? His name is Miguel Martinez. I have his toothbrush." Mex stopped speaking and Chase imagined the last time that toothbrush had been used. A private moment simply dealing with the normal hygiene of an ordinary day. "His brother brought it to me and I have no doubt that's who your murder victim is."

Sedona came and pushed him away from the refrigerator. Her brother moved like a zombie. "Would you like some tea?"

Mex didn't answer her. Instead he shuffled over to a chair near the window. "I also know the name of the woman. The one you found at the Ute burial grounds." Mex fell into the chair.

Chase understood that as hard as the information relating to the male was, this was infinitely more difficult. He waited.

"The woman's husband came to me. She was a young mother of two toddlers. He brought me her hairbrush but when I reached out to accept it he couldn't let it go. It was a part of his wife. Of the woman he loved. The mother of his children. His grip tightened on that hairbrush until I reached for an envelope to pull a few strands for samples. His tears were flowing down his face." Mex's voice trailed off. Chase knew he was remembering his own loss. "Her name was Anna. She was not only a wife and a mother, but also a resource in the undocumented community for assistance and counseling. Her husband told me she was responsible for at least a dozen young people graduating from high school."

Chase accepted both evidence envelopes, clearly marked with dates, times and names. "Thank you."

"I have more."

"More?"

"You need to talk to Efraín Madrigal," Mex continued.

"The kid from the bookstore? The one they call Tom Hanks?" Chase was in Cobalt Mountain Books at least once a month.

"Yep. That's the one."

"Why?"

Apparently the meds hadn't quite kicked in. Mex turned around and walked away.

Chapter Fifty-Eight

The Benavides Home
Tuesday, September 25

Daniel had trouble finding a place to park. Pickup trucks, delivery trucks and people took up every available space in front of the Benavides home. Daniel drove around the block and pulled his car in to the first spot he found, then walked back around and watched even more people arrive to help.

He saw the fire damage to the front of the house. The carefully tended flower garden had either been destroyed by the fire or trampled by the firefighters or the workers this morning. Whatever the cause, only mashed foliage remained. Chase said the fire had pretty much gutted the kitchen in the back. Guilt flamed in Daniel's chest.

Yesterday. It had just happened late yesterday afternoon. And already this morning the area hummed with the pounding of hammers and the conversation of people joined together to achieve a goal. Tejano music blared out of the biggest boom box he'd ever seen. The bouquet of flowers he held in his hand seemed pointless and weak. A little like how he felt about himself.

225

Elizabeth held a tray of hot coffee and cocoa in styrofoam cups for the people helping her family rebuild their home. "Are those for me?"

"No. Um... " He wanted to help her with her tray but the flowers nixed that idea.

"No?"

Why hadn't he thought to bring two bouquets? Two pointless and weak bouquets would be better than one. "They're, um... I brought them for your mother."

He couldn't believe his eyes. Elizabeth Benavides actually smiled at him. But the moment she saw him begin to smile back she wiped hers from her face.

"Mamá is around the back. She wants to make sure her kitchen is rebuilt top-notch. No corner-cutting for my mamá."

"Is there, um... anything I can help with?"

"Have you found my sister's murderer?"

"Not yet."

"Well, there's always that."

Daniel nodded and shifted his feet.

"You look awful," Elizabeth said.

Another nod.

"Take the flowers to Mamá before you mangle them beyond recognition. I have work to do." She moved off to a group of men unloading roof materials from a truck. Daniel watched as she moved effortlessly among them. Confident. Feminine. Strong.

Two bouquets. All it would have taken to make a miserable situation a little stronger would have been a second bunch of flowers. Never again would he arrive at the Benavides home with one pitiful handful of petals. Assuming of course he'd ever be invited back.

Daniel zigzagged through people to reach the back of the house. Neighbors were applying paint to the message on the garage, but they hadn't covered it yet. QUIT

TALKING BITCH affected him more than any other bit of graffiti or gang message he'd ever seen. Those words targeted Elizabeth. She didn't need this kind of crap. As a low boil of rage began to build in his gut, he realized he needed to regain a professional footing.

Ramona Benavides, sporting a hardhat pushed as far back on her head as she could shove it, stood outside the work area and gestured to a man with a clipboard. Probably an inspector. She obviously had the situation in control because the man, whose own hardhat bore the official county emblem, nodded as he made notes and checked off items when she pointed to them.

She glanced up and spotted Daniel. Without a word she turned her back to the county official and marched toward him. Daniel prepared for the worst.

"You! Detective!"

Daniel didn't move, certain he deserved whatever the woman needed to fling at him. He would have knelt on the ground if he thought it would help the short woman speak her peace to his face. But she didn't need his help.

"Look my house. Look these people. Here because of police. Here because of you." She stabbed the air with the same finger that had been pointing things out to the inspector a few seconds ago. But the rest of her hand was fisted. Angry. Accusatory.

"Yes, ma'am."

She sniffed. Crossed her arms in front of her. Swallowed. Exhaled.

"Who flowers for? Elizabeth?"

Two bouquets. Shit.

"No, ma'am."

"Who for?"

Daniel took a couple of steps forward and held the bedraggled bouquet out toward the woman. "I, um... brought them for you."

227

Ramona Benavides fell silent. A rosy hue and misty eyes appeared at the same time. She blinked her eyes clear and thrust out her hands. "Give. Maybe a vase did not burn."

Daniel handed the woman the flowers and her hands grasped his. Ramona had something else she needed to say to him. Whatever it was, he could take it. He deserved it.

"Elizabeth needs leave here. Take her for few minutes. Twenty, thirty. Okay?"

Ten minutes later, Daniel and Elizabeth sat at a table in The Coffee Pod. Sun slanted through the windows, highlighting Elizabeth's hair and reminding Daniel of that old television show where a normal girl suddenly announced her angel DNA. He could see Elizabeth saying the same thing.

"This is a bad time for both of us," Daniel said.

"Both of us?"

Daniel felt heat in his face but he persisted. "You are grieving. A major loss has tossed your life around like so much flotsam. And I'm in the middle of a complicated case. You can't be expected to have a clear head, and I can't focus too long on anything other than finding a killer or killers."

"Daniel, this might not be a good time but it is a time for us to bookmark and return to later. Then we can know what makes us laugh, what our favorite movies are, and maybe even share our dreams. And we will already know how we respond under pressure. If we end up with a relationship, we will have already gotten a lot of the hard stuff sorted out."

Daniel thought he might float away. She had said the words he wasn't able to, and she had put them together in a nonthreatening, open-ended, easy-relationship kind of way. He smiled and gave her a wink.

They finished their coffee in silence, then returned to Daniel's car for the ride back to the Benavides home.

Six blocks from their destination, Daniel spotted the black Mustang. "Get out." He slowed the car and pulled over.

"What?"

"You heard me. I need you to be safe. Quick. Get out."

"Not without you telling me why."

"See that black Mustang up there?"

Elizabeth nodded.

"It's involved somehow. You need to get out so I can follow them. Things could get dangerous."

"Involved? In the fire? In my sister's murder?"

Daniel didn't respond.

"I'm not getting out. I want to see what the people in this car have to show us. I want to know how they're involved."

"Dammit, woman! Get out!"

She crossed her arms in the same way her mother had earlier. He could pull her out but in the time it took to do that he'd lose the Mustang for sure. He watched as it made a left turn and disappeared.

"Fine. Then you need to sit tight, don't get out of this car unless I say it's okay, and follow every order I give you from this point forward. Do you agree?"

She gave a quick nod. "Yes. Now go. He's getting away."

* * *

Daniel followed well behind the Mustang. His plan had been to bring Robert Carlisle in for questioning today. What had the ex-con been doing in Elizabeth's neighborhood? Chase said he'd seen the car at the fire.

229

Had Carlisle come back to look at his handiwork? To threaten Elizabeth more?

All of Main Street and anywhere from two to four blocks on either side was the business district for Aspen Falls, the biggest section exactly in the middle of town. No surprise the Mustang headed down Main Street and parked in the first available space beyond The Coffee Pod.

Daniel checked his watch. A few minutes before ten. Robert Carlisle exited the vehicle and hitched up his pants. Still photos of suspects didn't have anything on watching them move. Daniel noted the steel-toed boots, hands that looked too large for Carlisle's slight build, and the way he checked out his surroundings. He cracked his neck as if he had all day, but his stance was wary and his eyes darted around. Another man got out of the passenger side.

The detective drove past the Mustang and turned left at the next intersection.

"What are you doing? You passed them!" Elizabeth screamed in his ear.

Halfway down the block Daniel made a U-turn and parked. Snapped off his seatbelt and checked his weapon. He considered calling for backup and rejected the idea. No use showing all of their cards when there probably wasn't a reason.

"Stay here." He didn't look at Elizabeth.

He heard her seatbelt unlatch. "Dammit, Elizabeth. Stay here. Stay safe. Stay out of my way. If you really want to catch the scum who killed Rachelle, you will back down and do as I say."

Daniel moved away from the car, tugged on his jacket to make sure his gun remained covered, and sauntered to the corner. He caught a glimpse of Carlisle just as he disappeared behind the building that housed Cobalt Mountain Books. Daniel jogged to the front of the building then slid down the narrow opening between the bookstore and the coffee shop. He slipped his weapon free, then stopped a good four feet from the edge and moved with a steady precision to the back corner.

A quick glance around the corner and he pulled his head back. Carlisle and the other man, presumably his brother, stood talking to a young Hispanic male in the delivery area behind the bookstore. The kid looked nervous as hell. Daniel watched, ready to intervene if necessary.

Carlisle handed a piece of paper the size of a business card to the kid and took a step back. Then he said something to his buddy and gestured in the general direction they'd come. The conversation ended and Daniel needed to get out of there fast. He double-timed it back around to the front of the building, holstered his gun, pumped past the still-closed bookstore, and slipped into The Coffee Pod.

From the front window of the coffee shop Daniel watched the two men get back in the black Mustang and take off.

When he got back to his car Elizabeth wasn't there.

Chapter Fifty-Nine

Cobalt Mountain Books
Tuesday, September 25

As Chase drove to the bookstore, he reviewed the meeting he'd had that morning. He had learned a lot about Mex Anderson from his sister and figured he'd learn a lot more from Mex himself. He and Mex had both suffered loss, but Chase couldn't imagine the horror of what Mex went through. To lose his entire family? There were a lot of reasons for depression, and Mex couldn't have picked a worse one.

He'd dropped off the hair samples and toothbrush at Jax's office earlier. The ME promised she'd confirm if they were a match to the John and Jane Doe as soon as possible. He knew better than to hope for anything anytime soon. This wasn't an episode of CSI.

Chase pulled up in front of the bookstore and saw the "Open" sign still swinging behind the door. When he entered Cobalt Mountain Books, a customer already had Efraín Tomás Hanks Madrigal fully engaged.

Damn. He knew the customer. Elizabeth Benavides. And she didn't act like she needed help finding a book. Efraín looked like he might toss whatever he'd eaten for breakfast any minute. Chase walked up to the pair, intent on getting control of the situation fast.

The door to the bookstore slammed open and Daniel Murillo stormed in so determined to get to Elizabeth he didn't see Chase.

Anger and fear hardened Daniel's features. "I told you to stay in the car. You could have ruined this investigation." Daniel spoke with controlled fury. "You could have been hurt."

"I saw those two men talking to this boy. I want to know why." Elizabeth squared off to face Daniel and she saw Chase. Her eyes flickered.

"Slow down. All of you," Chase said. "What two men?"

Daniel pulled up, sucked in a breath. He looked like he wanted to say something else but instead he exhaled. "Carlisle. And I think his brother. We followed them."

"You followed two suspects with a civilian in your car? A civilian I clearly told you needed to stay out of this?" He wanted something to hit. "A civilian you knew wouldn't? What didn't you understand?"

"Look, Chase—"

"Stop," Elizabeth interrupted Daniel, slapped her hands against her thighs. She blushed, looking like a little girl caught somewhere she knew she shouldn't be, but did not drop her eyes from Chase's. "This boy knows something."

"And that's what I'm here to find out," Chase said. "Is there somewhere we can talk?"

"All of us?" Elizabeth asked.

Chase looked at the other detective. Daniel shrugged. They would continue this discussion later.

Chase gave a quick nod and Efraín led them to a small community room that doubled as an office. The young man reminded Chase of a scared rabbit looking for a hole. "I need to leave the door open so I can hear customers."

233

Daniel turned, walked to the front of the store and adjusted the sign so it read "Closed." He flicked the deadbolt to lock the door. "Don't need to listen for anyone now."

Efraín sank onto a chair. "Am I in trouble?"

Chase waited until the boy met his gaze. "Should you be?"

A hesitation, a glance at Elizabeth, then a little shake of his head. "No, sir. I don't think so."

"Fine then. For now you're not in trouble. But we have some questions."

Efraín swallowed.

"What do people call you?" Chase worked to get the boy to relax.

"My parents call me Efraín. Almost everyone else calls me Tom."

"Tom?" Chase asked.

"My middle name is Tomás Hanks. My parents are fans." It was clear to Chase that the young man had explained this more than once.

"What name do you prefer?"

"Efraín."

"Okay, Efraín. How old are you?"

"Sixteen."

"How do you know those two men?"

The boy shrugged. "They've been around."

Chase tried to remember what it was like to be sixteen. Sixteen and as close to trouble as a gambler with a pair of dice in his pocket.

"Been around? You've never talked to them before?" Mex had given him the distinct impression that Efraín tied into the case somehow. And the Carlisle brothers definitely did.

"They've just been around you know? For a while." The young boy's gaze darted for the door.

Chase knew a stall when he heard one. He also didn't have time to help Efraín get on board in a nice gradual way. He decided to approach this kid directly. With a little bit of a punch to his psychological gut.

"Do you know what we're investigating?" Chase asked.

A slight shake of his head. "No, sir."

"Did you read about that body found in a dumpster late last week?"

"Yeah, but I don't know anything about that." Efraín looked scared.

"No ID. A young Hispanic male. We don't even know who to notify. His family still doesn't know he's dead. They just think he *might* be. Today I was given his toothbrush to try and make a DNA identification. His toothbrush, Efraín. Am I gonna need yours too?"

Efraín paled.

"He'd been carved up. Eviscerated." Chase paused. "I think those two men might have something to do with his death.

Efraín ran from the room. A moment later they could hear the gagging sounds of the kid tossing his cookies.

A lot of people go looking for trouble. For Efraín Tomás Hanks Madrigal, trouble had found him.

Chapter Sixty

Aspen Falls Police Department
Tuesday, September 25

Terri sat at her desk, more than one thing eating at her. Something about her visit with Leslie James yesterday didn't sit right, but she couldn't quite put her finger on it.

No doubt existed however about the other thing—she was in over her head. Carol Greene, Lily's grandmother, and her attorney, Krysta Corinn, had asked to meet with her this morning for breakfast. Because of the case Terri almost told them no, but something in Carol Greene's voice told her she'd better not.

After the waitress poured their coffees, Krysta Corinn got down to business. "We're concerned you might not be at the right place in your life to raise a little girl." The attorney laid it out straight and quick, protecting her client and keeping her billable hours to a minimum. No small talk this morning.

"What's your concern?" Terri tried not to think about the room she'd cleared out in her little home, ready for Lily to make her own decision regarding paint, window coverings and furniture. She tried not to think about the special shelf in the family room reserved for pictures of

Lily's mom and grandmother. Of her life before Terri. She didn't have a husband to offer as a father but that hadn't been an issue before. Could that be it?

"Your job is very demanding." Corinn gave Terri a direct stare. "There may not be room for a child."

First, Terri thanked her lucky stars she hadn't said no to this breakfast. It would have proved their point about having a demanding job and would have been one more nail in her coffin. Second, well, she got a little ticked off. "You've always known what I do for a living."

Carol Greene cleared her throat. "Yes, but I hadn't really considered your hours. Or what kind of element you might introduce Lily to."

Something had changed. Something had happened. There had to be more to this.

"Mrs. Greene, Ms. Corinn, all I can tell you is, assuming Lily will have me, I'm prepared to be her guardian. I know being a single parent isn't easy, but people do it all the time." Terri paused to look at Carol Greene. "Believe it or not, even police officers have been known to do it. The only things I can tell you are that I'm prepared to protect Lily, to be a role model for her, to help launch her into the world, and to love her. I'm also prepared to help Lily remember her roots. The family who loved her first."

Carol Greene looked a little uncomfortable. Corinn wore a poker face. *What the hell?*

"I think we all need to take a step back and re-evaluate what is best for Lily," the attorney said.

Terri pulled out more cash than her share of breakfast required and laid it on the table. "I'm sorry to hear you feel that way, but this is neither the time nor the place to discuss this in any kind of depth." She said good-bye and left—before they could make their re-evaluation on the spot and tell her no. They agreed to be in touch.

That had been two hours ago and Terri had been ripped to her core ever since. She wondered what had happened to make them suddenly doubt her ability—her commitment. Should she have stayed at the table and risked permanent rejection? Maybe she shouldn't have a child. Maybe she had no business wanting to be a mother. Maybe another family had entered the picture. One with both a mother and a father to offer Lily.

She forced her brain to get back to this case and consider her last interview with Leslie James. It took a moment but she got there. The doctor, the setting, James's words... some little element flitted just out of reach. Maybe a walk to clear her head would help her regain some focus.

The minute the fresh air hit her, Terri had the answer. Armand Fyfe. Rude, yes. Arrogant, no doubt. But underneath all of it Terri read subterfuge. Slime. A person of interest. And he worked in the ER. She did a one-eighty and walked back into the building. Skipped the elevator and took the stairs to her floor.

Once back at her desk she googled the man, found his address, and a few clicks later knew that today was his scheduled trash pickup. Without a warrant and sure he had something to hide, she needed to get to his house before the trash company made its rounds.

Terri wanted to talk to Dr. Fyfe, and some background information would give her the upper hand when they had that conversation. And with a guy like Fyfe, she could use all the surprise she could get. Even if it was refuse inspired. She hated garbage duty, but somewhere in his trash she might get lucky and find an item of interest.

Terri also wanted to talk to Carol Greene. Soon.

She grabbed her coat and some large plastic liner bags.

Chapter Sixty-One

Armand Fyfe's Residence
Tuesday, September 25

Terri threw her car in park and grabbed some gloves. Fyfe's house sat at the top of a fairly steep drive, at the bottom of which stood three large rubber bins, one piled with papers for recycling. At least that one would be easy. Terri gave thanks for people who recycled, including the man whose garbage she itched to get into. She didn't dare hope he also composted.

The smell coming from the containers told her Fyfe probably didn't compost. Based on the man's attitude, she couldn't really picture him as the gardening type. She fingered out a stick of gum to help with the gag factor, crammed it in her mouth, pulled on latex gloves, then grabbed the large plastic bags she'd brought with her and went to work. Too bad she didn't have a real reason to call out the CSIs for this little job. Desperate times called for desperate measures.

Less than ten minutes later, Terri tucked everything into the trunk along with her gloves, stuffed some fresh gum in her mouth and headed back to the station. She hoped there might be something, especially in the paper portion of her haul, that might give them some evidence. The arrogance of the man might just be his undoing. Assuming he had something to undo. Which of course, she knew in the cop part of her heart, he did.

She wanted to call Carol Greene but didn't want anything to interrupt their conversation. She needed to know why the grandmother of the girl Terri wanted to adopt—the same woman who had approached her with the idea to begin with—seemed to be having second thoughts.

That conversation would have to wait. The detective needed to detect. Even if it meant she had to sort through the garbage of a jerk. Things just might end on a high note today, she thought, at least as far as the case went.

She parked her car and popped the trunk.

Daniel pulled into the space next to her. "Need some help?"

"You have no idea."

Daniel checked out her trunk. "Please tell me this has something to do with our case. That this isn't crap from some ex-boyfriend or a neighbor you're gunning for." He grabbed one of the bags.

"None of the above. This here garbage is special order from Hollywood. You know how I feel about Johnny Depp."

"Please, Terri. Don't even tease. This is not the day for it."

"Okay. Help me haul these bags in, and while we sort through the crap, I'll tell you everything you want to know."

"You couldn't get someone else to do this?"

"It's just a hunch. But I think we might find a connection." She grinned at Daniel. "Plus I thought you could use some grounding."

Daniel shook his head.

"Have you seen Chase this morning?" Terri asked after they'd hauled the last bag in to the conference room.

"Kind of ran into him this morning, as a matter of fact. He's talking to the kid from the bookstore."

"Efraín?"

"Yeah. The one a lot of people call Tom Hanks."

"Why is Chase talking to him?"

"I think he's involved somehow with the case."

"Which one?"

"All of 'em. This one."

"The kid?" Terri shook off the idea. "No way could Efraín be on the killing end. You think he's a target?"

"Could be. That's why Chase is interviewing him. Backtrack, check out whether or not he's been to the ER, try to connect up some of these loose ends."

They each took a bag and began going through the garbage at opposite sides of the plastic- covered table. Evidence bags sat nearby in case they got lucky.

"Okay, wanna tell me why I'm gloved up and digging through a week's worth of someone else's crap?"

"There's something hinky about this guy. He's a doctor at Memorial, and aside from being an obnoxious asshole he's hiding something. And anyone around the ER who's also keeping secrets is someone I want to know more about."

"Jeez, Terri. That's all you've got?" Daniel stopped his search.

"Do I need to remind you about the time I helped you search a septic tank because you *thought* you'd seen someone drop something in it?"

"Fine. You got me."

They searched in silence then dumped the last bag open on the table. Paper products.

"Want to tell me why we didn't start with paper?" Daniel asked.

"Too easy. Besides, you're the one who dumped the first bag. And while I figured we might find something in the paper, that doesn't mean we could skip the other bags. You know that and so do I."

"I didn't know it had already been sorted for recycling."

"You didn't ask, so don't go all bitchy on me."

The two worked in silence.

"Well, looky here," Terri said.

Chapter Sixty-Two

Cobalt Mountain Books
Tuesday, September 25

"Are you doing a little better, Efraín?" Chase asked the young man.

Shaking, the sixteen year-old nodded. He took a sip of the water Chase had rounded up for him.

"It's just you and me now." Chase had sent Daniel and Elizabeth packing while Efraín threw up. He didn't need either one of them for this interview. Daniel needed to think about the decision he'd made earlier and Chase needed to calm down before addressing the younger detective about the danger he'd knowingly put a civilian in. The good news—if you could call anything good news—was that his detective had entered the bookstore visibly upset about Elizabeth's actions. Daniel had learned a lesson. It was Chase's job to make sure he wouldn't forget it.

"Do you need a few more minutes?" Chase asked the boy.

"Please. No."

"Which is it?"

"Talk. Let's talk."

"You're the one who needs to talk, Efraín. You need to tell me about those two men, about why they were interested in a young kid who goes to school and works in a bookstore. But first I have another question."

"Yes?"

"What's a sixteen-year-old kid doing working on a weekday morning?"

"I'm on a work-study program."

Common enough. Many families in Aspen Falls, in contrast to their wealthy neighbors, needed to have all of their family members contributing financially in order to make it.

"How does that affect your school work?"

"I've been an honor student for the last three years."

"Is there any question you want to ask me?"

Efraín's face pulled back, his eyes wide. "Me?"

"Sure. What would you like to ask me?"

Chase watched the young man's face begin to open. Watched as his brain searched for the best question.

"When this is over, can I go on a ride-along?"

Chase heard the request all the time and it always pleased him. Hell, he'd been the same kid twenty-five years ago. "Do you want to go into law enforcement?"

"No. I want to be a writer."

"I think a ride-along can be arranged. Now you need to tell me about the two men."

Efraín nodded, but this time with confidence instead of fear.

"They told me they needed my help. They said their mother is very ill. Dying. She needs a kidney. They said they believe I would be a match for her and could save her life. They also said they would pay me five hundred dollars for one of mine, but they needed my answer in forty-eight hours. After that the price they'll pay drops to two-fifty."

"Have you seen these men before?"

"No sir. Not before this morning."

"How are you supposed to let them know what you decide?"

Efraín pulled a business card from his pocket.

"They said I could not call them. Their cell phones could only be used for business. But they said they knew where to find me. They gave me this."

"Just set it on the table," Chase instructed.

Efraín dropped the card on the table as if it had caught fire. "Prints. I'm sorry. I didn't think... "

"Don't worry about it. We'll get your prints and eliminate them. Besides, we already think we know who the two guys are. We just need this to tie them to you and to our case."

"Really? I'm connected to a case?" The young man leaned forward, eagerness lighting his eyes.

How quickly teenagers forget. Fifteen minutes ago this kid's head and a toilet bowl were doing a dance.

Chase touched the business card lightly on the edge and turned it to read. One of those cards to remind you of your next appointment. *27/9* was written on the date line. *10* next to the preprinted a.m. Not much, but they now had a little more information. Whoever wrote this didn't use the American style for the date. Not exactly rare but not what he expected.

Where were those other Preston Clinics located? He phoned Terri. His call went to voicemail.

Chapter Sixty-Three

Aspen Falls Police Department
Tuesday, September 25

Terri carefully laid the crumpled sticky note to the side and walked over to another counter where she'd put some evidence bags. Daniel walked around the table to take a look.

Need new code—old one not working

"So? Why is this significant?" Daniel's eyebrows screwed up.

"Someone in the ER is ordering blood tests using a doctor's authorization code. I thought maybe they'd been hacked. Maybe it's a lot worse."

"Or it could be a note from his wife regarding their garage door opener."

"Could be. Or something else."

"Wait. You said blood tests?" Daniel asked. He walked quickly back to his side of the table.

"Yeah. You got something?"

"A staff memorandum for some meeting. An agenda item that might have a connection." Daniel fingered through the pile of items he'd already inspected. "Damn. I know I saw something." He shoved more papers around, careful not to mix them up with the items he still needed to examine.

"Here. *Medicaid / Blood Tests / Additional MD Support Required*. It caught my eye because notes had been made next to every other agenda item. But not this one."

"Great. Bag it. I'll run it by Leslie and see what she has to say."

Terri and Daniel went through the rest of the collected trash piece by piece but didn't find anything else of significance.

She stripped off her gloves and checked her phone. Three messages. Carol Greene, Krysta Corinn, and Chase. Ignoring the first two and the sudden tight sensation in her gut, she pressed the button to call Chase. Her job she could handle. Adopting a little girl? Maybe not so much.

"Daniel with you?" Chase didn't waste any time.

"Yeah."

"Neither of you were answering your phones. Tell him he needs to get back to the bookstore. His one and only assignment for the next two days is the safety of Efraín Madrigal, unless I personally pull him off of it."

"Is Efraín in danger?"

"He is. Now tell me why you weren't answering your phone and refresh my memory as to the locations of the other Preston Clinics."

After bringing Chase back up to speed, she asked him when he planned on coming back to the station.

"Right now I'm tailing Carlisle to see what he's up to. I picked him up by accident. I'll see what else I can learn before I bring him in for questioning. I have a feeling this guy isn't going to give up anything. Then I need to make a run to Aspen and pick up my father-in-law." He paused significantly. "I'll answer my phone if you call."

Chastised, Terri hung up, gave Daniel his instructions, and moved to a private location to call Carol Greene. She'd rather get any bad news from the grandmother she knew rather than the attorney she'd just met.

Chapter Sixty-Four

Tailing the Black Mustang
Tuesday, September 25

Chase had picked up the black Mustang by accident. He'd needed some nourishment before he drove to Aspen to pick Stuart up at the airport and decided to grab something at a fast-food place near the middle school. Before he could place his order in the drive-up, he spotted the Mustang pulling away from the curb in front of the restaurant. Thankful the lunch rush hadn't begun, Chase drove past the window, gave them a wave, and followed the car. Chase had very little doubt that Carlisle reported to someone further up the chain. No sense in getting his guard up.

He popped open the glove compartment and pulled out an open bag of Twizzlers. Six left. Probably better for him than fast food. But not as filling. He also grabbed a digital camera.

Carlisle drove back to the downtown area and parked by the drugstore. Chase found a spot in front of the bank, about a half-block before the drugstore, and watched Robert Carlisle sit.

One minute. Then two. No move to get out. Definitely something going on.

After four minutes, a Bugatti rolled around the corner and parked illegally. Chase loved those cars, but not necessarily their owners. The driver of this one walked briskly in his direction, then without hesitation slid into the passenger side of the Mustang. Less than a minute later the door opened and the man emerged. Chase had the camera ready and snapped several pictures.

Carlisle pulled out but Chase decided to wait and see if the Bugatti took him someplace interesting. Even in Aspen Falls, a multimillion dollar vehicle got attention. The car rolled through town, and even the glitz-hardened residents took notice. The business district behind them, Chase watched the car round a curve like butter on a warm plate. He imagined what it must be like to drive a machine like a Bugatti.

The car put on its left-turn signal and Chase drove on, not surprised. The car turned in to the Preston Clinic.

A patient? Maybe. A doctor? Maybe. A coincidence? Not a chance.

His cell phone rang.

"Waters."

Stuart Wentworth's voice filled his ear. "I'm landing in ten minutes. If I'm not your priority, I promise you, you *will* be mine."

Damn. Forcing a quick reunion for Bond and her father had better work. Chase continued on the back road to Aspen to meet the private plane from Chicago.

Chapter Sixty-Five

Aspen-Pitkin County Airport
Tuesday, September 25

Chase loaded Stuart Wentworth's carry-on into his trunk and closed the lid. Moments ago the two had shaken hands, done their version of a hug, and now Stuart sat in the car waiting for an explanation. The man had left his business, his home, his wife, and flown to Colorado at Chase's request.

Maybe Chase had overreacted. Maybe lack of sleep had made him turn this into a drama. Maybe.... No. He remembered the look in his wife's eyes as she told him the story. The pain etched on her face. He'd made the best move based on the information he had available. Time would tell if he'd made the right one.

The fifteen-minute drive home to Bond stretched before him.

"You're not going to tell me, are you?" More of a statement than a question.

Chase shook his head.

Stuart Wentworth half-mumbled. "It's bad or you wouldn't have called me. I wouldn't be here if it was a walk in the park."

Chase said nothing. Their conversation earlier this morning had told Stuart that much. Men didn't hold the wealth and power his father-in-law enjoyed by being stupid. He knew how to read people and situations. He could go from point A to a whole new alphabet without blinking, and getting to the truth was rarely a gamble.

Stuart Wentworth had made his first million before his thirtieth birthday. A marriage to a department store sales girl he thought loved him for who he was rather than what he had made him feel complete. The son she gave birth to put him on top of the world. No one could ever hope to have this kind of perfection. They named their little boy Jeremy.

Three days before his thirteenth birthday, Jeremy died. Stuart expressed his grief by throwing himself into work more than ever. In less than a year he tripled his fortune. Four years later, his name appeared on every list of "desirables," not only in Chicago, but New York and Washington.

Then Celeste got pregnant again. He thought he wanted another son. A son to replace the one he'd lost. He wanted a boy so bad he felt sure that's what he'd get. A boy he could try and get things right with this time. But it wasn't to be.

The little girl who held his heart from her first breath bore testament to the avenue of wealth for the young man of modest means. The bond market had changed his life—Bond changed the reason he lived.

Stuart Wentworth didn't share this story with Chase until after David's death. Until his daughter's marriage almost fell apart, even the existence of Jeremy had remained a family secret. Bond hadn't even known she'd had an older brother.

Based on what Bond told him last night, this family knew how to keep secrets. Bad ones.

The two men traveled the rest of the distance in silence. Not stressful exactly. But also not the comfortable companionship they'd forged over the years.

Chase pulled up the long drive to his house and took a deep breath. *Please let this go well.* He opened the door for his father-in-law, then followed with the man's overnight bag.

When they walked in the house, Bond had her back to them, putting something in the oven. "What are you doing home in the middle of the day?" She turned, then froze, eyes wide. Her gaze went from her father to Chase and then over her father's shoulder.

"Your mother didn't make this trip, sweetheart. Just your dad."

Bond swallowed and blinked several times. Then after another moment's hesitation, she gave a strangled cry and flew into her father's arms.

Chase took the luggage through the kitchen and down the main hall to the guest room. When he returned the older man, arms still around his daughter, nodded in silent thanks.

Chase reached for his wife. When Bond turned to him, her face blanketed with tears she hugged him hard. "I love you, Chase Waters. Thank you for bringing my Daddy to me."

Chase handed her his handkerchief and she wiped her eyes.

"Now get back to work." She gave him a squeeze and stepped back.

Bond tugged on her bathrobe, then touched a hand to her hair. "Dad, I'm sorry for the way I look. Why don't you unpack and I'll get dressed and put on a fresh pot of coffee or we have some sun tea." Bond was filling the space with words.

Stuart took his daughter's hand firmly in his and walked her over to the kitchen table. "Sit. Talk. I'm not going anywhere and neither are you until I know what's bothering you."

Chase's cell rang as he walked out the door.

"This is Raul Ramirez. I have some information for you."

The Santeria guy. From the frying pan into the fire. That's what Chase felt like, going from his father-in-law to voodoo.

"I can meet you at the same place in twenty minutes." Chase tucked the phone back in his pocket and refocused.

Chapter Sixty-Six

City Market Parking Lot
Tuesday, September 25

Chase worked to settle his stomach as he pulled into the City Market parking lot. It was unlikely that any information Raul Ramirez might have would be good.

He'd seen the worst mankind had to offer the world in the physical sense. From battered wives to abused children to broken bodies to eviscerated remains. But Ramirez represented something Chase could not fight against. He valued every man's right to believe in whoever or whatever his heart followed. That's what this country stood for. Still it left him feeling helpless.

The Toyota Camry sat idling at the far end of the lot. Smoke curled from the exhaust like a snake.

Chase pulled his car into the empty space directly across the parking aisle. He turned the engine off and waited. *Let this be quick.*

The driver's door opened and a flip-flop-donned foot appeared to settle on the asphalt. Ragged jeans followed and finally the skinny profile of Raul Ramirez.

Chase's gut did a strange lurch. Sort of a tighten and somersault at the same time. He swallowed.

"This will be the last time you and I meet," Ramirez said. "After today I'm out of your field of reference. You don't call on me and I have no obligation to contact you. Understood?"

"I didn't call on you today."

"My point. This is above and beyond, and I expect some gratitude."

An RV cruised the length of the parking lot toward them, probably looking for some hookups for the night. Chase watched the ambitious camper, ready for a surprise. Why Ramirez would stage an ambush he had no idea. But the situation remained tense and no way would he be caught unaware.

Chase eyed the little man. Ramirez had dark, intense and intelligent eyes. "Why did you call me?" he asked.

"I have my reasons."

"Look, Ramirez. I never wanted to contact you in the first place." Chase gambled on the fact that anonymity ranked high on the Santeria follower's wish list. "Your name came up—that's all. But I'm not after you or your group in any way, based on the evidence we've accumulated thus far. And I'm more than willing to let your name get dusty if there's nothing that points me back to it."

Ramirez froze, deciding. Whatever information Ramirez had would come out now or Chase would have to bring him in for questioning. That would take time, and Chase didn't even know if anything Ramirez had to say was important.

The voodoo practitioner stood in silent communion with whatever spirits he'd chosen in his life. Either he'd come across in the next few seconds or Chase would slip back into his car and move on.

"There's one name that has come up," Ramirez said.

Chase waited.

Ramirez sucked in a deep breath, held it, then expelled. "His name is Preston Adams."

Related to the Preston Clinic? Shit. If not, one more asshole to check out. Chase heard a ticking clock and wondered if Ramirez might have an interest in a bad outcome.

"He's dead," Ramirez said. "But he had a twin brother."

"Good for him."

"Preston died because he needed a new heart to live. Fourteen years old. Kaput. End of the road."

"It happens." But Chase listened with an intensity that made his head hurt.

"Brother's name?" Ramirez asked. "Are you interested in the brother's name?"

Chase didn't respond. His training was automatic. While a rookie might give in and answer the question, a seasoned interviewer would not. He waited, and by waiting kept the upper hand.

Ramirez looked like he wanted to kick someone but he took a couple of deep breaths and seemed to relax. "His twin brother, Presley, has made a fortune by providing medical answers to people who can pay for the best outcomes."

As in the Preston Clinic.

"You need to remove Presley Adams from circulation. His greed is unacceptable, especially as it invades the privacy we require."

"We're working on it, Raul. Believe me, we're working on it."

Ramirez shook his head, got back in his car and drove off.

Chase called Bond to check on her. No answer. He closed his eyes and breathed deeply. He really wanted to hear her voice. He'd have to try again later.

Next he called Chief Whitman's cell phone. "You should know I'm on my way to the Preston Clinic. I don't plan on pissing anybody off, but I do plan on getting some answers."

Chapter Sixty-Seven

The Preston Clinic
Tuesday, September 25

Clouds rolled over the mountains and the sky dropped closer to the earth. Gray tones replaced brilliant blue, and huge snowflakes began to feather to the ground. Chase sat in his car on the side of the road, a Twizzler stuck in his mouth. He would give Whit three more minutes to call him and tell him he had the go-ahead to appear at the Preston Clinic. Sometimes he hated the politics of this job.

Two minutes later, Chase put the car in drive and drove the last half-mile to the entrance. Go-ahead or no go-ahead, Chase needed to get some answers.

His phone rang. Whit.

The chief spoke first. "You're almost there, aren't you?"

"Just pulling up to the gates."

Whit sighed. "Good thing you're expected then."

This time he didn't need to use the intercom or wait. The gates parted like the Red Sea and he moved his vehicle through. As they had before, the second he'd cleared the gates they closed behind him.

Today he saw a stretch SUV parked in front of the clinic. He pulled up behind it, glad that this time his car was clean. One good thing about using a department vehicle—they washed the cars regularly.

The liveried doorman, probably some kind of security guard, watched him approach then opened the massive entry doors. Chase nodded his thanks to the man and moved into the lobby. A fire roared in the massive fireplace. Fresh flower arrangements, different from the ones that had been there yesterday, provided spots of color in the large room.

No one came to greet him so he wandered around. First he examined the artwork then the magazines. Still no one appeared. He paced a few times in front of the fireplace, walked the perimeter to see if he could hear any voices. Nothing. He figured they had hidden cameras in the lobby but they were well-camouflaged. The muted sound of a ringing phone caught his attention and he decided to see where it came from. He moved to walk down a wide hallway to his right.

"Detective Waters, I believe you're here to see me." The voice came from behind him and he spun around.

Bugatti man.

Chapter Sixty-Eight

Aspen Falls Police Department
Tuesday, September 25

Terri finished her paperwork, left a message for Leslie James about the meeting agenda item, and tried to think of something else she could do on the case. Anything. Anything at all.

Finally she decided she didn't want to call Carol Greene. She grabbed the extra jacket she kept in her locker and walked out into the snowy afternoon. Whatever bad news the woman had to say to her, Terri would make her say it to her face.

She texted Chase to let him know she'd be taking care of some personal business for a few minutes but would remain available in case of an emergency. Not a small part of her hoped an emergency might pop up in say, about four minutes, when she pulled up Carol Greene's street.

The snow had turned heavy and would soon be sticking to more than just the grassy areas. It looked like the high country might be in for a great winter season. Terri's skis, waxed and ready, stood like sentinels in her garage.

She didn't even know if Lily knew how to ski.

Her phone didn't ring. Terri checked it for messages or texts. Nothing. *Damn.*

What did her aunt always call times like these? Oh yeah—"come to Jesus meetings." Her aunt knew a lot about fear and religion. Not so much about making a little girl feel loved.

Terri had waded through a lot of baggage to make sure she wanted to be an adoptive mother to Lily for all the right reasons. She knew to the back of her spine, to the deepest place in her heart, that she could make a difference for Lily. Terri's reasons were for Lily and not for her. Well maybe a little for her, but more for what she could give—in the love she had to give—rather than what she could get.

She tucked her car into a parking place two doors down from the Greene home. She was ready to fight for the little girl, to make sure Lily had every hope of a strong future and wouldn't be saddled with some family member who would want to cut off her light and force her into their own ideal of a perfect child. Terri pushed open her door.

Movement on the walkway in front of Carol Greene's home made her pause. A familiar figure moved with quick purpose from the house to a car parked on the opposite side of the street, got in and took off. Terri stared, fighting to place the individual.

One of the things most cops got good at involved recognizing the same person in different, often surprising, places. Like the perp who showed up at a parent-teacher conference, or a judge spotted in a strip club. Terri hadn't exactly mastered this, but she knew when she'd seen a face. And she'd seen this one before. But where?

She settled back in the car, unwilling to proceed until she figured this out. She mentally reviewed the last few cases she'd worked, the people she'd seen and places she'd been to in the last few weeks. Lunches with friends—including wait staff and other people in the restaurants—the night she went to the movies by herself because she really wanted to see that film, newspaper articles she'd read that contained photos, memos and informational bulletins and emails she'd received at the station for BOLAs. Someone. Recent. *Who?*

The ER. The last time she'd been there, Armand Fyfe had made himself a target by his attitude. There was another employee who stood at the nurse's station and watched as she and Leslie James went for coffee.

What business did an Aspen Falls Memorial Hospital employee have at the Greene home? Had Carol taken a turn for the worse?

Terri opened her door again and raced to the front door. She rang the doorbell and waited. Knocked. Waited. Pulled her cell out at the same time the front door opened. Carol Greene stood there looking as healthy as she had at breakfast but with a very curious expression. Terri's heart rate slowed.

"I saw the healthcare worker leaving your house and I thought… I thought—"

"Well as you can see, I'm doing fine," Carol Greene bristled, her voice tight.

Terri took a breath and allowed herself to smile. "For that I'm glad."

Carol's face softened. "I believe you truly are."

"Why was he here? Is Lily okay?"

"Lily is fine." Carol opened the door for Terri to enter. "Frank is the son of my sister's stepdaughter. He's one of those lost souls who is trying to find his place in the grand scheme of things and having a tough time. Thankfully, for the last year or two he seems to have settled in well at Memorial."

The two women stood, uncertain and uncomfortable.

"Did Frank happen to see you?" Carol asked.

"I don't think so."

"Not that it makes any difference, but I'm just as glad not to have the confrontation."

"Confrontation?"

"Frank is the one who came to me initially to tell me about your history."

Chapter Sixty-Nine

The Preston Clinic
Tuesday, September 25

Chase turned to face the man who stood several feet behind him. "I'm afraid I'm at a disadvantage." No outstretched hand. Nothing. Bugatti man did not appreciate the presence of one of Aspen Falls' finest.

"My name is Presley Adams, Detective. I own this clinic."

"It's quite impressive. I appreciate you taking the time to meet with me." Chase knew Whit had presented an either/or case to the clinic representative he must have spoken to a few minutes earlier. Diplomatic but firm. *Speak to my detective or run the risk of further scrutiny— maybe even some press.* Always know the weak spot.

"What is it you want to know?"

"Is there somewhere we can speak privately?"

Presley Adams looked around at the empty lobby but a surreptitious glance at one of the paintings where Chase assumed a camera was hidden made him change his mind.

"Follow me."

Presley Adams led Chase down another wide hallway with soft lights and art niches on either side. The thick carpet completely absorbed the sound of their footsteps. Adams turned a corner and walked to a set of eight-foot-high carved mahogany doors. He entered a code on a keypad hidden behind an ornamental piece of wood and the doors swung open. Once inside, he walked to his desk and pressed a button. A control pad rose on his desk and he pressed in another code. Chase wondered if he had just enabled the audio-visual system or disabled it. It didn't matter.

"Please, Detective Waters. Have a seat."

Two dark brown leather club chairs sat in front of the massive desk. Chase sat and tried not to run his hands over the buttery leather. He pulled out his small notebook.

"I understand you have some questions. I can give you only a minute or two so I suggest you ask them quickly."

"Tell me about the transplant side of the clinic."

"What specifically do you want to know?"

"Do you do many?"

"We do. We have an international reputation that attracts not only very wealthy, very ill patients, but also highly skilled doctors and surgeons."

"Where do you obtain the organs you use?"

"Well, Detective, that's an entirely private matter between the patient and their medical providers. The vast majority of our donated tissues and organs come through UNOS, just as for most hospitals. But our patients are often able to make private arrangements that don't directly concern the clinic."

"So the clinic never provides the organs?"

"I didn't say that. We have contacts in countries all over the world, and it would be morally reprehensible for us not to access them if it means we can save a life. The clinic, in those cases, merely acts as a conduit. Once again

Detective, it's a matter between our patients and their doctors."

The man rekeyed his code into the control pad on his desk, pushed another button and the doors swung open.

"That's really all the time I have at the moment. If you have any more questions, my secretary would be happy to schedule an appointment."

Chase stood and walked to the door, tucking his notebook back in his jacket pocket. At the door he turned and waited for some kind of response from Adams.

"Yes?" Presley Adams asked.

"Nice Bugatti."

The confusion and momentary panic that flashed across the man's face gratified Chase more than he would ever admit.

Chapter Seventy

The Greene Home
Tuesday, September 25

How would this Frank person from Aspen Falls Memorial know anything about Terri's history? Terri felt cornered, guilty for things she should feel no guilt over. The edges of the entryway she stood in blurred and went gray.

"What exactly did Frank tell you, Carol?" She fought to stay grounded in the moment.

"He told me enough about your past to raise a concern about your suitability to parent Lily."

Terri's hand tightened on her purse strap, every ounce of frustration flowing to her fingers. She had learned years ago, long before her police training days, how to control and compartmentalize her emotions.

"What, exactly?" Terri asked.

Carol Greene moved to straighten an afghan, placed precisely on a chair just inside the living room. She pulled the beautifully patterned blanket off the chair and began to refold it, checking the corners to make sure they were aligned perfectly. Her cheeks spotted with color. "He said you had an abortion when you were fourteen."

How did anyone know this? Somehow he'd gotten access to sealed records.

"That's true, Carol." Terri stood firm, her voice strong. "But I don't see how that would make me unfit to adopt Lily."

"Maybe it doesn't, but it does suggest that as a child you were never properly parented."

Terri closed her eyes. Carol Greene's words were shades of her aunt, and yet she didn't believe the woman standing in front of her would ever be as extreme as the stern woman who Terri had lived with for almost six years.

"My parents loved me very much."

"And they died when you were twelve."

Terri pushed away memories of her parents, their devotion as well as their deaths. Deaths caused by a drunk driver. Carol Greene's words had begun to lift the lid on the box but Terri slammed it shut. Another place and time. Not now.

"Once again, Carol, I don't see how any of this has any bearing on my desire—on my ability—to adopt your granddaughter and be there for her. None of what you have said could possibly—"

"What about the mental hospital?"

A cold wave washed over Terri, her lungs emptied of air. Terrible memories vied for her focus, insisting she lose herself to their vivid lure. But she had spent hard months, even years, learning what she gained and what she lost if she allowed herself to be a victim.

Terri swallowed and took a deep breath. "Can we sit down? I think we need to talk."

269

Chapter Seventy-One

Aspen Falls Middle School
Tuesday, September 25

Angela retrieved her favorite black jacket from her locker and pulled it on. She flipped her long hair out of the collar as she looked in the small mirror on the inside of the locker door, licked her finger and rubbed some ink off her cheek, then popped in her earbuds and did a quick search for the set of songs she wanted to listen to on the way home.

"You going to the party Friday night, Angela?" Keaton strode up behind Angela and opened the door wider so she could check her lipstick. Or pretend to.

"My parents haven't decided." She felt like such a baby. And Keaton looked even older than the fourteen she'd just turned. She looked sixteen, at least.

"That's too bad. But you know what I heard?" The other thing about Keaton—she always knew the latest gossip.

"What?"

"The really big party—the biggest party of the year—is tomorrow night."

"Wednesday? A school night?"

"That's what makes it so big. No babies. Probably some college guys. It's right off their campus."

Keaton gave her the details and suggested that Angela try wearing some lipstick Wednesday night. And mascara.

In the parking lot Angela looked around for Hailey's car. It was kind of hard to find with the snow. Heather's sister had promised them a ride home after school—way better than taking the bus—as long as they were both at her car when she got there herself. She didn't want to have to wait for them.

Angela spotted Heather waving at the end of a row of parked cars. Nice. She jogged over to her friend.

"Guess what!" Both girls said at the same time, then fell into giggles, their breath frosting in the cold air.

"We absolutely have got to go to that party," Angela said.

They spent a couple of minutes talking about what they planned to wear.

"Shhh," Heather said. "Don't say a word to Hailey. I don't think she'd like the idea of us going to one of *her* parties."

Chapter Seventy-Two

Cobalt Mountain Books
Tuesday, September 25

Daniel paced around the bookstore, pulling books from the shelves, thumbing the pages, and shoving them back in. Who had the time to read all these books anyway?

Something gnawed at Daniel. Something he should have figured out earlier. *Crap.* He hated this. He should be working the case. Chase could have gotten a couple of uniforms to offer protection. Instead, it was Daniel who watched the kid.

Efraín knew his job and he knew the bookstore customers—most by name. After greeting them as they walked into the store, he almost always had something in mind for them he knew they'd like. Without exception, they bought the book or books they'd come in to get, along with the one he recommended.

"You're really good at this," Daniel said. "You could sell anything."

"I can sell books. I love them. I want to be a writer."

"No kidding."

"You act like you've never met someone who wanted to be a writer."

"That would be correct."

"Especially a Hispanic kid from the wrong side of the tracks."

"I didn't say that."

"Didn't have to." Efraín squinted his eyes at Daniel. "What do you like to read?"

"I um, I don't have time to, um—"

"You kind of like that girl who was here, don't you? Elizabeth? Follow me."

Less than a minute later Daniel looked at the book in his hands. "What kind of title is *Like Water for Chocolate*? And am I supposed to be impressed because it was written by a Hispanic?"

"Trust me."

Daniel bought the book.

The evening employee arrived and Efraín updated her on new arrivals and customers he thought might be coming in after they got off work. She slid a couple of questioning glances in Daniel's direction but the kid ignored her.

When Efraín pulled something up on the computer, the elusive piece Daniel had been missing a few minutes ago roared big and bold into his brain.

"Efraín, do you have to go home right away?"

"Not necessarily. But I do need to let my mom know where I'll be."

"Good. Call her."

Efraín shook his head. "That won't work."

"Why not?" Daniel's patience had left the building.

"We don't have a phone."

Daniel, brought up short with sudden realization for the second time in less than a minute, processed the information. "Okay, fine. We'll go by your house, you can talk to your mom or leave her a note or whatever, then you and I need to get to the station."

273

Daniel punched a number in his cell phone. "Terri, I need you to pull a warrant for me ASAP and send a couple of uniforms over to the ER and get the main computer they use. You should have enough between Leslie James and Fyfe's trash. I want that computer and I'll be at the station within the hour. Oh, and get me the name and contact info for their head IT guy, in case I need it."

He had to move the phone away from his ear. He waited until the high-pitched static in the form of his co-worker's screeching slowed before settling it back against his head. Terri vented as well as anyone he knew.

"One computer will do. Thanks." He disconnected before his hearing could become permanently impaired.

"C'mon, young Hemingway. We need to lay down some tracks."

Chapter Seventy-Three

The Preston Clinic
Tuesday, September 25

Edward Sloan sat in the chair, pressed into his wife's hospital bed, head resting at her side. He held her hand while she slept.

Friends and family hadn't understood that Diana couldn't have flowers in her room, so the lobby of the clinic soon filled with colorful arrangements, from simple daisies to dramatic exotics he couldn't name. In her room, a stack of get-well cards they'd gone through together sat on the table next to her bed. A simple pile of paper illuminated by soft lamplight that represented the love of so many people. She'd grown tired before they could read them all.

The snow had almost stopped, leading to a day that had been busier than most with visits and phone calls from family and friends. Maggie had run interference for them when needed, but Diana had been so happy to catch up with everyone that Edward allowed it to go on a little longer than he should have.

The clinic—the staff and surroundings—were everything he'd been promised and then some. But the room's elegant appointments didn't mask the mechanical hiss of machines that kept his beloved alive.

Or cover entirely the sound of his weeping.

Pressure on his back. He jerked up to see an angel standing behind him. No, not an angel. A nurse. He wiped the tears from his face.

"Mr. Sloan, would you come with me, please?"

She turned and crossed the room to the door. Waited for him to follow.

In the hall after the door had closed on its silent hinges, she held out her hand. "I'm Nancy Collins, Mr. Sloan. I'll be helping care for your wife."

Edward Sloan, not used to people seeing him vulnerable, shook her hand and mumbled a thank-you.

"Dr. Frederickson would like a word with you in the conference room."

"Now?"

"Yes, Mr. Sloan. If it's not inconvenient."

Once again she turned and began walking away from him. He followed.

The clinic hallways were decorated like a fine hotel. Patterned, bordered carpet—with such thick padding that pushing wheelchairs would be almost impossible— stretched between butter yellow walls. Mahogany wainscoting and crown molding framed both the walls and the occasional table that featured more fresh flowers.

Nancy Collins paused outside a closed door and knocked. She pushed it open, nodded to the occupant, then stood aside for Edward to enter. He heard the soft click of the door close behind him.

Edward Sloan was used to conference rooms—he'd been in enough of them over the years. This one however, looked more like a large dining room. He made eye contact with a man dressed in a respect-me-I'm-a-doctor white coat, standing next to a sideboard.

"Mr. Sloan, I'm Dr. Nathan Frederickson. I'm the administrative doctor on staff at the clinic. Although I don't have direct responsibility for the patients, I do get involved in the communications with the families." He gestured to two small settees in the corner. "Please."

A pitcher of water and two crystal glasses sat on a tray near them. Frederickson righted the glasses and poured them each some water.

"I want to make sure you have the complete picture of the patient's condition as it now stands." The doctor took a sip.

Edward nodded.

"Her heart is wearing out, Mr. Sloan. The mechanical intervention that keeps her alive is now a contributing factor to her death."

Edward dropped to the settee. He'd heard it all before. Once was one time too many.

"In the event Dr. Jackson hasn't been clear, she doesn't have much time. If we are unable to obtain a suitable replacement organ soon, I'm afraid there will be nothing more we can do for the patient."

"Her name is Diana."

Dr. Nathan Frederickson's face went blank. He didn't understand.

Edward gritted his teeth. "Is there anything else, Dr. Frederickson?"

Unused to being dismissed, the doctor sat speechless while Edward Sloan stood and moved to the door.

He didn't turn around. "Just have an operating room available at all times. For Diana."

Edward made his way back down the long hallway. He'd grown weary of the supercilious attitudes of the medical profession. So many of them tried to cast larger shadows than normal human beings could. They did so because on some level it worked for them.

His own shadow had shrunk in the last few months. He was one man—one broken man—without his wife. Two years ago when Diana had her first transplant operation, they had prayed together about the life that had to be lost in order to spare hers. When matching organs—typed rare—had become available, they'd felt blessed by God.

Circumstances were different this time, and Edward Sloan understood the ramifications of his latest decision.

Someone healthy would have to die in order for his wife to live.

This time he wasn't praying.

Chapter Seventy-Four

The Madrigal Home
Tuesday, September 25

Daniel's patience was as taut as his nerves. Who knew this scrawny high school kid used his own money to pick up groceries on his way home? By the time they made a stop at City Market, Daniel wanted to yell at someone. Maybe one of these days he'd experiment with that meditation stuff to try and find inner peace. Well if not peace, at least to calm down a little. But not today. Too late for today.

Efraín gave him directions. Daniel could have plugged the address into his GPS, but at least this gave them something to talk about.

"Turn right here."

Daniel swung a right and drove down a dark road. The snow had been tracked by cars, but no plows would be out for just a couple of inches. If there were street lights here they weren't lit.

"This is my house." Efraín indicated a small clapboard structure that looked like a good gust of wind would lay it flat. Daniel parked the car and followed the boy down a dirt path to a side door. On closer inspection, the clapboard had recently been painted a sort of mustard-orange color and the windows sparkled. The house might blow over in a heap, but it would be a clean, maintained heap.

"Does your family own this house?" Daniel asked.

"No. We rent. But we sometimes can pay less when we fix things. My dad is good at fixing things. We've lived here for as long as I can remember."

They walked into the kitchen and three sets of eyes looked up from schoolwork to see who had come home with their brother. Politeness and respect for their guest kept them silent.

Efraín introduced Daniel to his mother. She said his father had found a day job and probably wouldn't be home until after dinner. When Mrs. Madrigal learned what Daniel did for a living, her face closed up. Her responses became either a nod or a shake of her head while she cast suspicious glances in Daniel's direction. When Efraín told his mother they were leaving and he would be home later the woman froze, then grabbed her son's arm and pulled him into the next room.

Daniel heard rapid Spanish spoken low and intense. Efraín's responses were even more muffled. Then silence. The children working at the kitchen table fidgeted in their seats but said nothing. Daniel needed to get to the station, get to that computer, and still do what he'd been told to do by Chase. Protect Efraín. About to interrupt the discussion in the adjoining room, Daniel stopped short when Efraín reappeared with a backpack and nodded toward the door.

They drove to the station without speaking. Daniel put the car in park.

"I'm sorry for the way my mother behaved."

"You don't need to apologize. I should have spoken to her myself."

"It wouldn't have done any good. She worries too much."

"She's a mother."

When they got to the conference room their team had made into a base of operations, Daniel saw a computer tower sitting in the middle of the table. *Yes!*

Daniel set to work, absorbed in what the memory could tell him. Even the deleted items. Especially the deleted items.

Damn. He needed the IT guy. The data he wanted access to was stored on the hospital's server, not the individual computers. Thank goodness Terri had gotten him the contact information and included it in the warrant. He picked up the phone.

* * *

Three hours later he looked up to see Chase watching him.

"Hey Chase, I'm getting the connection between Memorial and Preston. You'll—"

"Do you have any idea what time it is?"

"Um... shit. The kid."

"I arranged for a uniform to take him home thirty minutes ago. You ever hear of dinner?"

"But you said—"

"I know what I said. The kid might be in danger but not tonight. Mostly I needed you to cool your heels for a couple of hours after that stunt you pulled with the Benavides girl."

Chapter Seventy-Five

Aspen Falls Police Department
Tuesday, September 25

Chase passed the printouts to Daniel. The two men sat alone in the team meeting room. Between Terri's hunch, Daniel, and the IT guy, they had found the link between the emergency room at Aspen Falls Memorial Hospital and the Preston Clinic. Every seven to ten days the blood test results ordered by Armand Fyfe for ER patients were sent to a computer at the clinic location.

"Bring Fyfe in now. I want to talk to him," Chase said.

"Already done. The good news is we got him at home so there's no warning to whoever else might be involved at the ER. The other good news is he made quite a scene. If we don't find something on him to tie him to this case, we could probably hold him for obstruction of justice and just being a genuine ass."

"Is he here?"

"They just got our visitor settled in the interview room about five minutes ago."

"Good. We'll let him sit a bit. Have you seen Terri?"

"I've been babysitting, remember? But she must've hustled some kind of butt to get a warrant for this computer and have it here as fast as she did. Plus she got me the IT connection I needed."

Chase took out his cell and saw the text message from the other detective. That was six hours ago. "What time did the computer come in?"

Daniel checked the paperwork. "It was seized at four thirty."

Chase retrieved another package of Twizzlers from his drawer.

"Good work, Daniel."

"Thanks."

"Are you going to see Elizabeth Benavides when this is over?" Chase made two points by asking this question. One, he understood the attraction between the two people. Two, Daniel's best move for his career did not involve taking Elizabeth with him on any more tails.

The other detective shrugged his shoulders but the rust color in his face couldn't be dismissed.

Chase laughed. "Okay, then. Why don't I go talk to the charming Dr. Fyfe?"

Chase and Daniel walked to the small space adjoining the interview room and checked the video equipment. Two screens showed separate views of an anxious Armand Fyfe. An audio check confirmed good sound. Fyfe inhaled and exhaled so hard Chase thought he might hyperventilate.

He took a few more minutes to watch his subject. Smallish with a thin build, dark curly hair slashed with gray, he looked more like a lab rat than the doctor in charge. Chase figured the man had taken a few hits as a kid because of his last name. He'd grown up in a time when people knew about Barney Fyfe, the bumbling sheriff's deputy on television. And with Armand as a first name? Chase guessed the guy had a pair to make it through high school, let alone college and medical school.

A moment later he knocked politely on the door and entered the interview room. He knew exactly how to play this.

"Dr. Fyfe, I'm Detective Waters. You are here because of some cases we're investigating, and I have a few questions we need you to answer."

Chase watched anxiety flee from the man's demeanor, replaced by arrogance.

"You have no fucking right to do this to me."

"Actually we do." Chase pulled a chair out from the end of the table and sat it on the same side as Fyfe at an angle. He sat down and crossed his legs.

Armand Fyfe pushed his chair further away and pressed deeper into it. "I am a respected doctor at Aspen Memorial Hospital. I pay my goddamned taxes and don't break the law. I've done nothing illegal. You are risking a hell of a lawsuit that will ruin your shitty career and fuck up your life for the rest of the time you might have left. But then, maybe you already have a fucked-up life and wouldn't notice much of a difference." Fyfe took a breath. "You and your assholes have pissed up the wrong rope."

"You are making my day, Dr. Fyfe."

"Excuse me?"

"You heard me. With every delightful word you utter, my day keeps getting better."

"Fuck you."

"Perhaps I should explain." Better and better. Chase loved interrogating suspects, and Armand Fyfe already ranked as one of his favorites. He couldn't wait to bring this guy down. But first he wanted to toy with him a little.

"I'm waiting, and with each minute I piss away here on my day off my lawsuit against your little shit-ass department ticks up by one mil."

The little man reminded Chase of the wolf in the children's story about the three pigs. Fyfe huffed and puffed, threatening to blow the AFPD house down. This called for a little more rope.

"My apologies for inconveniencing you, Dr. Fyfe."

"You said you would explain this abominable behavior."

"Yes, I did," Chase said. "We're investigating some particularly brutal murders."

"*Hell-lo*? I'm a doctor. I'm no fucking murderer. I don't even know anyone who's been murdered."

"Oh, but you do."

"Who?"

"How many patients do you see in a typical week, Doctor?"

"I don't see wha—"

"How many?"

"I don't know. One hundred? Two hundred?"

"And how many of those patients require blood tests?"

"That all depends. I never order unnecessary tests, if that's what you're getting at."

"According to the computer data we have, you order more blood tests than all of the other doctors at Memorial put together. And I don't think it's a coincidence that a fair number of the patients for whom you've ordered tests are later murdered. Do you?" Chase watched the color leach from Armand Fyfe's face.

Twenty minutes later, Chase left Dr. Armand Fyfe alone to contemplate where his actions—and his greed—had led. More importantly, Chase left with the name of the ER employee who had arranged to lease the good doctor's computer access code. Fyfe hadn't ordered the blood tests himself. He'd just leased out his access code. *Idiot.*

Chase made sure Daniel had been able to commit everything to video, then went to the front desk to complete some paperwork. Knowing that what's written isn't always read, he told the officer on duty to release the man in Interview Room Two at ten o'clock. Releasing Fyfe temporarily was a risk he was willing to take.

Chase had what he needed.

Chapter Seventy-Six

The Preston Clinic
Tuesday, September 25

The serrated words of the administrative doctor ripped Edward Sloan's soul into a ragged, bloody mass. "She's weaker tonight."

Welts raised on his heart. Edward Sloan sucked in a lungful of air and reached for one of the chairs at the long polished table. He was beginning to hate this room at the clinic. The grayness of the day had seeped into the air of this space. Now it crawled inside him. The snow may have stopped, but the chill it represented had stuck.

When he'd come back after a short break for dinner, Nancy Collins had met him in the flower-filled lobby. Told him Dr. Frederickson wanted to speak with him in the conference room before he saw Diana. She didn't bother to show him the way again.

"We're doing everything we can to keep her strong enough to withstand surgery, Mr. Sloan. But if we don't find a suitable donor in the next few hours, I'm afraid the patient won't be able to handle the trauma associated with a long operation."

Edward didn't bother reminding Nathan Frederickson of his wife's name. It hadn't worked before. Frederickson was a computer, not a healer. Edward closed his eyes. Healers with empathy and compassion hadn't worked no matter how much money he spent. Now his money was buying impersonal automatons he would never invite into his home.

So be it.

The doctor was seated at the far end of the table, a clipboard in front of him. A china tea service on a silver tray sat nearby. Only one cup, Edward noticed.

With a pen, he checked something off then looked directly at Edward for the first time. "It isn't that we aren't fully prepared to do our part, should the opportunity present itself. It's simply that we are trying to do the kind thing here and make certain you are prepared for all plausible eventualities."

Edward nodded, but the *kind* medical professional had turned his attention back to the checklist. Which, Edward Sloan guessed, contained the task of this very conversation. One less thing for the dear doctor to deal with this evening.

He turned and left the room, shoulders sagging with unshed tears and unlived dreams.

Martin Jackson had left him a message this afternoon, and Edward hadn't yet returned his call. Their old family doctor had probably phoned to discuss the same thing. The delivery would have been different but the message essentially the same.

Edward Sloan wanted to pray for good news. For a heart that was as good a match as the previous organs were. And for it to come through legitimate channels. But he knew if he began praying he would pray for a heart from any source, including the other sources he'd put in play. Sources that had required him to harden his own heart in order to use them. Praying meant he'd have to talk to God, and he didn't like the idea of talking with God right now.

Like changing clothes, Edward threw off the hopeless desperation Frederickson seemed adept at providing. A cloak of doom tailored by lawyers and statisticians designed to protect the investors and the heartless administrative professionals who ran this best-in-the-world level of care private clinic. In place of gloom, he powered up a current of optimism before entering Diana's room. He couldn't let his wife see how close he was to giving up.

Edward stopped short of Diana's door, gave himself a shake and pumped up his posture. Got an image in his mind of taking Diana away on a lavish holiday once this was behind them and her health restored. She loved the ocean. He'd find a private beach with crystal water and white sand. Edward could hear her infectious laughter and watch as the sparkle in her eyes rivaled the sun glinting off the water.

He opened the door.

Chapter Seventy-Seven

The Sloan Residence
Wednesday, September 26

Edward Sloan pushed the off-button and laid the phone on his desk. It was almost two thirty in the morning. Light pooled and spotlighted the mechanical instrument, the sleek modern lines somehow mocking the tradition of inlaid mahogany and leather on the surface of his desk. Shadows pressed in from the rest of his study. Shadows pressed in on his mind. He took a sip from his drink.

There had been no good news from any of his sources. He had people in China, India, prisons around the world—all looking for something that could make them rich. But a heart from a donor with the same rare blood type and other matching issues as Diana's remained elusive—while time collapsed around them at an alarming speed.

Edward Sloan did the only thing he had left to do.

He made one more phone call, then fell to his knees.

* * *

He'd been dreaming about Diana. Just before she got sick the first time. The dream felt so real he looked over to the space next to his in their bed. His head fell back on the cool pillow and he closed his eyes. So real...

Edward had critically wounded his wife. They both knew it but neither talked about it. He'd almost killed their marriage—nothing would ever be the same. They both knew that too. The purity of their commitment to one another was gone forever. They were devoted to each other, but the sanctity of their marriage was spoiled.

Because of him.

Somehow he'd justified the affair. He was a man. He needed more than his wife was willing to give him (no matter that she'd given him all she could, including the very heart failing her now). He was wealthy and successful and he'd been honest enough to suggest to Diana what he was going to do. It made no difference that she didn't believe he'd do it. Now all these years later, he couldn't for the life of him come up with one reason to validate what he'd done. Edward had risked losing the best thing in his life. He couldn't live without Diana.

He often wondered if after his infidelity, his wife had felt okay to pursue her own relationship outside of their marriage. He had no proof one way or the other, but he never felt she had. And there was always the possibility, small though it might be, that his actions—his choices— had contributed in some way to Diana's illness. He'd read studies that indicated unusual or prolonged stress could lead to catastrophic illness.

If he could take it back—every bit of it—he would. He'd been so foolish.

Edward fell back into a troubled sleep.

The ringing of his telephone caused him to lurch up in bed. He glanced at the bedside clock. Oh God, no. Please, no.

"Sloan."

"Dad, I'm sorry about the time difference but I just got your message."

Eddie. In Japan. Not the hospital. "Hi, son."

"Is she that bad?"

Edward choked back a groan. "It doesn't look good. Unless we find a compatible heart in the next few hours, maybe a day, we're going to lose her. Get here as quickly as you can."

"She's always loved you, you know."

Something about the way Eddie said it. Did his son know what he had done all those years ago?

Chapter Seventy-Eight

Aspen-Pitkin County Airport
Wednesday, September 26

Chase pulled up at the airport, and his father-in-law unlatched his seat belt. "Thank you for coming, Stuart. I know your visit meant a lot to Bond." Hours of talking, touching and tears had begun the healing in his wife that should have happened decades ago.

"You love my daughter and for that I will always be grateful."

The man had aged in just a couple of days. A shadow had fallen across his features—pulled them to a sad place. Chase understood. He'd seen it often in the faces of survivors. Hell, he'd seen it in the mirror.

Chase didn't know if Stuart had spoken to Celeste since his arrival and didn't feel comfortable asking. The relationship between Bond's parents only affected him as it affected Bond. And for now his wife had received the time and attention she needed from her father. The rest could wait.

He retrieved Stuart's overnighter from the trunk, then handed the wheeled luggage off to the older man and held his hand out for the customary clasp and shake. Instead

293

Stuart pulled him into a tight and awkward hug. When they broke apart, Stuart's eyes had pooled with tears. He blinked and when they spilled onto his cheeks he didn't bother wiping them away.

Stuart Worthington walked toward his private plane, shoulders stooped, his overcoat dragging unnoticed on the ground.

Chapter Seventy-Nine

Aspen Falls Police Department
Wednesday, September 26

"It's ducks-in-a-row time, detectives. We need to make sure we're all on the same page, have all of our bases covered, and... if I could think of one more crappy cliché, I'd puke it up now." Chase hauled in extra donuts and muffins and three grandes—each geared toward the particular tastes of the recipient—from The Coffee Pod.

"I think we're almost at the end of this thing." He set the food and drink down, and hands appeared as if by magic. "Terri, when you've had a sip and a bite, would you take the board?"

"I've got it," Daniel said. He pulled a fresh whiteboard on rollers from the storage closet and set it next to the others, prepared to write.

"We have a couple of different motives here," Chase began.

"Money," both Terri and Daniel said at once.

"And?" He paused. "Think about it. What would prompt someone to offer money—maybe a lot of money—for a body part?"

"Fear," Terri said.

"Yeah, well... fear of loss maybe. Or death. But I submit one of the other motives is love," Chase said. "Of course love doesn't give us the same legal clout as money in this instance, but it bears thinking about."

Daniel looked a little confused. "So it's money, right?"

"Right."

"Money for who?"

"Presley Adams. The Preston Clinic is named after his brother." Chase got up to get another muffin, vaguely concerned he couldn't remember having eaten the first one. "Adams has an extremely wealthy clientele around the world. Wealthy enough that they made him a millionaire in his own right a few hundred times over. And he would do anything to build up their loyalties, not to mention his bank accounts."

"He fills a need," Daniel offered.

"Exactly."

"And in this case," Daniel continued, "there is no way supply can ever exceed demand."

"Bingo."

Terri continued the familiar case wrap-up with the team while Daniel wrote madly on the whiteboard. "He needed a supply source who would be a match for a majority of his clients but who wouldn't be in a position to seek help from the authorities if things went bad, or even if they didn't."

Daniel stopped for a moment and then in a soft voice—almost reverent—"Illegal immigrants. People who generally live well within all the laws of our country, except for one. But it's a big enough one that they will stay underground at all costs."

"I'm willing to bet that every mutilated corpse that has been found in our region in the last two years, especially if they're Hispanic or Latino, is someone who lived under the radar. Whose family and loved ones could never come to us for help or answers. I've requested records from every jurisdiction contiguous to ours." Chase checked his watch. They couldn't even begin to apply for arrest warrants until they could convince a judge they had probable cause.

"And our tie-in to the Preston Clinic?" Terri asked.

"Aspen Falls Memorial Hospital," Daniel said.

Terri shifted in her seat and pursed her lips.

Chase tipped his chair back and then let it pop back to the ground. He leaned forward. "Look Terri, Leslie James is not the head of the ER. More important, she not only doesn't have anything to do with these murders, she helped us get a handle on them. She'll survive whatever fallout occurs."

Terri nodded but didn't look any more comfortable.

Daniel kept writing. "We have evidence that a doctor, Armand Fyfe, accepted payments for his access code in order for blood tests to be requested. We know they were all ordered by Frank Dumont, a physician's assistant who not only ordered the blood tests of uninsured Hispanics who came into the clinic, but also sent the test results directly to Presley Adams."

Terri sat forward on her chair. "And Presley Adams then compared them to the current needs of his wealthy clients from all over the world. When he could make a match he moved ahead."

"Enter the amazing Carlisle brothers," Chase said. "Bobby and Sammy would do anything for a buck. If the donor target doesn't go along with the cash-for-organs scheme, or if the body part required sustains life, they do a quick grab and the target is never seen again."

"Unless they turn up in one of our dumpsters," Terri said.

Chase crumpled a napkin. "Yeah, there's that."

"We have the Carlisle brothers offering money to Efraín and meeting with Adams. Right?" Daniel asked.

"That's right. Hard to miss a guy in a Bugatti."

"We also have them at the scene of the fire at the Benavides house," Daniel added.

"Problem," Terri said.

Daniel didn't like the sound of that. "What?"

"The Benavides family is here legally."

They fell silent. Chase cursed to himself. He couldn't have been wrong about this case. He couldn't have been. Did this put them back at square three? Or even square zero?

"I know the answer," Daniel said.

"Well?" *This better be good.*

"The Benavides family is an exception to the rule."

"Rule? What rule?" Chase asked.

"If you're Hispanic, live in that neighborhood, and have to use the ER when you're sick, the rule says you're undocumented. That means you're fair game to Presley Adams."

"Okay," Chase said. "I can buy that. But why wouldn't Adams at least hesitate? Consider the possibility that even though they were Hispanic, lived in that neighborhood, and went to the ER, they were also citizens who would raise a fuss?"

"Think of Mrs. Benavides. Left up to her, they never would have contacted us. We are not to be trusted, even by people who have lived here for generations. There's too much negative lore. The authorities have proven time and time again that power corrupts, even on a small scale. The idea of 'us versus them' is so engrained, it wouldn't matter if they lived in a mansion and your sister cleaned their toilets." Daniel's face turned that rusty color Chase had seen earlier. "Sorry."

"Don't be. What you're saying is that if it weren't

for—"

"If it weren't for Elizabeth Benavides, we might not be here right now. Unlike the others, she was willing to come to us and speak up."

"She's an exceptional woman," Chase said. "We need to put together arrest warrants, and I'm gonna tell you now we're going to have a hard time convincing a judge that an ER employee, a doctor, and Presley Adams are responsible for the murders. And without them we can't even get to the Carlisle brothers. They all need to come down together."

"And if we can't get them all at once?"

Chapter Eighty

Aspen Falls Cemetery
Wednesday, September 26

Chase and Daniel stood on the perimeter of mourners gathered to say goodbye to Rachelle Benavides. Although the old oak tree next to them had lost most of its leaves, a few scudded over the patches of unmelted snow and still-green lawn. Clouds pushed and shoved across the sun, a giant mirror ball mottling the earth as the tears mottled the faces of the family and friends of the young woman.

The detectives didn't try to hide the fact that they were examining and cataloguing every person in attendance. Chase didn't expect to see anyone tied to the murder here. Not really. This was not the kind of killing done for narcissistic pleasure. But they were cops, and just as autopsies were revealing, memorial services could be as well.

"See anything?" Chase asked.

"Nope."

"You're carrying around those flowers like you thought there wouldn't be any at a funeral."

Daniel looked away but didn't seem all that embarrassed about the bouquets he held in his hands.

Chase stiffened. "Black Mustang. Three o'clock."

The car moved slowly down the crowded driving lane but didn't stop. When it disappeared around a curve, Chase and Daniel gave one another a nod and moved into action. Daniel dropped the bouquets and with as little fanfare as possible the two men moved through the crowd to stand at either end of the Benavides family. They were ready.

The priest continued in a mesmerizing combination of Latin, Spanish and English—enough of each language where each listener could get the gist of what he was saying. No translators required. It was a special kind of *pochismo*, something that extended beyond a blend of just Spanish and English.

Elizabeth seemed aware of their presence. Her parents were too wrapped up in grief to see beyond their pain. Their son, Robert, sat stiffly between the older couple. He'd been able to get leave for an immediate family member's death even though he served in a combat zone. He looked dazed. Chase imagined that if the soldier had considered his family sitting around a gravesite, he thought it would be his rather than his youngest sister's. The young man had probably been more shocked by this violence than by anything he'd encountered so far in his military experience. Very few war casualties were carved up so completely by the enemy.

Chase was about ready to relax when he saw a figure. Daniel drew to attention as well. The man didn't stop at any of the graves but bisected them to come to a halt directly in Elizabeth's view. There he stopped. Spread his legs and placed hands on hips as if he were willing Elizabeth to look in his direction.

At the same moment Elizabeth looked up, both Chase and Daniel began walking around the final resting place of Rachelle Benavides to approach the man who had

301

challenged the sanctity of a funeral. Who was only there to threaten. By the time they'd rounded the gravesite and mourners, the brazen interloper became aware of their approach. He looked in turn at both detectives, flagged them with his middle finger and walked away. No harm, no foul, he seemed to say.

Bullshit.

Chase and Daniel returned to their positions. The priest, to his credit, had not missed a beat in his multilingual ceremony. Then it was over, and time for the family members to pay their last respects over their departed loved one.

Mr. Benavides took a shovel full of earth and turned it into the grave. Ramona Benavides did this same thing, visibly working to keep her shoulders back and her body from crumpling. Robert took his turn and remained true to both Catholic and military tradition. Then it was Elizabeth's turn.

The woman rose from her chair next to the grave and reached for the shovel handle her brother passed to her. Rather than digging a bit of the piled earth to pour on top of her sister's coffin as her father had, as her mother had and as her brother had, she raised the shovel over her head and turned to look at the people standing in silent expectation of custom.

She seemed to look each person in the eye. "You loved my sister. You know this isn't right. We should not be here today burying what's left of her body." Her voice was strong even though tears streamed down her face. She looked in the direction the threatening man had slithered away to and then turned her face to look directly in Chase's eyes. "These people have gotten away with *unspeakable* things because they've done them to people who *will not speak*. No more. It is over." Her face crumpled and she folded to the ground using the shovel as a pole to slide down. Her brother and Daniel were each at her side in an instant, helping her up and guiding her to her chair.

The priest made some closing comments and said a prayer. This time all in Spanish. When several people began tossing single flowers into the grave, Daniel went back to the old oak and retrieved his bouquets. He waited until most of the mourners had paid their respects and quietly took his place at the end of the line. As he passed Elizabeth, he gave her a bouquet. The second went to her mother. The third one he offered as a sign of respect and loss to Rachelle.

Chapter Eighty-One

Aspen Falls Police Department
Wednesday, September 26

This was the part of police work they never show on television. The hours of boredom where nothing happens. The wait. Whether you're a traffic cop or on surveillance or getting arrest warrants to bring down some truly bad guys, the wait makes you want to scream.

Chase had left the team meeting that morning and gone directly to Whit. For this next step he knew they'd need the backing of the Chief of Police. The big guns. Terri had worked a minor miracle to get the warrant for the ER's computer and server, but this—requesting warrants to arrest several people including one of the wealthiest men in Aspen Falls—could make the most assured cop feel like a rookie. Careers were on the line. Nobody rushed to help.

Now it was just a waiting game, hoping for a judge to grant them the warrant. Daniel and Terri were throwing crumpled bits of paper at each other, both detectives even more quiet than usual.

Chase called Bond for the third time that day to check in.

"Chase, I'm fine. You don't have to keep calling. Really." Bond did sound good. Like her old self. Almost.

"I'm worried."

"You're bored."

"Caught me." Oh God, he loved this woman. "Kids in bed?"

"Yep. We need to talk about the party Angela wants to go to this weekend. I'll call the parents tomorrow, and if they're both going to be home I think we should let her go."

Chase felt the usual cramping in his gut whenever he had to let one of his kids grow up a little more. The world he knew and the world they knew could collide in some very bad ways. Bond tried to make him find balance and reason, but what the hell good would balance and reason do if another one of their children died? Where would balance and reason be then? "We'll talk after you confirm with the parents tomorrow." With any luck the parents wouldn't know anything about the party and that would be the end of that.

Whit walked in the room and immediately had the attention of everyone.

Chase spoke quickly into the phone. "Gotta go. Don't wait up."

"We have one last hope," Whit said. "Every other available judge has said they want additional probable cause before committing their names to a warrant. Judge Lane has been on vacation but is expected home within thirty minutes. I'm heading to his house myself and will let you know."

"We'll be ready to go."

Less than forty-five minutes later, Chase got the call from Whit.

"Go get 'em."

Chapter Eighty-Two

Aspen Falls Memorial Hospital
Wednesday, September 26

Terri waited in the parking lot for the patrol officer who would assist her in the arrest of Dr. Armand Fyfe and Frank Dumont. She didn't anticipate any trouble she couldn't handle, but a bit of backup wouldn't hurt.

A car with the Aspen Falls Police Department's logo pulled up next to hers. A female officer nodded in Terri's direction and exited the vehicle.

"Detective Johnson? I'm Officer Thomas. It's a pleasure to meet you." The younger woman held out her hand. "I understand we're making two arrests in the ER?"

"That's right. Both male. Armand Fyfe, a doctor, and Frank Dumont, a physician's assistant."

"Let's go. I'll follow your lead."

Fifteen minutes later a sputtering and still arrogant Armand Fyfe sat handcuffed in the backseat of the cruiser while Officer Thomas began writing her report using the laptop locked on the front console.

Terri secured Frank Dumont in the back of her car and walked over to Thomas's window. When the officer saw Terri the window whirred down. "I just want to thank you, Officer Thomas. That went as smoothly as any arrest I've ever made. Good job."

"Thank you. And it's Linda."

Terri gave the officer a smile, then slid into the driver's seat of her vehicle and started the car. She needed to get a few things off her chest but didn't want to blow an opportunity. She turned on a recorder and announced her name, Frank's name, the date, time and location. He'd been Mirandized before leaving the building but she read the list of warnings and rights again. He didn't respond. She stated his lack of response for the recording. "Well, Frank. It's just you and me now. Funny how that happened, isn't it?"

No response.

"Huh. I thought you were the talkative type. You sure talked a lot to Carol Greene."

Silence.

"You thought telling her that crap about me would what... scare me away?"

"Stupid bitch."

"What then?"

The spit hawked from the backseat missed her. Terri smiled. "Let me try this one. You didn't want any nosy cop hanging out at family gatherings. Maybe get too close to your business. Ask too many questions about where you got that extra money."

The silence this time spoke volumes.

"Now see, Frank. A couple of things. First, we were on to you long before you and I could have ever met around the backyard barbecue. That would simply never have happened unless you got out on parole or something. And second, Carol and I talked through everything and we're cool. Not, of course, that it's any of your business."

"You can't prove a thing."

"Wrong again. Computers give up a lot of information these days. And so do scared doctors."

"Fyfe didn't say a thing to me."

"You keep digging your hole deeper don't you?"

"You must be talking about Fyfe. You arrested him."

"Why would he have said anything to you?"

Silence.

"The reason he didn't is because he thought we'd leave him alone because he gave you up."

"Fuck."

"Make that past tense and you're right."

Chapter Eighty-Three

The Presley Adams Residence
Wednesday, September 26

Chase knocked on the front door of Presley Adams's mountain mansion, the uniformed officer with him tense and visibly anxious even in the dark. He knocked again and rang the doorbell. Light washed the shadows away and a moment later the intercom popped to life.

"Yes?" A woman's voice. Accented.

"Ma'am, we're with the Aspen Falls Police Department." It would go a lot easier if she'd open the door and let them in.

"Is something wrong?" Swedish?

"Yes, ma'am. There is. Would you please open the door?"

"Show me some ID."

Chase took out his creds and held them up to the camera as steady as he could. He heard a heavy bolt land home and the massive door swung inward.

"Please come in." She had blond hair that was almost white. Nice looking in a forced kind of way. Chase thought she'd probably had some work done in one of the Preston Clinics.

"We're here to see Presley Adams," Chase said.

"He's gone."

"Where did he go?"

She shook her head. "I don't know. He called me from the clinic yesterday afternoon and told me to pack a bag for him, bring his passport, and arrange for someone to drive his car home."

Damn it! Yesterday afternoon. The man could be anywhere. A nice Swiss bank account and Presley Adams could do anything—be anyone—he wanted.

"What is your name?"

"My name is Kristina Bjorg. What is this about?"

"Ms. Bjorg, we have a warrant to search these premises and to arrest Presley Adams. Would you please show us his study? Then this officer will wait with you while I take a look."

The woman began to shake. She lifted her hand in a ghostlike point down a long hallway, then her eyes closed and she started to crumple. Officer Duncan caught her as she went down.

"Get her some water then stay here with her." Chase nodded toward the part of the house likely to hold a kitchen. "Be quick about it." He waited until he heard the sound of water running then started down the hall in the direction Kristina Bjorg had pointed.

The study stood silent and cavernous. For all of the security in place at the clinic, Adams had surprisingly little at his own home—that false sense of security mountain resort living often brought on.

Chase turned on the lights and moved to the desk. He wished Daniel could be here to take a look at the computer, but maybe he could get some information on hard copy if he could figure out where to look. When he opened the first file drawer he sighed in relief. Not only a lack of security inside the home but organized as well.

That didn't make up for him skipping the country, but it did provide some encouragement.

Three filing cabinets didn't reveal much, other than numerous bank accounts and real estate holdings. Clinics in all of the places Terri had learned about from Leslie James, but so far nothing to incriminate Presley Adams for anything other than being a rich bastard. Chase kept up his search.

His cell phone buzzed. Terri. "Did you make the arrests?"

"Taking them in now."

"Good. I'm at Adams's house. He skipped."

"Damn."

"Yeah. Yesterday. No need to rush getting the information out. He's gone."

"You find anything on him?"

"Not yet. If you want to handle the interrogations on your guys, go ahead. But stop if you run into any problems. Have a uniform do the taping."

"I already started on the PA. We had some personal things we needed to discuss. Don't worry, it's on tape and I caught him a couple of times. For the in-house interview, I'll ask the uniform who assisted me with the arrests to handle the recording."

Chase went back to his task at hand. Where would Presley Adams put something important? He didn't seem concerned about actually hiding anything. Chase walked over to the liquor cabinet and opened the doors. Crystal and bottles—but something didn't look right. He closed the doors and reopened them. The interior should be bigger. He ran his hands along the exterior of the cabinet then shoved the bottles over a little on the inside. There. He pressed. A panel slid open to reveal a hidden cache. Inside Chase found bundles of hundred-dollar bills, two passports with Adams's picture but other names, and a leather-bound notebook. He set the cash and passports to the side and took the notebook over to the desk.

Names, dates, medical issues, payments—everything. The journal began more than two years ago. Easily a hundred people. Pages and pages documenting the donors and the recipients by name and blood type. Most of the donors' names had a cash figure associated with them. Anywhere from two hundred to five thousand dollars. Some of them simply said N/A. He looked for Rachelle Benavides or José Sanchez and found them near the end. The blood test results from the ER patients at Memorial were also there. Twenty new names had come in last week. Potential body parts ready to be harvested for the right amount of money.

He looked for Efraín Madrigal's name. He saw the young man's name spelled out with an offer of two hundred to five hundred dollars indicated, and a split second later he froze.

No. He must be reading this wrong. He blinked and felt his heart crashing around in his chest like a captured lion.

Chase put his fingers on the page and followed them along the columns. Under remarks. *There.* Two names that made his world eclipse to a sliver. *David Waters. Angela Waters.*

* * *

Think. Think. Read this again. It didn't make sense. Why would the names of two of his children be in this kind of register? He forced himself to read carefully. Slowly. Understand the words. Determine the implication.

He sat and pieced together the information. It didn't take long. The records were thorough.

313

Two years ago a current client of the Preston Clinic had been the recipient, through legitimate means, of both a lung and a kidney, and was apparently very lucky to have found a compatible donor. She had a rare blood type that made it nearly impossible for her to find a match in order to receive what she needed now. A heart.

When Chase and Bond had signed the form to allow David's organs to be donated, they were not allowed to know the name of the transplant patient. Somehow Adams had gotten access to that information. Under the remarks section, David's name indicated he'd been the previous donor. The best possible match therefore was David's sister, Angela. A great deal of money had already been paid to the Preston Clinic as a deposit, with an even more significant sum to be paid upon a successful heart transplant.

The precise ledger indicated that Diana Sloan had checked into the clinic Monday night.

Panic seized Chase. He pulled out his phone to call Bond. The phone hadn't even rung when he cried out, "Answer, answer!"

"Hi, honey. Still waiting for those warrants?"

"Where's Angela? Go check on Angela." The image of the black Mustang crawled into his brain. The Batmobile. The dumpster. Rachelle Benavides.

Angela.

"Chase, what's wrong?" Bond asked, but he could tell she was moving. On her way to their daughter's bedroom. He held his breath.

"She's right here, Chase. I told you. Both girls were in bed when you called a little while ago. You worry too much."

Chase pictured Bond approaching Angela's door. Hand on the knob. Turning. His entire world drilled down to what was happening in his home while he stood in an evil man's study—helpless. He was aware of his heartbeat, his breathing, the hairs on the nape of his neck.

"Chase, everything's okay. She's in her bed."

He squeezed the words out. "Check her, Bond."

"I don't want to wake... *oh my God, Chase! It's pillows! She's not here! Angela is gone!*"

Chapter Eighty-Four

Wednesday, September 26
9:41 p.m.

Heather had picked her up at the end of the driveway earlier than ever before, but Angela's dad wasn't home and her mom was zonked. In case her mom or dad did check on her later, she'd taken extra special care to arrange her bed to look like she was asleep.

Angela felt pretty with the lipstick and mascara she'd put on in the car. She also felt grownup. And just a little scared. As often as she and Heather had snuck out, they'd never gone to a party or anywhere they absolutely knew for sure their parents would be dead against.

The music made her tummy thump and kids were laughing and shouting all around her. Everyone was drinking and a few people were hooking up in the corners. She wanted to relax a little more and not stick out like a baby.

Heather came up behind her holding two glasses. "Here, take one." She held one toward Angela.

Angela had to shout. "What is it?" Angela took one of the tumblers and held it up to her nose.

"Mostly pop, but some guy added a little bit of booze to each."

"What kind of booze?"

"How should I know?"

Angela sipped and watched her friend do the same. She was pretty sure the face Heather made mirrored her own. "Look, I'd say just put them down, but then someone else would just give us something even worse. Let's hold onto these and walk around."

Heather nodded and the two began to circulate through the crowded house.

After a while, Heather wandered off to dance with Randall Sprinkleman, a senior at the high school. Angela saw some other friends and went to hang with them for a few minutes. She wished there was a guy here she was interested in.

Someone touched her sleeve. "Excuse me." She heard the shout in her ear. "Are you Angela Waters?"

She turned and looked into the face of an older man. Well, older than any of the kids who were at the party. He smiled even though the rest of his face looked very serious. "Uh-huh."

"I have a message for you."

Oh, no. Who knew she was here? Had Mom or Dad found out? No. If they had, they'd be here in person and they wouldn't be asking anyone to excuse themselves. "Who from?"

"Can we go outside? I can't hear myself think in here."

"Can't you just tell me?"

"I promised him I'd make sure you understood that he was running late and didn't want you to leave before he got here."

"Who?"

The man shook his head. "Please. I don't want to keep shouting."

Could it be from that cute new boy in her science class? He'd said something about looking for her at the party. Angela nodded and followed the man outside.

Maybe this guy was his older brother. Angela trailed behind him through the front door and out onto the lawn where it was quieter. He'd looked over his shoulders twice to make sure she was still behind him. Far enough, she thought. Angela stopped and waited for the man to turn around and deliver the message, but he waved her toward him. She took two steps and decided something wasn't right.

Angela turned to walk back inside when two powerful arms wrapped around her and a moist cloth pressed over her mouth and nose.

* * *

She woke up in the backseat of a car. Her hands and feet were tied up and all she could do was wiggle a little. Her head hurt and she couldn't think straight. They must've drugged her. She thought she might barf.

How long had she been out? She had a hard time judging time in the best circumstances. But this? Impossible.

Two men argued in the front seat. Something about a necklace. Without warning the car jerked wildly and her head and shoulders fell to the floor. Tires squealed. She called out but her mouth was gagged.

Angela prayed for help. She knew it was one of those groan-type prayers—only hers was more of a shriek inside of her head than a groan—she hoped it would do.

It was hard to breathe and she felt hot. She forced her body to go slack and tried to think. Where were they taking her? Were they going to rape her? She needed to gather as much information as she could if she had any hope of escape.

The car lurched to a stop and the passenger side door opened. She heard the music. The party! They were back at the party. Maybe they'd let her go. Maybe they were just trying to scare her. Teach her a lesson.

The passenger door slammed shut and the car took off. She could tell there was only one other person in the car now. The sudden quiet was eerie. Somehow scarier.

The car shifted, first one direction and then another. Whatever road they were on was a winding one. She almost gagged. They could be anywhere.

The vehicle slowed down and made a left turn. She expected a bumpy gravel road but the ride remained smooth. They stopped. The driver was talking to someone outside. She heard gates opening and the car pulled forward.

A moment later they went down a steep hill. Reverberation noises told her they'd driven into some kind of structure. Probably a garage. The engine turned off and a door opened and closed.

She heard the snap of a lock and felt the door nearest her head swing wide. Cool air fell onto her face. Hands grabbed her under her arms and jerked her out of the seat. She decided to pretend she was still out.

They laid her on a gurney or something similar. A moment later she heard the clatter of metal on cement, and felt her head explode in pain.

"Easy with the merchandise, idiot."

"What's it matter?"

She heard a giggle and then smelled someone's sour breath. Felt heat by her face. Rather than try to pull away she willed herself to remain still.

"You've caused me a lot of trouble, bitch." She tried not to flinch as the hot, low words slapped her face. "I'm hoping this won't be easy for you."

"Does she need more load?"

"Nah. She's out of it. And besides, a little pain is good for the soul." The sour stench lessened. "Get her inside."

Wheeled onto an elevator. Up. Gurney bumped out and pushed on something smooth—like tile. Light flared and receded through the cloth that trapped her eyes.

The gurney slowed. Stopped.

"This the girl?" Fingers touched her wrists. Like feathers. Firm feathers.

"Yeah."

"Leave her."

"Fine with me." The kind of sloppy footsteps her parents hated receded. She could hear her mom's voice in her head, "Pick up your feet when you walk. Do you want them to fall off?"

Something pierced her skin. She wanted her mom.

Chapter Eighty-Five

The Preston Clinic
Wednesday, September 26
9:48 p.m.

Edward Sloan gave a nod to the two men talking in the hallway at the clinic. The senior of the two, the administrator with the clipboard, had just told him they were moments away from life-saving surgery for Diana. Or "the patient" as he continued to refer to his wife.

The ecstasy he'd expected had fallen short. There was an unanticipated heaviness he'd realized with the news. *What had he done?*

Still, it meant he'd have his Diana with him longer. They could take that vacation to some place warm. Some place with white sand and waves that would wrap around their bodies infusing warmth and affirming life. They would make love under the stars and believe in tomorrow.

The tears that welled in his eyes were not from gratitude toward a power higher than himself. They weren't as much tears of relief as they were of cost—what he had paid to make this event a reality. Not in terms of his fortune but his soul.

He gathered himself outside the closed door of his wife's room. He told himself that if not for his efforts she would have died. Edward focused his mind on the shine her eyes held and the sureness her presence gave his heart. He couldn't afford to think of anything else.

He pushed open the door.

Filtered moonlight sifted like diamond dust—or maybe a sword—through the windows. His love lay motionless, dwarfed in her illness even by the small bed. Machines pumped and pulsed and pinged around her. She should have been surrounded by the songs of angels—she was that precious. Instead of an angelic choir she had the plunks and planks, beeps and gasps of mechanical equipment.

Edward pulled a visitor's chair close to her bed and reached for her hand. His life connected here. With her. She both anchored him and set him free.

What he had done was right. What he had done had saved two lives, not just one. Saving Diana meant saving himself. That's what he had to remember. That's what he had to focus on.

A tear slipped down his face and dangled on his chin before it fell to the blanket that provided warmth for his Diana. For the woman who made everything possible.

Because of the steps he'd taken, everything would be as it should. His children would have a reason to come home for the holidays. He would have a reason to go home every night. He closeted any feelings of remorse. The single most important part of the universe lay in front of him now. Ready and open to the health and added years he'd been able to provide.

Edward rose to kiss her on her forehead and leave the room to wait. Wait for the miracle that would restore his wife to him. As his lips touched the smooth skin, it felt cool and a little other-worldly. He pushed the discomfort the contact created aside and started for the door.

"Edward." Her whisper pierced him.

He turned in his tracks and felt himself pulled back to his connection. His name, uttered in more breath than voice by her lips, was a glorious command for his presence. He found the chair again, pressed her hand into his and leaned close.

"Diana, I'm here."

The barest suggestion of a squeeze scored his heart.

"Edward, I know you love me."

"With all my being."

"You have given me everything I ever wanted."

"There's more to come."

He couldn't be sure but he thought he heard her breath catch in between the rhythmic pumping sounds.

"Please, I—"

"What do you need, darling? Whatever it is I'll make it happen. Eddie's on his way home."

"I want to go."

"We will, sweetheart. Just as soon as you're better, we'll go wherever you want."

"Let me go, Edward."

"But—"

"I know what you've done. You need to stop it. Now."

The air exploded from his lungs. How could she possibly know the arrangements he'd made?

Each word took concentration and tremendous effort. "I know you too well, Edward. I saw it in your face."

He pulled her hand to his lips. "We'll be happy, Diana. Together."

"Neither of us could ever be happy at the expense of someone else. You know that as well as I do. You've just gotten lost in all the fear."

He wiped a tear from her cheek. "You're all I've ever wanted. You're all I've ever needed. I don't think I could go on if you weren't in my life."

She closed her eyes and lay still. His skin sunk into his bones and his world froze. *No!*

Her eyes opened. Lids hung heavy, shuttering the light Edward desperately wanted to see. "Please... trust me. Trust God. Let me go." She squeezed his hand. Hard. Surprise at her sudden strength engulfed him.

She let go, fingers slack, and looked into his eyes. "I'm so tired. Do you love me more than life itself?"

"Darling, you know I do."

"Then trust me. More than life itself. Trust me, Edward. Love me. I'm ready."

"Oh, God. I can't—"

"Promise me. Stop this. Stop what you've put in place." Her hand loosed its grip. Her head sunk deeper into the pillow. She pushed the last words out. "Promise me."

"I promise."

A smile creased her face. Not a big one. But Edward saw it. He would see her smile—this smile—forever when he closed his eyes and thought of his Diana.

He sat and waited, his love pushing out volumes of tears through his eyes. He barely took breaths. His heart barely beat. He waited.

Until *her* heart no longer beat. Until the end.

Edward Sloan fell into an abyss he thought would never end.

When Diana's heart stopped, Edward pushed to his feet and moved to the door. He would find the administrator and tell him the patient had died. He would keep his promise.

Chapter Eighty-Six

Wednesday, September 26
10:17 p.m.

The Carlisle brothers weren't home when Daniel arrived at their apartment building, so he was forced to troll for the Mustang.

He'd been driving for about twenty-five minutes looking for the black car when he got the request to follow up on a missing girl. Every other available officer had been sent to respond to a call because a kegger had gotten out of control at Rocky Point. Daniel would look for the Carlisle brothers some more after he took the initial report. He sure hoped it was just some teenager ticked off at her parents, and not a repeat of Rachelle Benavides.

Daniel turned off the ignition in front of the house where the call had originated. Loud party music punctuated by shrieks of laughter filled the air. A girl missing from here? How could anyone tell? A noise ordinance would go into effect at eleven o'clock so even the most easy-going neighbors were likely to take action and call the police by eleven-fifteen. Daniel didn't plan on being here that long.

A small group of about seven kids stood on the front lawn. He looked at them carefully. Young. He'd be willing to bet there wasn't a legitimate driver's license among them.

A young girl took a step toward him. As she did, a figure who had been in shadows a little farther down the street straightened up to look in their direction, stuffing an object into his shirt pocket.

There was something familiar about him, his body shape, the way he moved. The bookstore! Samuel Carlisle!

The older brother took off running. Carlisle had a head start on Daniel but the big man was pretty much a lumbering giant and Daniel closed the gap quickly.

One well-timed lunge and Daniel tackled Samuel Carlisle to the ground. He put a knee in the man's back and cuffed him. "Well, Sammy. I've been looking for you. We need to talk."

He hauled the heavy man up to his knees and then to his feet. Samuel Carlisle remained quiet but compliant as Daniel directed him to his car.

The young girl stepped into their path. "Wait! You can't leave without getting the information about my friend."

Daniel continued to shove Carlisle toward the girl, who backed up as they moved forward.

"Wait! My friend's dad is a detective!"

Daniel froze. "Who are you talking about?"

"Angela. Angela Waters. Her dad is Mr. Waters. Um— Detective Waters."

When Carlisle heard the girl's name his body stiffened and he flinched away from Daniel.

Daniel tightened his grip on the man's arm and spun him around. He got so close to the face in front of him he could count the eyebrow hairs. "You'd better start talking. And you'd better start talking now."

Carlisle shook his head. "I don't know nothin'."

"You're done, Carlisle. If you want to avoid the death penalty, you'd better tell me where Angela Waters is." Daniel couldn't begin to imagine having to break this kind of news to Chase.

"I told ya, I don't know nothin'."

Daniel pushed Carlisle over the hood of his car, forcing his head onto the metal. "Tell me now, do you want gas or a needle? I want to make sure and get it right."

"You're too late, anyways."

Daniel felt a hot rush of hate and fear flood his veins. Too late? These were the guys who were buying organs from undocumented immigrants. The only reason they'd kidnap Angela was for the same thing.

He put Carlisle in the back seat and called Chase.

Chapter Eighty-Seven

Wednesday, September 26
10:31 p.m.

After hanging up the phone with Bond at the Preston residence, Chase told Officer Duncan to secure the house until either he or one of the other detectives could return. "Tell Ms. Bjorg she's going to have to stay somewhere else. Let her pack a few things, but stay with her."

He'd also called Terri and told her to meet him at his house. Daniel was still on the missing girl call before continuing his efforts to track down the Carlisle brothers.

Chase broke every traffic law in the state to get home. He needed to see Angela's room for himself. When he walked into her bedroom, Bond flew into his arms. He held her for a moment then told her he needed to look around.

He satisfied himself that no one had broken into her room. Her window was sealed tight and she had in fact put some clothes and extra pillows under the blankets to make it look like there was someone asleep in the bed.

He willed himself to calm down. His daughter had sneaked out of the house. Maybe that was all. He wondered how long that had been going on. "Okay, it may not be as bad as I'd feared. Angela left here on her own." He looked at Bond. "Wasn't that party Friday night?"

"It was, but that doesn't mean there wasn't something going on tonight."

There had been enough secrets between them. He didn't want to freak Bond out, but she needed to know what he'd found at the Preston residence. He was trying to find the words when his cell phone rang. It was Daniel.

"What's happening? Did you get the brothers?"

"Samuel. We got Samuel. But Chase, you need to get to the Preston Clinic."

"I can get there a little later, Daniel. I'm taking care of something at home right now."

Daniel beat Chase to the news and then some. "Angela's been abducted."

When Chase heard those words the strength poured out of his body. He fell onto Angela's bed. "Talk to me."

"Angela is the missing girl I was called out on. Samuel Carlisle and his brother grabbed Angela from a party. I've got Samuel and we're on our way to the station. I'll hand him over and join you, but you need to get to the clinic now. I'm sure that's where they've taken your daughter."

Chase clicked off the phone and punched to his feet, adrenaline replacing utter fear. "Angela's in trouble." Bond stood for a moment in the middle of the room, her entire body shaking, then began to tumble to the floor. He caught her and laid her gently on the bed in the middle of the pillows and clothes his daughter had arranged. "I need to go. I'll call you."

He tore down the stairs and out to his car. When he peeled away he called Whit. "You need to get me some backup at the Preston Clinic. Pull guys away from that damned kegger. They've got Angela."

"Hostage?"

Chase choked in a breath. "No." He forced himself to breathe again. "Donor."

Chapter Eighty-Eight

The Preston Clinic
Wednesday, September 26
10:53 p.m.

Chase pulled his car up to the gate and tried to think beyond this barrier. Surprise was not an option. His baby was inside. Were they cannibalizing her body at this minute? Were they ripping organs out of her to sell to someone else? Was his sweet daughter lost forever?

No time. He put his car in reverse and backed up a good distance down the drive. He prayed that the car and its momentum would be more than the gate could stand. He threw the gear into drive and floored it, careful not to let the engine grab too much air. When his car approached the gate he closed his eyes. Somewhere in his awareness he heard a guttural scream rise out of the sound of the engine and the scraping and the other sounds of impact. So much for a surprise attack.

The airbag exploded and Chase frantically shoved it aside. He didn't let up on the accelerator as he powered the car toward the clinic entrance. He was barely aware of throwing the car into Park before he flung open the door and sprinted to the entry doors of the Preston Clinic.

331

He should have taken the tour. He had no idea where the operating rooms were. Where was the security? Surely a place as buttoned-up as this would have security up the wazoo.

Chase made a calculated guess. A one-story building meant that probably most of the patients were on the main level. He pounded down a flight of stairs to the basement level.

The lower level was every bit as plush, but even more quiet, with a feeling of isolation. Chase made sure no one was waiting to challenge him and took off in a direction he could only hope would lead him to the operating suites.

About fifty feet down the hallway, the light quality shifted. Soft incandescent light fed into fluorescent glare. Chase processed the difference. That had to be it. Automatic double doors followed by another set of doors convinced him he'd found the surgical area. His fist hit the wall-mounted door opener with enough force to knock it free of the wall.

The first room on his right stood dark and empty, but a rush of activity drew him farther down the hall. Frantic movements in an OR were not good signs.

He charged into the room and drew to a stop, confused. Where was the surgical team? Only two people stood before him in scrubs.

Why only two people?

The answer slammed into his brain. Because they had no intention of keeping this patient alive.

Angela lay motionless, restrained. Horrible, tight wheezing sounds strangled the air above her as she fought to breathe. He rushed to his daughter. Her pulse was thready and she was unresponsive.

Chase found his voice. "What did you give her?" He forced his focus to include the other people in the room.

One of the two people he'd surprised slipped behind him and broke into a run before Chase could stop him. The sound of slapping rubber soles sounded down the hallway as he fled. The second person backed away like a cornered animal, eyes darting over the surgical mask.

"What in God's name did you give her?"

A woman's voice came from behind him. "Just a sedative. A little Versed and something to knock her out."

Chase spun toward the speaker. A woman stood in a defiant stance, her scrubs saying she belonged. Daniel stood behind her and shoved the woman a little farther into the room. She was handcuffed. A pinched face reflected the anger that had chewed her up and spit her out.

"We didn't kill her. She's fine." Hard features reflected a hard soul. The woman's lower jaw jutted forward. Chase had seen this before with suspects they'd caught. The perception criminals often held—that everyone was against them—turned otherwise normal people into despicable human beings. Her eyes squinted, like she was trying to protect the hatred she held. Only it wasn't working. Hatred leaked out of every pore on her body. "I don't know why you're doing this to me. I haven't done anything. I just work here." She tried to jerk away from Daniel's grasp. I've never done anything."

"What exactly did you give her to 'knock her out'?"

"Fentanyl." She backed away from Chase, who seemed to suddenly scare her more than the detective at her back. "Hey, don't blame me if there's a problem. I just follow orders."

When Chase heard the name of the drug, he knew what had happened.

Chapter Eighty-Nine

The Preston Clinic
Wednesday, September 26
11:17 p.m.

Chase didn't have much time. He tried to remember what he'd learned in the paramedic course he took after David died. He raced to the anesthesia cart and yanked open the drawers, throwing medication boxes to the floor until he found an ampoule of Albuterol. Rifling through the other compartments, he found a face mask and nebulizer. He squeezed the medicine into a reservoir and connected it to the oxygen system. After he placed the mask over Angela's face he turned on the flow of oxygen. He could see the mask mist with each struggling breath.

He scanned the room. Where was the code cart? Every operating room had one. But this wasn't every operating room. There was nothing typical about this place.

Chase fought to not scream the words. "Where's your med room?"

The nurse turned a blank stare on him.

"Where are your resuscitation drugs kept?" Now, he was screaming.

She continued to stare.

"I need a code cart!"

The sound of sirens reached them.

"It's across the hall."

Chase ran to the door.

The nurse, in an almost sing-song voice said, "Won't do you any good. You need a key."

"No, I don't."

His first effort to force open the locked door with his shoulder made his vision go gray. He shook it off, backed up and kicked with every muscle his leg possessed. The door cracked. One more kick and it popped open.

They knew so much about his daughter. How could they not know she was allergic to Fentanyl? The brightly lit room with cabinets and cases and two refrigerators was clean and organized. Chase zeroed in on the red metallic cart with the defibrillator on top. Prayed it was properly stocked. He found the Epinephrine, Solu-medrol and Benadryl in the top drawer. He grabbed some Zantac from another cabinet on his way out the door.

His hands shook as he drew the Epi dose into the syringe. Once the needle cleared the plastic stopper, he slammed it into Angela's thigh. Plunger depressed. Medication delivered to muscle. *Please, God.*

He held his breath. Waited.

Please, God. Their family had risen from the ashes once before, but losing a second child would render them in a wasteland without a road. Without hope.

Chase knew now that protecting his family went beyond him. He couldn't do it alone. He needed a little help from a more powerful source. *Please, I promise. I'll go to church. I'll talk to you more. I'll do anything. I'll quit doubting.*

He watched as the wheezing from Angela's chest eased with each successive breath. Her body visibly relaxed. He injected the steroids, Benadryl and Zantac, into the IV. He'd done it. All of that online reading, discussion with doctors, and plans he'd made in his mind that he'd thought he'd never have to use. He'd done it.

Sirens rent the air. Rather than symbolizing the loss of a son, they marked the saving of a daughter. He could live with that.

Chapter Ninety

The Waters Home
Thursday, September 27
2:49 a.m.

Chase fought to control himself. Bond sat on the sofa cradling Angela in her arms. "What in the world were you thinking?" He tried not to shout the question.

Her answer was a sniff.

"Do you have any idea how close we came to losing you tonight?"

Bond looked at him. "That's enough. You don't need to terrify her more."

"Maybe we didn't terrify her enough."

Angela pushed away from her mother. "I want to know why. Why do you think someone wanted to kill me? I've never hurt anyone."

Bond pulled Angela back to her chest and began to rock. "Shhh... you're safe now."

For a moment Chase watched as his wife and oldest daughter melded into one another. He felt much as he did when Bond was pregnant—separate and ineffective. Then later when Angela was sick and he didn't know what to do and Bond filled the gap with an instinct and naturalness he would never achieve.

He went to kneel before them. "The danger is over, but you deserve to know why it happened."

Angela locked her eyes on his. He felt energy and natural curiosity in her gaze, but mostly he felt her trust and his own obligation as her father.

Bond shifted. "Chase, maybe later would be better."

"No," Angela said. "Now."

Chase took a breath. "Do you remember why David died?"

"Sure. His heart. Something about the electric pulses being off."

"It's called Long QT Syndrome. It's genetic. Your mom had a brother who had the same thing. And I had a sister. After David died, we had you and Stephanie checked specifically to see if you were affected. Thankfully, neither of you were."

"So?"

"So we thought you were safe. We thought our loss, as horrible as it was, would be limited to your brother."

"Are you saying I'm sick now?"

Bond hugged her tighter. "No, honey. You're not sick. You're perfectly healthy."

Chase cleared his throat. "When your brother died, your mom and I made the decision to donate his organs. It was the right thing to do." Chase made sure he had both Angela's and Bond's attention. "*It was the right thing to do*," he repeated.

Chase grasped one of Angela's hands. "You and David share a rare physical makeup, but while your brother's heart was affected, yours wasn't. You were unique in every way David was, but your heart was strong. *Is* strong."

Angela's eyes widened. "Someone wanted my heart?"

"Yes." Chase decided she didn't need to know the details. She didn't need to know that if things had happened in just a slightly different time frame, his daughter's heart would have been transplanted into the same body her brother's organs had gone to two years ago.

Chapter Ninety-One

Thursday, December 7

Chase thought about the lives the recent events had impacted. He'd personally made a call to Skizzers at his sister's house to let him know it would be okay for him to come back to Aspen Falls. His sister had told him that Stephen had entered a drug rehabilitation program out of state. Chase expressed his hope that it would be successful.

Terri had confided in him that she was trying to adopt a young girl. Chase offered whatever personal recommendations he could to make sure that happened for her. It was supposed to become official after the first of the year. Hopefully they would have some transition time to deal with the loss of the girl's grandmother.

Daniel and Elizabeth were in the young stage of love. Ramona Benavides thought the sun rose and set on the young detective. Daniel had been back to Cobalt Mountain Books three times to buy more novels by Hispanic authors.

Chase and Bond had found an entirely new level of closeness. One of these days Bond would probably be able to have a discussion about the past with her mother, but the time wasn't right.

Bond's parents, Stuart and Celeste, had embarked on a two-month vacation. One that Stuart had confided to Chase might heal the rip in their marriage. Bottom line? Stuart Wentworth loved Celeste Wentworth. Chase had to swallow his words more than once. But who was he to make the rules of life?

He and Bond had a wonderful dinner with Jacqueline Taylor and her new significant other, Scott Ortiz. Between all of the medical jargon, they were lucky to stay in the conversation.

Mex remained a mystery. Chase felt certain that over time, the two of them would find a way to get to know each other better. The man was haunted, but he was stand-up and solid.

The DNA results for the two bodies hadn't come back yet, but Chase's money was on Mex.

He pulled the current copy of the *Aspen Falls Register* open to the article he'd just read and read it again:

MISSING—Former Aspen Falls resident and prominent international businessman, Presley Adams, has been reported missing in Los Cabos, Mexico, where one of his companies recently opened a new private clinic. Adams has been named as a person of interest in the recent murders and abductions of several people in the Aspen Falls area. Four other people are pending trial.

The Preston Clinic in Aspen Falls is under new ownership.

In an unrelated story out of the same region of Mexico, the continuing battle with various drug cartels has Mexican officials reeling. A larger army, more money, and Santeria are blamed for the failure of the Mexican government to bring an end to the cartels.

Chase folded the newspaper and tossed it on the counter. He didn't believe for a minute the stories were unrelated.

Acknowledgements

The Missings is the result of a complete rewrite of a manuscript I wrote a couple of years ago. That one was the result of a complete rewrite of an even earlier story. The original, although it bears next to no similarity to this book, was arrived at with the support of The Writing Girls—author Kelly Irvin, author Susan Lohrer and Angela Mills. They are gifted writers in their own right, and I'm proud to count them as friends.

I received assistance for medical issues from author Jordyn Redwood, and crime scene information from author Tom Adair. If there are any errors related to either of these aspects, I assume full responsibility. Both of these people are experts in their fields, gave me their considered opinions, and then I tried to make them work for the story.

The police chief in Aspen, Colorado, Richard Pryor (yes, that's his real name!) helped me with some tricky problems with the plot—including my need to have a civilian involved in the investigation. Elizabeth would not have been as much fun to write if she had to be pathetic and mourn on the sidelines.

Carol Myers is my cousin, and I asked her to read the scene with Birdie to make sure I nailed the Eastern European language challenge. I remember my Great-Grandmother, but Carol spent much more time with her and came back to me with a thumbs-up.

My first readers were wonderful. Bestselling author L.J. Sellers, author Lala Corriere, Kel Darnell, Kathleen Hickey, Joni Williams and Gail Swift helped me get it ready for an editor. Each one of these women lead busy lives and I appreciate them tackling an unedited manuscript just because I asked them to, and each one of these women contributed to the final result. My gift to them is a brand new ending to the story they read all those weeks and months ago.

This was my first time working with Jodie Renner. She is a terrific editor and made me feel like I had a collaborator extraordinaire. She found things that needed fixing and areas that needed expansion, and then she sat back patiently while I applied her advice or convinced her to let me have my way. She made the editing process thoroughly enjoyable. With Jodie, it was very much a collaborative effort that spoiled me, taught me and stretched me. And she did it all without changing my voice. She was also one of my biggest encouragers. Because of Jodie, *The Missings* is a better story.

Patty G. Henderson worked her magic once again for my cover design. Patty tweaked and emailed and tweaked and emailed and tweaked some more. Maybe it's because she's in Florida and I'm in Colorado, but I didn't get the sense she rolled her eyes or sighed even one time. She just wanted me to be happy. That's what I call a partner!

And last but not least, in order to attempt to provide readers with an error free reading experience, Krysta Corinn Copeland applied her keen eye to my manuscript looking for strange little problems. If any exist in this version, it is not due to her oversight but my negligence.

For more information regarding organ donation, begin with United Network for Organ Sharing, or UNOS. You can find them at http://www.unos.org. If you are not currently an organ donor, please carefully consider the final gift you might have to help greatly improve, or even save, the life of another person.

Finally, I want to acknowledge those of you who read *Red Tide* and told me how much you enjoyed it. You gave me the heart to do everything again. Thank you. Without you I would simply be spewing words into a vacuum, and how much fun could that be?

.

RED TIDE

Peg Brantley

1

To my mom, who loved and believed in me even when she wasn't here.

Happy birthday, Mom.

To my dad and my sister who showed me it could happen.

And to my husband, the Love of My Life, who has waited patiently

for the done-done version.

"And all the waters that were in the river were turned to blood. The fish that were in the river died, the river stank and the Egyptians could not drink of the water of the river…"

Exodus 7:20-21 New King James Version

Chapter One

Sometimes the dead shouldn't stay buried.

Jamie Taylor ducked under an aspen branch. Sometimes the dead needed to be unearthed, exposed, examined, and prayed over.

And sometimes, mulchy, worm-filled graves were not meant to be their final resting places. Places where secrets remained hidden, held fast to rotted flesh and dry bones.

"Never," Jamie said. "People are not meant to be buried in unmarked, unremembered tombs. Not as long as I have anything to say about it." She and Gretchen had begun their search in earnest when the golden retriever alerted next to a mountain laurel. There, Jamie found a small, fragile piece of stained cloth. She marked it with a utility flag so the crime lab tech could photograph and bag the bit of evidence, and then she moved on with her dog, spirits high with the promise they'd find what they were looking for soon.

Hours later, physical exhaustion gave way to punchiness, and her certainty flagged to a dull depression. Jamie signaled to Gretchen with a light tug on the lead. "Time for a break." The golden gave her a look that said, "Not yet," but Jamie knew Gretchen would go until she could go no further.

"I need some water, my sweet. And you're getting some even if you don't consider it a priority."

Jamie hiked a few feet up and behind the ground they'd already covered and settled onto a flat rock, her supply pack at her feet. She dug out water for the two of them and surveyed the field they'd been searching since early that morning.

Field... more like prairie. She and one other handler were searching a hundred acres of high country meadow. Beautiful. Until you were forced to navigate the rough and rocky terrain hidden beneath the grasses.

They were looking for the body of a forty-two year old woman, missing for over a year. Her husband, finally drunk enough to tell his dirty little secret to a woman he'd met in a bar, said no one would ever find the body. The woman, after thinking about it for a while, became sufficiently terrorized to go to the authorities.

Analeise Reardon deserves a proper burial. She deserves to be prayed over by people who love her. Her parents, and her three children, deserve to have some closure. "And her damned husband deserves to have his arms cut off at his elbows and stuffed up his ass for starters," she mumbled.

Painful memories of Jamie's mother's murder flooded her thoughts and her breaths grew shallow and quick. Her ribs compressed until they felt like strong, bony fingers squeezing inside her chest. Her vision blurred, and instinct—born of deliberate practice—forced her to shake her head to shatter the tension. She pulled a breath deep into her lungs, then forced air out. *Inhale. Calm.*

This wasn't the first time Jamie and her dogs had participated in a search for a body as a result of someone who had decided divorce cost too much time, money and trouble. It also wouldn't be the last. People never failed to disappoint her.

Jamie's gaze travelled the edge of the field and she found a visual she might never have seen as part of the original search plan. Even Gretchen, working the

6

established scent cone pattern, might not have picked up something that far out of the search area.

"C'mon girl. We've got a grave to find." She stowed the water and tucked her supply pack out of the way on her back. Her soil probe slipped easily from its holder, a sort of magic wand to use on her quest. Gretchen gave her a look that in a teenager would have involved rolled eyes and stood, ready to get back to work.

Jamie keyed a number into her cell. "It's me. I've got an anomaly. Grasses." She recorded her present coordinates on the handheld GPS she'd splurged on last summer and began the hike over to the area she'd spotted where the grass grew lush in comparison to nearby vegetation.

The path she took brought her back to the primary search area, then up again, almost fifty yards. Sure enough, a small area of prairie grass was growing thicker and darker and higher than anything else around it. Before she could sink her probe all the way into the earth to create the first breathing hole, Gretchen dropped to the ground. Full alert.

Nearby the song of a meadowlark filled the mountain air.

Sometimes, with a little help, the dead don't stay buried.

Chapter Two

Gray walls, gray ceiling and floor, poured concrete table and chairs—all blended together to eliminate any visual stimulation. Colorado's Supermax prison facility didn't waste any funds on interior design. The lack of color made the stink of sweat and urine seem touchable. Assistant Special Agent in Charge Nicholas Grant hated it here.

He dry-swallowed two oxycontin tablets, his sixth and seventh of the day, no longer certain his back condition bore any relevance to his need for what he euphemistically referred to as "pain management." Now however, wasn't the time to consider his motivation for popping the pills. It hadn't been the time for close to two years but he didn't want to think about that either. He tapped the amber plastic bottle in his pocket, assured by its presence and the control it represented.

The semi-public area was eerily quiet compared to other parts of the penitentiary. But rather than tranquility, the air spiked with anger, resentment and distrust. No one left here the same as when they came in. No one. Not even him.

Prior to his arrival, the prison authorities had checked out and cleared the wall-mounted camera and recording equipment. No extra feeds to an unauthorized receiver were in place and everything tested in working order. So far technology had chronicled his failures on this case. Maybe today it would record a success.

Before beginning the interview, Nick was glad to have somewhere to go to complete his mental preparation and give his subject time to stew. Inmates measure their freedom, such as it is, in inches. *When the guards brought Leopold Bonzer into the interview room and secured him to the cuff rings, his incarcerated ass would be about as mobile as a sick snail on a slow day.*

Nick wandered back up to the security screening area in between two of the guard towers and settled on the corner of an unoccupied but cluttered desk that was already piled with stacks of forms, folders that looked like they had been pulled from a filing cabinet and dumped, unopened sleeves of Styrofoam cups, two canisters of powder for hot chocolate and a few old *People* magazines.

Nick worked to stay on good terms with all of the guards in this part of the prison. Over the years he'd popped in and out enough times to know about births and deaths, marriages and divorces. He knew which guards were die-hard Bronco fans, which ones followed the Rockies and even one who secretly pulled for the Redwings.

"Thanks for getting me the contact request list for Bonzer so fast." Nick fist-bumped the guard. "You'd think after all this time even the tabloid reporters would know they can't have access to inmates here." Sensational stories sold papers. And a serial killer who admitted to murdering fourteen people was pretty sensational. A serial killer who wouldn't give up the location of thirteen of those bodies and to whom no other members of the media had access was especially prime.

The tenth anniversary of the sentencing for Leopold Bonzer loomed a little over three months away. It had been Bonzer's bad luck to get caught red-handed. He'd killed a postal worker vacationing at Maroon Bells, and then got stopped on his way to dispose of the body. The murder of a federal employee on public land received the attention of the FBI, and Nick had smelled more blood from his very first meeting with the suspect. He hadn't quit in ten years. *Be damned if I'll quit now.*

Slow to give up, the supermarket rags had continued to cook the Bonzer story at a slow spin, like a pig on a spit. They fanned the flames just enough to get a little sizzle, especially on the anniversary of his sentencing, but never so much that the story had dropped into the flames and smoldered away to an ashy memory.

The guard nodded and looked at Nick. "Some guys, their families try to get in to see 'em even when they know they can't. Bonzer's family, if he's got one, is smart enough to have cut him loose. Your guy is almost as big a media draw as our resident terrorists in H-Unit." The prison guard leaned back in his chair and used a toothpick to dig out what Nick assumed were remnants from his lunch. The man sucked some spit, then motioned to one of the camera images with the tiny wooden pointer. "They're loading him in now, Agent. What's your plan this time?"

Nick tensed his jaw. *Is that a smirk? A dig at my lack of success over the last ten years? Professional, not personal, right? Don't let this guy get to you. He's a friggin' security guard for crying out loud. Besides, he has a point.* He shrugged. "Wish I had a plan. Nothing's worked so far. He's looking for some kind of deal in exchange for details on the bodies but I've got nothing to offer. He doesn't even want to try to negotiate his way to a different facility. Claims he's happy here."

"I'd help you if I could. You're different from the other feds we're expected to work with, and if I could think of something to get you what you need, I'd do it. So would most of the staff here. You want to help those families, not just move your own career a rung up the ladder. And it's pretty clear the Bonzer case is more of a career killer."

A sudden wave of doubt poured over Nick. His success rate at the bureau put him near the top, but the one criticism he'd endured review after review was that he might be too soft. His superiors claimed he got too involved in his cases and failed to maintain enough professional detachment. *But if you don't care, why put your life in jeopardy in the first place?* The day he developed "professional detachment" would be the day he would know he needed to get out.

Nicholas Grant thought about the parents and other family members who had lost loved ones at the hands of Leopold Bonzer. Even with his confession to their brutal murders, there would always be one huge loose end for thirteen families. The lack of a body always fosters impossible images and irrational ideas in the minds of a mom or dad, a lover or friend. Until he could give them irrefutable proof, unquestionable evidence that a life had ended, hope would push to the surface.

Chapter Three

"Well, if it isn't Agent Grant." The clean-shaven man wore his wrinkled prison uniform as if it were a thousand-dollar suit.

"Hard to believe I surprised you, Bonzer, seeing as how I'm the only visitor you get other than your legal team. And how long has it been since they were here?" Nick set two frosty cans of soda pop on the table in front of him. He opened the top on one, then purposefully sat so he could cross his legs while Bonzer's ankles remained shackled.

The inmate swung his head to the side, arched his neck and rolled his shoulders, flexing as much as his confine- ment with his wrists in the table restraints allowed.

A stretching snail. "Feeling confined, Bonzer?"

Bonzer fixed Nick with a glare. He took a breath. Released it. Another breath. Release. "You know I like my privacy." His right eye twitched and the fingers on his right hand fiddled.

"How big is the window in your *private* cell?" Nick took a long swig from his can, his gaze not leaving Bonzer's face.

"A perfect four feet."

"That's four feet *wide*. How high is it?"

12

"I told you. I like my privacy."

"Four friggin' inches, that's how high. See much of the world from your room at this hotel?" Nick popped the top on the other can and shoved it across the table, then called the guard in to release Bonzer's hands from the restraints.

"Go to hell!" Bonzer took the can. Held it in front of him, temptation warring with pride. His eye continued to twitch.

When Nick went through his training he heard stories about Supermax prison, but he'd seen some pretty tough correctional institutions in his time and figured the stories for so much hype. His first visit here to meet with Leopold Bonzer almost ten years ago had opened his eyes.

Supermax, officially known as the United States Penitentiary Administrative Maximum Facility—or ADX— housed some of the worst criminals the Bureau of Prisons offered. The Alcatraz of the Rockies remained the most restrictive and punitive federal prison in the United States. Mafia family members, terrorists—homegrown and otherwise—drug kingpins, white supremacists and gang leaders all resided within its walls. Even a few serial killers, including a physician who got off on poisoning people, made Fremont County, Colorado their home.

Most of the cells were furnished with a desk, a stool and a bed, all poured concrete. If a prisoner attempted to plug his toilet for whatever reason it would automatically shut off. Showers were available in each cell, but they ran on a timer to prevent flooding. If a prisoner earned a few privileges he might have a polished steel mirror bolted to the wall, an electric light, a radio, and a black-and-white television that broadcast recreational, educational and religious programming. Other than the mirror, each privileged item was remotely controlled so the inmate never actually came into contact with them. Even though people often compared Supermax to

13

Alcatraz, its namesake never imagined the security this prison would boast, nestled in a valley at the foot of the Rocky Mountains. A multitude of motion detectors, cameras placed in every conceivable location, fourteen hundred remote-controlled steel doors, twelve-foot-high fences topped with razor-wire, laser beams, pressure pads and attack dogs all made Supermax one of the most secure facilities in the United States.

Nick believed the attack dogs were the real dissuaders. Dogs were predators. Carnivores. At their core they lived to rip open flesh and devour warm, raw meat. Other prisons might have them, but he could only imagine the extra genetic encoding the dogs at this prison must have.

"Heard the dogs barking lately?" The words were flippant, casual, but Leopold Bonzer had been badly mauled by a dog as a child. He'd endured seven surgeries: one to save his life and six more to give him a reason to live. Nick could relate.

The usual venom glinted from Bonzer's eyes, but Nick saw something else in them too. Something new flickered behind the mask. There'd been a shift of some kind. He would wait and think this development through before he chose the direction this interview would take. And maybe in the meantime Leopold Bonzer would give him some kind of clue. If he did, it would be the first.

Nick sat back, sipped his cold drink and considered his options. Two minutes of quiet might feel like two hours to a restrained prisoner alone in a room with a fed even if that prisoner spent hour after hour alone. Nick thought, *Maybe especially if that prisoner spent hour after hour alone*. Nick reached into his pocket and pulled out a pair of fingernail clippers. He didn't really need a manicure, but it would give him something to do while he waited. Weapons weren't allowed into the interior of the prison, but clippers still passed the innocuous test.

He pretended not to notice Bonzer trying to twist on his seat, or hear him sucking air between his teeth or even when he hocked a wad of spit and who-knows-what onto the floor near the door. Instead he focused on getting just the right shape on his pinky.

When Leopold Bonzer's face reddened, then emptied of color almost as quickly, Nick slowly closed his fingernail clippers, rubbed them free of smudges and tucked them back in his pocket. For the first time in a very long eight minutes, he looked directly at Leopold Bonzer.

Bonzer narrowed his eyes then arched his back a fraction of an inch. "I might want to talk about relocating." Nick nodded but said nothing. Instead he leaned forward, put both elbows on the table and rested his chin in his hands.

Bonzer said, "I might be ready to give you what you want... for the right *hotel*."

A million questions played through Nick's head, but he didn't dare interrupt the process. "I'm listening," Nick said.

"Not today. Next week." Bonzer's eyes brittled with intensity. You get me the paperwork so I can look at it... let me see you sign it in front of me. I'll want confirmation from my legal team that it's a done deal. Then I'll talk."

About the Author

A Colorado Native, Peg Brantley is a member of Sisters in Crime and Rocky Mountain Fiction Writers. She and her husband make their home southeast of Denver, and have shared it over the years with a pair of mallard ducks named Ray and Deborah, a deer named Cedric and a beloved bichon named McKenzie.

Peg loves hearing from readers. If you'd like to learn more about Peg, or get in touch with her, you can go to her Facebook Author page at
https://www.facebook.com/PegBrantleyAuthorPage
or her website at
http://www.pegbrantley.com
or her Amazon Author page at
http://www.amazon.com/PegBrantley/e/B007P35G
WW/ref=ntt_dp_epwbk_0

Made in the USA
Las Vegas, NV
01 May 2021